What Not to do When Wooing a Witch

ISBN-13: 978-1-961802-30-8

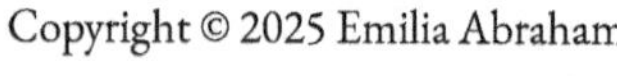

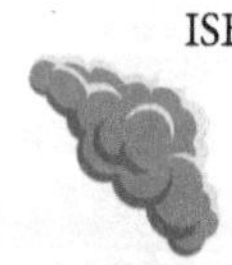

For those who are too loud, too excited, too much—
I hope you find the one who thinks you're just right.

Content Considerations:

Adult Language
Sexually Explicit Scenes
Witchcraft
Demons

CHAPTER ONE
DIMITRI

A closet would be a horrible place to die.

No windows. No room. No exit. At least not in this particular closet. I've searched for a handle, but there isn't one. Door, yes. Knob, no. A sliver of light filters through a gap by the floor.

The first time I was here, I tried to peek underneath. Instead, I got stuck between the door and the wall. and had to dislocate my shoulder to get out. Thank fuck I'm a demon so the pain didn't last long. Hurt like a son of a bitch when I did it, though.

I used to enjoy my time here. It's cozy, albeit a little cramped with the boots and random boxes. I swear I sat in a cauldron once. My ass slipped right inside, and it took a bit of maneuvering to get out. I thought about calling for Omen, but he's busy with his witch. Or rather, avoiding his witch.

I sigh, leaning against the fluffiness of a winter coat. At least, I assume it's a winter coat. Doesn't really matter to me as long as it's soft. My eyes flutter closed, and I let my mind wander. Hopefully nothing weird will happen this time around. I've only been sucked in here a couple times, but I don't see that changing anytime soon.

Counting in my head to keep track of time isn't helping my boredom. Time topside isn't the same as in Hell, which makes it hard to figure out. A couple minutes in a closet isn't so bad.

Except it's getting a bit exhausting being summoned up here, then thrown back into Hell. And half the time I'm so disoriented, I have no idea where I am.

If I'm being honest, I fucking hate this. My head won't stop spinning. I'm perpetually exhausted. My magic's on the fritz and I feel like I'm losing my mind. These moments in between being tossed around dimensions are a little reprieve from the disorientation. I just wish I had longer to recharge. Eventually, I'll flame out. I suppose that's more of an Omen thing. I'd be more likely to shock out—is that even a thing? I've never been pushed far enough for my magic to overwhelm me. I wonder what it's like... not enough to actually try it.

"Fuck," I groan as a familiar swoop in my gut hits me. Before I know it, I'm whisked away into the void. I groan again, though no sound comes out. In here, I'm nothing more than energy. My magic is the only thing keeping me in some semblance of order.

After what feels like an eternity, I'm dropped into a cage. My muscles scream and my head swims. My knees buckle and I crumple to the dusty floor. At least I'm in Hell. I remember being sent down here for something or someone, though I don't remember what. Or who, I suppose. The place is empty now.

"You've got to be fucking kidding me," I wheeze as I push myself upright. I kick the door to the cage, but it doesn't budge. Leaning against the wall, I close my eyes and focus on my breathing.

This summoning thing is for the birds. It's disorienting and painful, though not surprising. I spent a couple years in the void, trying to figure out the different dimensions, what it was made of, what it did to demon bodies. I didn't discover the meaning of life or anything like that. I did find that magic linked us to our souls, keeping us somewhat intact. At least enough to get us to our destination. Problem was, that discovery led me down the rabbit hole of why demons have souls, which led to how soulbounds work. From how Omen's acting, I wonder if that little tidbit will come in handy sooner rather than later.

I've been dealing with this for...weeks? Months? With the time difference between Hell and topside, I have no idea. I just know I can't take it much longer. A nervous energy runs down my arm, and my fingers flicker. I shake out my hands and sparks fly everywhere. They fizzle out, leaving a soft pulse of electricity behind. I glance down and sigh at my glowing hands. I'm fucking cursed. That's the only explanation.

My head thumps back and my mind shuts down. I don't know how long I'm out before a clanging in my head jolts me awake. When I pry my eyelids open, Omen paces in the cage with me.

"Omen?" I croak, and his shoulders tense. He's been riding the edge for weeks now. One of these days he's going to explode more than he did when I accidentally touched his little witch.

"Start talking, Dimitri," he growls.

"Uh, welcome to the cage?"

He snorts, not bothering to face me. His fingers wrap around the rusty bars, and his knuckles turn white. Maybe he'll burst into flames and melt the metal.

"What a clever name. Who thought that one up?"

"Triton, of course. He sent me down here to...get someone. Then I got that weird tingly feeling again, and *bam*, I was in a closet. Spent a couple minutes in there, too terrified to come out on account of what happened the last time I was in a random person's house, which wasn't so random seeing as how it was your—"

"Get to the point," he snaps.

I press my lips together and adjust my shoulders to ease the ache. I wasn't going to call her his girlfriend or anything. He's clearly still pissy about my little side quest into her house. It's not like I had a choice. Someone's been tossing me across dimensions, and I don't know how to stop it. Maybe I should ask his witch about it. She seems to have enough witchy knowledge if she figured out how to summon a demon.

"Okay, touchy. After that, I felt the tug again, and *bam*, I was

in here. 'Cept now the door is locked and I'm on the other side of it. Don't know what happened, but I've just been waiting for someone to come get me. I thought it'd be quick."

I'm not about to tell him I passed out. He's got enough on his plate without dealing with my problems. Besides, between the two of us, I'm the laid back one—the one who goes with the flow and doesn't get bogged down with all the extra stuff.

He turns, his brows pulled low. "How long have you been down here?"

I shrug. "Don't know. I keep getting pulled back to the human realm. It was disorienting. I'd come back and eventually I couldn't handle the magical trip. I'd pass out, come to, get shoved into limbo—"

"I get it. You don't have to overexplain everything, Dimitri."

I wince, then shoot him a tight-lipped smile. It's hard to remember he doesn't like excessive chatter. With him being gone so much, though, I don't really have anyone else to talk to. Most of the others give me a wide berth. Never bothered to figure out why.

Omen's hand flutters by his side as I push to my feet. "You know I didn't mean—"

"I know. Forget sometimes. Mind going a mile a minute. Sometimes it's hard to slow down. Take out the unimportant bits. You know," I mutter. He doesn't need me piling on when he's clearly going through the shit.

"I do." The corner of his mouth twitches. "So, knock it the fuck off. How did I get down here?"

I shrug again. He won't like my answer, anyway. I don't even know how *I* got down here. Him being sent to the cage doesn't make any sense either.

"Maybe you should flame out. See if that pops the lock or something." My knees buckle, and I cover my faulty bones by leaning against the wall. I wonder if he can see the exhaustion.

"You could have shocked the shit out of it."

I hold up my hand, and the soft glow from earlier weaves

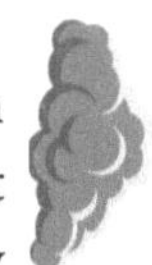

through my fingers and pulsates slightly. Apparently, my little nap didn't do much to fix my magic or my exhaustion. Eventually, I need to figure out if I'm actually cursed.

"Pretty, but not particularly useful," he says, pulling me from my thoughts.

"Careful, or I'll steal your girl." I wrinkle my nose. "Too soon?"

He huffs, turning back to gaze through the bars. "Be glad she's not here or we'd have more trouble than we can handle."

A soft meow pierces the silence stretching between us. Omen groans, though I can't figure out why until I spot the small cat padding from the shadows. Squished face, stubby legs, and fluffy black fur with white paws. Fucking adorable.

"Look how cute she is," I coo. Omen mutters something, but I'm too distracted by this creature. "Shit. Omen? I think she's hurt?"

He rushes over, though I don't know what he's going to do for the thing. She doesn't look like a typical cat. She winds around me, and I turn with her, then run my fingers through her fur. Omen drops to his knees behind me and I tense. He's not a cat person, and I'd rather he not punt the little thing into a black hole.

"Where?" he snarls as he manhandles her.

"She looks like she ran into something. Cats' faces aren't supposed to look like that," I mutter as she meows. I snatch her from him and cuddle her to my chest.

"First of all, it's a he. Second, that's just his face. I think Clara rescued it or something."

I snort, then swallow down my humor. "Let me get this straight, your little witch has a cat, which probably is a familiar—"

"Or she rescued it."

"You're freaking out about it being hurt, but you hate cats. And you're still clinging to the fact you don't care about Clara?"

He's too deep to keep thinking he isn't tied to her. She was able to summon him for a reason. We're too far up the chain of command for things like this to happen. I don't fully understand why he's fighting it. If I'd found someone who wanted me around, I'd cling to them. Probably too much, and then they'd kick my ass out when I smothered them with my constant presence and excessive chatter.

Omen huffs, glancing off into the corner I curled up in however long ago. "I never said I didn't care for her." His nostrils flare as my gaze catches on someone loitering on the outside of the cage. "I'm just acutely aware of the risks of getting involved with a witch."

"Uh, Omen?" I grimace when Clara steps into the muted light just outside the bars.

Of course he doesn't heed the warning in my tone. "None of which has anything to do with her personally. A witch doesn't belong in Hell. If she'd just get rid of the summoning circle...fuck, if she never chalked it in the first place, we wouldn't be in this mess."

Hurt flashes across her face before she lets out a soft sigh. Omen tenses, fear and hopefully some shame build in his dark eyes. The last place I want to be is here while he bumfuddles his way out of this situation. I have no idea how Clara got down here. It's not like Hell has public tours. Half the time the new crop of demons who come up get lost within the various dimensions down here. Then again, Clara isn't a normal witch.

When Omen doesn't move, I nudge him with my foot and hiss his name. Pain stabs into my temple, and I dig my fingers into the cat's fur. He doesn't seem to notice. Clara's talking, but I can't make out the words. There's a high-pitched whine pulsing in my head. Omen grabs the feline from my arms, and I make a sound in the back of my throat. I don't think it's actual words, but he doesn't stop.

Nausea bubbles in my gut, and I swallow over and over. I'm cursed. It's the only explanation for whatever the hell is happening to me. Whoever's fucking with me needs to knock it the fuck off. I'm going to lose myself if I don't figure this shit out.

Clara's voice cuts through the pain. "I'm not taking the cat, Omen."

"I'll take him," I croak, and flames burst from the top of Omen's head. "Or not."

He drops the cat in my lap once more, and I wonder if I won anyway. I don't really have time to take care of a pet, but I could make it work. Even if he looks like he got stopped by a brick wall to the face. My head swims and my eyes cross. I pull in several deep breaths, wondering if they'll notice me if I puke all over the floor.

They're bickering again, and I tune them out while trying to get my shit together. It's not until there's a clanking of metal that I focus on them once more. The door's open and Clara's wiggling the handle up and down. Whether she merely opened it or used some witchy powers, I don't know. From the look on her face, I doubt she does either. I let out a chuckle at Omen's affronted face. Electricity zips through my veins, and my stomach flips.

"Well, shit," I wheeze as the cat jumps from my arms.

Sparks crackle across my skin as I'm shoved into the void once more. My body goes numb, and I barely feel anything when I hit the floor. When my mind shuts down, I embrace the darkness.

CHAPTER TWO
MARI

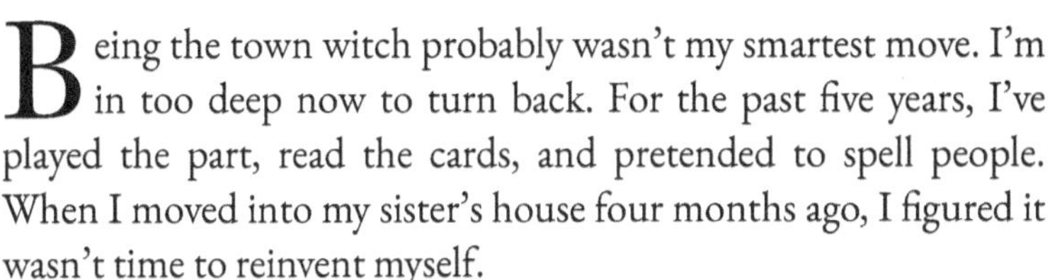

Being the town witch probably wasn't my smartest move. I'm in too deep now to turn back. For the past five years, I've played the part, read the cards, and pretended to spell people. When I moved into my sister's house four months ago, I figured it wasn't time to reinvent myself.

None of it is real, though. I thought it'd be easy to fool people since I'm an actual witch. Turns out, it's a lot harder than I imagined. Doing witchy things while not accidentally doing something actually witchy hurts my soul in a way I wasn't prepared for.

It's times like these I wish I could curse humans. The man in front of me gives me the ick. I'm pretty sure he deserves boils or bedbugs. Something to put him in his place. I plaster on a fake smile, reminding myself I don't know this guy from the man in the moon. He could be fine and is just having some bad luck.

I wave my hand around, my large sleeves billowing around me. "You'd like to summon the spirits? For what purpose, my child?"

"I need to convince my girlfriend to take me back. I've tried everything else, but she's not caving. Figured this might work."

"I'll need more information...in order to summon the right spirits. Why did she break up with you?" Because I know she broke up with him. It takes everything in me not to show my

emotions and keep the ethereal voice I adopt for these interactions.

He winces, then covers it with a smirk. He hems and haws, finally settling on the ridiculous excuse of lying to her. Which is code for he cheated. Definitely an asshole. Even if I desperately needed the money, I wouldn't help him. My morals won't let me. Now to find a way to get out of this without jeopardizing my reputation. I may not need his money, but I still need to pay my bills. Especially if I have to take time off soon.

"You should know, this isn't guaranteed. Also, there are risks... for you," I murmur.

"What kind of risks?" His voice wavers, and I sweep around him to put the round table in the middle of my front room between us.

"Oh, the usual. Boils, hauntings, unwanted attachments. Some demons like to meddle as well. Oh, and there's a small chance your balls will shrivel up like grapes withering on the vine," I say wistfully as I stroke the fake crystal ball. "So, shall we begin?"

I almost burst out laughing at the absolute horror blossoming across his face. He clearly didn't think about the consequences. If I were to turn my witchy powers on him, I doubt I'd be able to do even half of what I said. I've never even met a demon. I'm pretty sure they exist, but they don't just pop over for tea.

"Fuck that." He makes a break for the door, tripping over the threshold, then down the porch steps.

"Oh no. Come back," I call softly as I pad across the floor to shut the door behind him. I flick the lock just for good measure. "Douche canoe."

I peek out the front window, trying not to move the curtains. The last thing I need is them gossiping more about me. Except I'm pretty sure no one talks about when they make appointments. I'm kind of their last resort when shit goes sideways in their life. Thankfully, my client, if I can even call him that, is hurrying away. He trips over the crack in my front walk, and I stifle a cackle.

He's an asshole of the highest sort. He said his name was Jeremiah, but I think that was an alias. Most people use one even if I know who they are. Living in a small town, it isn't hard to know everyone. Even me, who didn't move here until recently, recognizes most of the residents. I doubt I'll be seeing Jeremiah around as much. Good riddance.

I collapse onto my couch and rest my head back. There are a million things I need to do today, but I'm exhausted. Between running this sham of a business and searching for the book, I don't have any energy left. I've spent too many months trying to track down the damn thing while keeping my powers under lock and key. Now, I don't think I have a choice. I'm going to have to start using some of the magic flowing through my veins to find it.

"You just had to make this hard, didn't you?" I grumble as I push to my feet. "Never could make my life easier."

I stomp from the living room, eyeing the closet door as I pass. There's no use putting off going in there. I chucked most of the odds and ends of being a witch in there as soon as I got here. It was too much of a temptation to use the spells or the candles or the potions.

I could have made things easier on the townsfolk, but then they'd know I was actually a witch. They'd blow my cover, and eventually there'd be stakes and burning, and I'm just too tired to deal with all that. Besides, I didn't want to use anything to find the book other than the brain rattling around in my head since the circle my sister left behind was a bust.

Should I be looking for an ancient text said to be forged within the deepest pits of Hell? Probably not. Am I going to stop searching? Nope. It's the only lead I have to find my sister. Most people, witch or human, would understand. Then again, most of them would have good intentions when it comes to a sibling. When I find mine, though, we're going to have words. Very short, angry words.

I finish in the bathroom and walk by the closet again on my way to the kitchen. I swear there's been knocking on the other side late at night. One time I could have sworn I heard someone cursing from inside. I wasn't about to check. Whatever happens in there isn't my business. Though, I suppose it's about to become mine soon.

As I pop a mug of cold coffee I brewed hours ago into the microwave, there's a knock on my front door. My shoulders slump, and I shuffle my way around the small dining table to peer out the window overlooking my yard. I wait, knowing my deflection spell will guide them back enough for me to see them. When no one appears, I narrow my eyes. If the spell ran out of juice, I'm going to be pissed. I was told it would take years of full moons before it would wear off. There's another thud, but I can't figure out where it comes from.

The microwave beeps behind me, and I shake my head. If I didn't know any better, I'd say I was having auditory hallucinations. My aunt always said it ran in the family, not that I saw any evidence of it. Didn't spend much time around anyone other than her and my sister, though, so I suppose anything's possible. Our other aunt disappeared long before our parents died. Maybe the rumor started with her.

I grab my coffee, wincing at the burn the cup leaves on my fingertips, then make my way to the living room. I struggle to haul the chair in front of the closet while holding my mug. A heavy sigh leaves me as I plop down and stare at the door. My nails clink against the porcelain as I contemplate how to open it. Just turning the knob would do the trick, except I'd have to deal with the magical fallout. I really don't want to get knocked on my ass or spend the next seven to ten business days wallowing in bed while my magic goes haywire.

"If only I would have thought this through beforehand," I mutter.

Except I wasn't thinking. I was pissed and overwhelmed and beating myself up for shit out of my control. I spent too long trying to recreate Lark's summoning circle and figure out where she went. By the time I gave up, I was so drained I threw everything in the closet and magicked it closed. At that point, I thought I'd never open it again. If I want to do it the right way, I'll have to wait for new candles to be delivered. Unless I want to call Jeremiah back here. I could use some of his blood. Little problematic, I suppose.

"Welp, no time like the present."

I push to my feet and set my mug on a side table. Cracking my knuckles, I bounce on the balls of my feet as I try to psych myself up. I have no idea what'll happen. I can't put it off, though. With the sun setting, I need to do this soon.

Instead, I bail, rushing from the room. For some reason, my feet carry me to the office. At least I think it was supposed to be an office. My sister turned it into something else completely. I left the space as Lark did, with the half-burned candles lining the windows and the summoning circle on the floor.

I stare at the white chalk, careful not to smudge it any more than it already is. I don't know if this is a summoning circle, which is why I need the book. It's the only spell I know for sure is in that cursed object. I'm sure there are all other sorts of nefarious spells and potions in it.

I can't even imagine what else Lark might have dabbled in. She always gravitated toward subjects we weren't supposed to. She'd scribbled down spells late at night underneath her blankets, a flame flickering from her fingertips. It wasn't until I caught her sneaking a dark arts book of spells into the house that I started to get worried. I warned her she'd go too far one day. She'd stir up shit we weren't allowed to stir up.

And now I'm afraid she's done exactly that. I can't be sure, though. The only way I'll get answers is if I can get the book, fix the circle, and follow her to wherever she went.

Finding anything else in this room isn't possible. I dig my nails into my palms and pull in a calming breath. It takes me a minute to gather a bowl and one of the black candles. I should use some

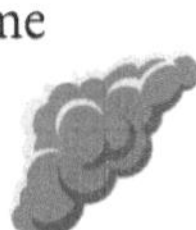

oil as well, but I'm pretty sure I stuffed that in the closet. This'll have to do. Setting all this up might not do a damn thing.

I flip off the circle before I flounce out of the room and back to the closet. Once I set everything up, it takes me a full minute of snapping my fingers for a soft flicker of flame to ignite the wick. I let out a heavy sigh and roll my shoulders to ease some of the tension. I've never spent so long without using my magic. I was afraid I lost the ability. I don't know if that's a thing, but if could happen, it would happen to me.

"Come on," I mutter at the fire, then remember I'm supposed to be gathering good vibes or whatever. "Be nice and don't knock me on my ass. I'd also prefer to keep all my hair. Fuck me, I really should have done more research before I sealed this bitch. Um, deliver something good. A breakthrough perhaps. Yeah, that'd be great. I'd rather not gallivant all over by myself searching for this."

I swallow hard, then wrap my cold hand around the knob. Heat sears through my palm and I attempt to yank it away. A tendril of purple shadows winds its way around my wrist and snakes up my arm. Despite it not hurting, my chest still tightens. The spell I used must have strengthened over time. It's the only explanation.

Something pounds on the wood from inside and the door violently rattles. I grip the knob tighter and squeeze my eyes shut. It'll be over soon. It has to be or my magic will eat me from the inside out. Already it's bubbling in my veins as the tendrils wrap around my throat. Just because they're not strangling me yet, doesn't mean they won't. My lip quivers and I grit my teeth, determined not to cry.

Time warps and nausea crawls its way up my throat. Then the world shuts off. At least, that's what it feels like. Silence permeates the space, and a shiver rolls down my back. The flame wicks out, plunging me in darkness. After a momentary panic, my vision clears and moonlight filters through the window.

I twist the knob and the door bursts open. I fly back as the smell of sulfur mixed with something sweet swirls around me. My back hits the chair and the whole thing tips over, taking me with it. A purple haze fills the air, hissing like a smoke grenade. When I try to get up, something hard crashes into me, and I let out a terrified scream.

Frantically, I shove at the heavy thing crushing my body. I thrash around, though it doesn't do anything. Whatever magical bullshit grew in the closet shouldn't be attacking me, yet here we are. I won't go down without a fight. At the very least, I'm going to go out screaming my bloody head off.

I hit something soft, and the thing above me grunts. I freeze, my palm pressed against something warm...something that feels like skin. The smoke clears enough for me to see the outline of a man—creature—being. One with small horns poking from black hair and dark grey skin.

He grins, revealing a row of sharp white teeth. "Whoops."

CHAPTER THREE
DIMITRI

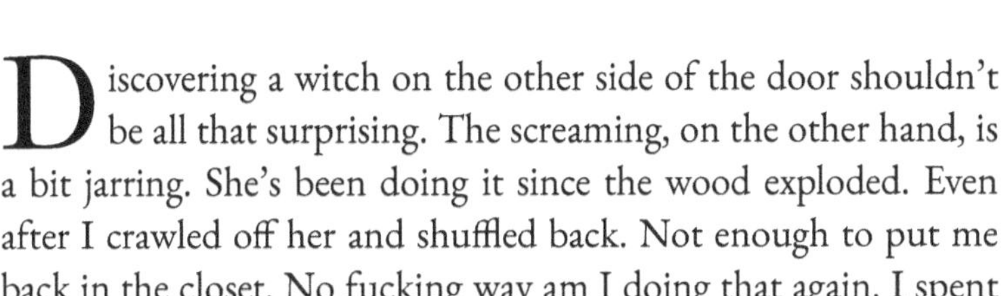

Discovering a witch on the other side of the door shouldn't be all that surprising. The screaming, on the other hand, is a bit jarring. She's been doing it since the wood exploded. Even after I crawled off her and shuffled back. Not enough to put me back in the closet. No fucking way am I doing that again. I spent enough time in there.

"Can you stop?" I wince as I shove my fingers in my ears. They're ringing and I'm going to get a migraine. Not entirely sure if demons can get migraines, but I'm not willing to risk it.

"Seriously? You break my door, wreak havoc on my life, and crush me with your heavy ass and expect *me* to stop?" She paces in front of me, and I exhale heavily.

"Wait, you think my ass is heavy?" I crane my neck to look at my ass. It's the same size it's always been.

"That's what you got out of—" She yelps, and I swing around in time to see her feet flying over her head as she crashes into the chair.

"Well, shit," I mutter, shuffling closer to help her up.

She holds up her hands, and I stop. "I'm fine."

She winces as she pushes to her feet. Huffing, she stomps across the hardwood floors and light floods the room. As much as I wondered what was on the other side of the door, I don't give two shits about the space. Not now that I'm staring at her.

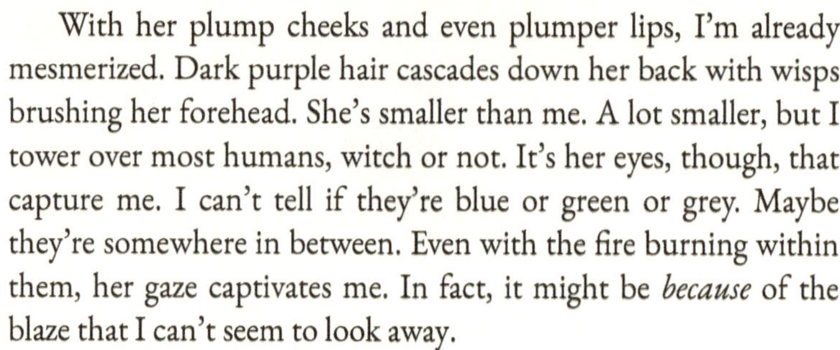

With her plump cheeks and even plumper lips, I'm already mesmerized. Dark purple hair cascades down her back with wisps brushing her forehead. She's smaller than me. A lot smaller, but I tower over most humans, witch or not. It's her eyes, though, that capture me. I can't tell if they're blue or green or grey. Maybe they're somewhere in between. Even with the fire burning within them, her gaze captivates me. In fact, it might be *because* of the blaze that I can't seem to look away.

"You're a spitfire, aren't you?" I murmur. Immediately, I wish I could stuff the words back in. If the look on her face is any indication, she's about to start hitting me again.

"Who are you? *What* are you?"

"I'm a demon. Name's Dimitri." I bow, though I don't know why. Maybe it's habit. Except when I met queens in the past, I never bowed. They didn't deserve such deference. Most of them were catty bitches who just wanted to get back at shitty men. I didn't blame them, but it didn't make me want to defer to them.

I clear my throat as I straighten. "And you are?"

"None of your business. How'd you get in the closet?"

I shrug, though she doesn't seem satisfied with that. "Demons can be summoned—"

"I didn't summon you," she snaps.

"Well, I didn't just pop up topside by myself, spitfire. I was perfectly content in Hell. Why isn't there a handle on the inside?" I glance behind me at the door still hanging open. Still no way to get out if she closed it again.

She makes a frustrated noise in the back of her throat and pokes me in the chest. I didn't even realize how close she got, and it takes everything in me not to do something I'll probably regret. I really like all my appendages attached to my body, and she seems like the type of witch to retaliate before thinking.

"I'm the one asking questions, demon," she snaps.

I glance down at her finger still buried in my chest, wishing I wouldn't have worn a shirt. "It's Dimitri."

She throws her hands up and paces away. I strain to make out

her mutterings, but she's too upset to speak clearly. Plus, I'm pretty sure my hearing is wonky from the blast. I don't know what she felt when I tumbled out of the closet. Based on the redness splashed across her cheeks, now would be a bad time to ask.

"So, where's your circle? Is it *in* the closet? Because it was too dark in there every time I got summoned." I wander closer to my temporary prison, still worried about being sucked back in.

"I never summoned you. I don't have a circle." Her voice breaks at the last word.

I raise an eyebrow as she avoids my gaze. All the fight seems to have gone out of her. It's then that I notice the dark rings under her eyes and the slight tremble in her hands. I may have thought this was a fun little banter session, but she's clearly going through something.

I clear my throat, and she glances at me, then away. "Are you okay?"

She scoffs. "As if you care. You're a demon."

"Don't know much about demons, do you?"

"I know you're..." She frowns as she scans me from head to toe. "You're grey. And from Hell. And a demon."

I fight off a smile. "So almost nothing. Got it. Well, in order for us to come topside, we need a conduit. From what I understand, the only one left is a summoning circle, which can be found in certain witchy texts. I suppose it's probably passed down from generation to generation, but it's been a bit since I last spoke with a coven leader."

"Witchy texts?"

"Oh yeah. There used to be more of them, obviously. Then that whole burning thing happened. Add in the Alexandria debacle and you lost a lot. That was about the time we started keeping records. Actually, that was Karma's idea. It was a pretty good one, but don't tell her that. I'll never hear the end of it." I sigh heavily. "An-y-ways...you don't have a circle? You a coven leader?"

"A coven—wait. You think I'm...no." Her hand slashes through the air. "No, no, no. This isn't a meeting of the minds. We're not bridging the gap between witches and demons. We're not going to try to bring our...species together in some grand gesture to save humankind or some bullshit."

I tilt my head as my mind fixates on her calling us different species. Sure, she's closer to humans than demons are, but we're largely the same. Mostly. Kind of. We have the same parts even if they don't work the same way all the time. Plus, we both have magic.

I shake my head and smile ruefully. "Wasn't asking you to bridge a gap or save humanity, spitfire. Just wondered how I got here."

"Well, I can't answer your questions. I have enough problems on my own."

"Like the douche canoe who was cheating on his girlfriend and she rightly dumped his ass? Seems like you handled that problem perfectly fine."

Her eyes grow wide. "You heard that?"

I nod, fighting another smile. "And that weird breathy thing you did with your voice that's notably absent now. It's a nice touch, I gotta say."

Her nostrils flare and her eyes narrow. "I don't have to explain myself to you, demon."

"Again with the demon? I'm beginning to think you're not listening to me. It's Dimitri. Not even a hard name to pronounce, really. Also, you're going to need it soon."

"Why on the great mother's green earth would I need your name?" she spits out.

"To send me back to Hell. Or if you needed to summon me for something."

An expressionless mask slips over her face. "What could I possibly need from you?"

"My best friend was summoned to open a jar of spaghetti sauce, so honestly it could be anything." I shrug when her mask slips into incredulity. "I don't make the rules, honey. I just break 'em when needed."

She worries her bottom lip, and I can't help but fixate on it. Whatever she needs, it won't be easy to get it out of her. I shouldn't care. I've got enough on my plate without taking on someone else's issues. Especially a cantankerous witch's issues. Except there's a heaviness in her eyes that's hard to ignore. With Omen dealing with Clara and Triton up my ass about taking on more responsibilities, I really could use the distraction. Besides, I like being topside.

When the veil between our dimensions thins, I happily bounce between the two. Never enough to put me down like these little sojourns have lately. I like discovering new food and watching humans interact. They're fascinating, really. I used to feel the same way in Hell. There was always something new to find down there. Getting away to explore new dimensions now isn't as easy. I don't mind training the new demons coming up the ranks or tracking down rogue dragons. It just gets monotonous after a while. Add in Ludovic never giving me a fucking day off and I just want to get away.

"I don't need your help. How do I send you away?" she says, pulling me back to reality.

"Um, I'm not entirely sure." I grimace as she scowls at me.

"You said I needed to know your name to send you to Hell, yet you don't know how I can accomplish that?"

I tilt my head from side to side, wondering how to explain this. "I know how to deal with a witch who used a summoning circle. For one who doesn't? Not really. Unless you're dealing in the dark arts or whatever they call it. Did you make a deal? I can work with that. In fact, I can deal with a lot of things."

"I'm sure you can," she mutters.

I smirk, though she's avoiding my gaze. "Definitely can help with most of your issues."

She shoots me a sardonic smile. "I'll pass. Go away."

I glance down, waiting for my feet to disappear or the familiar swoop in my stomach. Nothing happens. I cross my arms over my chest and let out a heavy sigh. Exhaustion hits me hard, and my body sways as my vision blurs. The last thing I need is to pass out in front of her. She'd probably throw a rug over me and pretend I was just part of the decor.

"Why don't you just say *begone demon* and we'll see if that works." While I might enjoy our banter, I won't last much longer.

"Are you—nope. Fine. Begone demon."

The swoop attacks my gut, yet something's wrong. I can't quite put my finger on what as I'm whisked off to the void. Whatever curse I'm afflicted with didn't go away when the closet opened. I just need to rest. As soon as I get some sleep, everything will right itself. I'll probably never see the witch again. That thought shouldn't bother me, but for some reason it does. I'm too tired to figure out why.

My feet slam into the hallway outside the door to my apartment. Bits of obsidian scatter across the floor. I barely make it through the entrance before I dry heave on the tiles. When I'm finally able to breathe again, I push to my feet and stagger toward my bedroom.

Omen calls his place a house, but that always felt weird to me. It's a house within a building within a dimension within Hell. It's not exactly like other worlds. There are layers upon layers of magical places to stay. At least I had the good sense to ward my space from visitors other than Omen. I wouldn't put it past some demons to just pop in whenever they felt like it.

I collapse into my bed while my head swims. I'll either end up falling asleep immediately or puking all over my sheets. There will be no in-between. As my eyes flutter closed, a strange tugging in my chest jolts me upright. Exhaustion swamps me and I flop back once more. Whatever curse this is, I need to figure it out quick.

Maybe the little spitfire witch could cure me. It's my last thought before darkness takes me.

CHAPTER FOUR
MARI

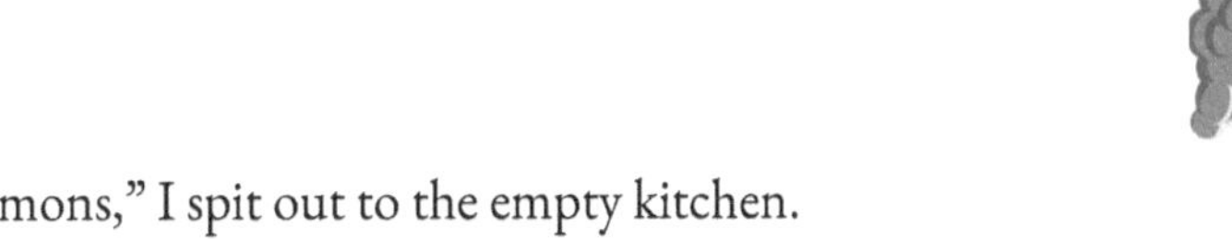

"Demons," I spit out to the empty kitchen.

I slam the lid on the pot filled with simmering soup. It won't be ready for another half hour, but my stomach rumbles out its displeasure, anyway. I put off eating too long. Again. One of these days I'll remember my body can't run off spite and caffeine. Today's a wash, but there's always tomorrow. Or next week. It's always better to start new habits on a Monday.

"I swear if he shows up again..."

Except I promised myself I wouldn't be thinking about Dimitri—*no, the demon*—yet here I am, still cursing his lingering presence in my mind. If he would have just left when I first told him, I wouldn't be in this mess. I don't know what bull honkey he was shoveling about not being able to leave. I didn't summon him. I had no control over where he went or what he did. That thought should probably terrify me.

Regardless of whether or not it was my sister's summoning circle that brought him here, I've stayed far away from it. I thought about using magic to seal it like I did with the closet. It's the only link I have to finding her, though. Unless I could find the book. Dimitri, *the demon*, mentioned other texts. He was pretty much babbling by that point so I'm not entirely sure if I believe him. Plus, he's a demon. They can't be trusted.

Still, he wasn't what our mother described at all. He wasn't

ten feet tall or wearing the bones of witches he'd devoured. His horns weren't huge and curling around his head. Nor did he seem to have wings or a tail. He didn't even have blood red skin made of the hardest substance within hell. When he fell on me, he was hard, but no more than a human. And his flesh was grey, though I'm pretty sure I spotted a hint of purple.

"The same color as my hair," I murmur, then shake my head.

No use making connections between us. We're not connected. At all.

If anything, he's linked to my sister. She's the one with the faulty summoning circle. She's the one who was dabbling in dark magic. She's the one who took a little fight and went off the deep end in retaliation. Bitch.

As soon as I find her, we're going to have some words, then I'm going to kick her ass. She always goes to the extremes in every aspect of her life. From when we were nine and she was convinced she could surf down a raging river to investing all her money in some random digital investment. She never thinks things through and expects me to save her ass. Every. Fucking. Time.

It's exhausting, but I'm not about to leave my little sister to the wolves. Or the demons, I suppose.

The lid rattles, bringing me back to the present, and I rip it off, then drop it on the counter. Thoughts of my mysterious demon filter through my head once more. I tap my finger against my chin as I stare at the steam curling off the soup.

He'd probably know how to find the book. I don't have to tell him the whole story. He doesn't even need to know *which* book I'm searching for. Maybe he's got some hellish library I could...no, that would require me to *go* to Hell. I'd do a lot for my sister, but dying just to find a book, then to come back as some type of specter and...no. That wouldn't work at all. Perhaps the demon could help, though.

Huffing, I press the heels of my hands into my eyes. Pressure has been building in my head all day. No amount of hot showers or cold compresses has helped. I finally broke down an hour ago and took pain meds, but they haven't touched the pounding within my skull. It's been like this every day since I unsealed the closet. I unleashed the magic, and it's burrowed its way into my body, sucking the very life from me. Hence the soup.

I added as many herbs as I could think of to calm the magic inside me. The scent of creamy potatoes and fresh basil wafts through the air, and I inhale deeply. One of these remedies has to work or I'm going to lose it. I can't handle the constant ache much longer.

"This is all that demon's fault," I mutter. "Excuse me, *Dimitri*."

I spit out his name like the curse that it is. Should I be tempting karma by being an asshole about him? Probably not. I figure she can't wreak much more on me, anyway. She's been fucking with me for a lifetime, no matter how good of a witch I was. She's just got it out for me.

Slowly, I ease myself to the floor and prop my elbows on my knees with my head in my hands. A groan leaves me as my heart beats in my ears.

"Problems, spitfire?" His deep voice rolls over me.

"I'm fine," I whisper. I'm not even surprised he's here. Three days isn't nearly enough time for things to go back to normal.

"Are you on your period?" he asks gently.

I drop my hands, ready to yell at him, or burst into tears, I don't know which. Except his gaunt face stops me. His dull black eyes don't seem to be able to focus. Yet there's a compassion in their depths I've rarely seen before in others. I didn't really think about demons being able to feel things like sympathy. Especially while they're suffering like Dimitri clearly is.

"What happened to you?" I ask, though the words come out soft and slightly pathetic—not concerned. Definitely not.

He gives me a half-hearted smile as he crouches in front of me. "Nothing a nap won't fix. You?"

I could lie. Or say the banishing words to get him to go away again. Hell, ignoring him would probably do the trick. He

reminds me of a puppy, eager to please and hyperactive until you rebuff them. Then they hide with their tails between their legs. For some reason, I can't do it.

"Headache," I murmur, then wince as the edges of his body blur. I don't know if it's my vision or some demon-y thing. Demonic? Demon-y? Is that even a word? I dig my knuckles into my temples and wait for the pulsing to subside.

"Seems more like a migraine. It's sucked all the fire right out of you, huh?" He pushes to his feet and peers into the pot. His nostrils flare as he inhales deeply, then hums as he exhales. "I'm not one to invite myself to dinner, but I have a feeling you'll break something if you're left to your own devices."

I roll my eyes, then squeeze them shut. "I'm perfectly capable of taking care of myself."

When I peek at him, he's swirling the ladle around. "I'm sure you are, spitfire."

"Why the hell are you calling me that? I have a fucking name, you know."

"Except you haven't *told* me your name. And while I could call you witch, like you call me demon, it's a bit demeaning to strip you down to the magic inside you."

Heat floods my cheeks, and I mumble something even *I* can't understand. It's halfway between an excuse and an apology. He lifts his hand while still leaning over the pot. I swear if he gets any closer, he'll stick his nose right in and snort the soup. If he ruins it, I just might cry. I can't take one more setback.

He snaps his fingers, and I grimace. Such a small sound shouldn't hurt as much as it does. A bowl appears in his hand, and he hums a happy tune as he dishes himself some herby goodness. I drop my chin to my chest, bracing myself to push to my feet. I should tell him to get the fuck out. Except I already dismissed that idea. At least I think I did. My head hurts too much to remember.

"Up you get," he murmurs, and his hands slide under my arms. I don't even have it in me to care.

"I can—"

"I know you can. Doesn't mean you will. You can banish me after some soup. Because if you do it before I get to taste it, I just might cry."

He tries to guide me toward the small breakfast nook, but my feet won't work. Maybe I am cursed. I know magic demands a cost. It was hammered into us by our aunt since we were young. Except I'm not supposed to be the one suffering. Maybe that's why Dimitri looks so gaunt. I don't know if demons take on the magical burden when shit goes sideways. I'd ask him, but I'm afraid I'll puke all over the floor, and I doubt he'd clean it up.

He scoops me up, and a strangled cry leaves me. He shushes me like I'm a child throwing a tantrum. By the time I open my mouth to cuss him out, he's already settled me in the chair and whisked away. A bowl appears in front of me, and the sweet scent wafts through the air. I inhale, letting the familiar smell comfort me.

"Well shit," he breathes, and I glance up. Dimitri's wasted no time digging into the soup, and he's too preoccupied to notice my attention.

I drop my gaze to my own bowl and gather my spoon. Only his occasional muttered exclamations and the utensils hitting the ceramic punctuate the silence that settles between us. I probably should be more freaked out. Or worried he's about to eat me. Instead, there's a sense of calm I haven't felt since I discovered my sister missing. I'll chalk it up to the food and the migraine.

"I didn't realize you could eat human food," I murmur, and his spoon clatters into the empty bowl.

"Now why would you ruin a perfectly good meal with that question?" He scowls at me, then shakes his head.

"For once, I wasn't trying to be offensive," I snap, though my ire is muted.

He rolls his eyes, then stomps his way to the pot to refill his bowl. "Weren't you taught about demons? Thought witches had training and books and all that."

He drops into the chair once more and immediately inhales the food. I almost point him in the direction of a measuring cup but stop myself.

"We're not friends," I mumble. "We don't need to have a heart-to-heart. Just eat your soup and then you can leave."

He tilts his head back and forth. "*Or...*"

"No, no *or*. We're just going to eat in silence, then go our separate ways. You should be grateful I'm feeding you in the first place. Actually, you should be grateful my body hates me and I can't fight back."

"Wasn't fighting you, spitfire. I'm not exactly in a position to do anything other than eat and pass the fuck out." He taps the spoon against the rim, then stops when I glare at him. "What do you know about curses?"

"Uh, they're shitty?"

"Obviously. Do you know how to break them?"

I shrug, then wince at the tightness in my shoulders. "Depends on the curse. Just like the price of dark magic."

"You realize it's not really dark, right? It's about balance—"

I hold up my spoon. "Do not lecture me."

"Except you—"

"Well aware. But do you honestly expect us to go around explaining balance and neutrality every time we talk about the other side of magic? What a ludicrous notion. I swear, every time some yahoo comes along, they think they know better than us. Even when I'm faking it, making up all the rules, they still want to argue."

He sits back and crosses his arms. I resist the urge to do the same. Instead, I tuck my knee closer to my chest and huddle over my bowl. I forgot—forgot that he's a demon, that he could crush my skull with one hand, that he could smite me. Wait, I think that's the other guy. Whatever, a demon could probably do it. He was right when he questioned how much I knew about them. My aunt always said the words were best left unspoken. Lark and I always thought she meant it literally. Maybe she was wrong.

"Seems to me you could use some education on demons." He holds up his hand when I start to object. "And I could use some help with curses. Wouldn't it be better to work together instead of bickering? From the looks of it, you could definitely use some help. I'm sure I don't look much better."

"Well, that was insulting," I mutter, glancing away.

He gives me a look I can't decipher. "We could help each other."

"No," I snap as I push to my feet and gather my dishes. I'm halfway to the sink when he sighs heavily.

"Why not?"

I drop the bowl onto the counter and spin around, planting my hands on my hips. "You hid in my closet for weeks—"

"Wasn't hiding," he mutters.

"You crashed into me when I finally opened it."

"Didn't really have a choice."

I plow onward, trying to ignore his interruptions. "Then you acted like my house was the new vacation spot."

"I'd probably pick the beach for vacation. Or the moun—"

"And then you showed up tonight without warning."

"Not my fault."

"Would you stop?" I cry, and the fight drains out of me. "I don't know who you are. Or why you were in my closet. Logically, I should be terrified. I should electrocute you or something. I should be cowering under the covers waiting for the thing that goes bump in the night to eat me."

His lip twitches, and I swear if he makes some dirty joke I'm going to hex him—see how his pretty face looks covered with oozing boils. He'd probably pull it off somehow. Pretty bastard. Maybe that's what I'll call him since he insists on giving me a nickname.

"You know, if we helped each other, we get to know each other. And then we wouldn't be strangers anymore."

I narrow my gaze at the note of desperation in his voice. Questions roll through my mind. What's his motive? Why is he so

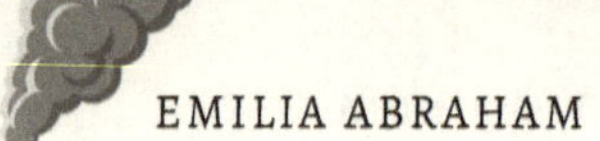

insistent? How does he keep getting in here? The longer I stare at him, the more pile up, yet I shove them all away. I don't need answers. I need a shower and a nap and a break.

"I'd rather be strangers. You can begone or whatever," I say, waving my hand as I stumble from the kitchen.

I don't really care if he's here when I come back or not. I just can't be bothered. As I get in the shower, though, I realize how nice it was to eat with someone else. Getting used to it would be disastrous. I vow not to think about him ever again.

CHAPTER FIVE
DIMITRI

I wonder at what point I should tell her I didn't disappear.

As the shower starts up, I let out a heavy sigh, then push to my feet. I gather up my dishes and take them to the sink. I end up puttering around her small kitchen instead of venturing into the rest of the house. She looked sick, and I doubt she'll want to clean up this mess when she's done avoiding me.

I find containers shoved into a cupboard for the leftover soup. By the time I've put it away and wiped down the counters, I'm exhausted. Bouncing between dimensions is tiring at the best of times. Add in a curse and even these simple tasks drag me down.

As I rinse the bowls, a squeal erupts from the bathroom down the hall. At least I'm assuming it's the bathroom. Maybe I shouldn't have turned on the hot water. Quickly, I stick everything in the dishwasher, thankful I actually spent time topside. Otherwise, I'd be out of my depth here.

With nothing else to do, I wander through the archway, past a staircase leading to what I assume is a basement, and finally into the living room. A table is set up in the corner with an obviously fake crystal ball and a set of regular playing cards. When I get closer, I see a paper propped up with a list of her services. They're all ridiculous and not things witches do. At least, I don't think they do.

It's then I notice the picture at the top. A crescent moon with

a name—*her* name. Mari Mystic. Laughter bubbles up within me, despite the tightness in my muscles. From the short encounters we've had, I'm not surprised by her ridiculous choice of a name. Her services, though, leave something to be desired.

"Love potions. Banishing weeds and vermin. Time travel. Prevent balding?" I snort, then bite back a groan as pain lances through my temples.

The nap in Hell helped, but it wasn't enough. Nothing seems to be enough. The closest I've been to any semblance of peace was when I was eating. I doubt it had anything to do with Mari's presence. She was cantankerous at best.

Despite her rejection of my proposition, I still believe she's the key to overcoming this affliction. I'm fully convinced I'm cursed at this point. Providence practically confirmed it. Not that she's very forthcoming about such things. Omen's sister plays her cards extremely close to the chest. It's annoying how alike she and Omen are.

There's a tug in my gut, and I brace myself to be whisked away to the next place. When nothing happens, I drop to the couch and lean my head back. My eyes flutter shut, and I fold my hands over my stomach. I'll only rest until Mari comes out and sends me back to Hell properly.

After the world's shortest nap, a pillow smacks me in the face and jolts me awake. A string of incoherent curses leaves me as it tumbles off my lap.

"Get up and get out," she snaps, then stomps from the room.

I push to my feet and follow her down the hallway. I'm not about to bust into her bedroom, but I don't want to get attacked again. I pass several closed doors and fight back curiosity. If she wasn't so pissed at me for merely existing, I'd peek inside the rooms. Maybe they'd reveal some of the secrets she's keeping. I can't bring myself to invade her privacy like that, though.

Her door looms ahead, and I stare at the dark wood. I don't know whether to knock or wait for her to come out again. Sighing, I end up rapping my knuckles lightly. A muttered curse filters through the air, and I fight a grin. Maybe she is making me feel better. I fix my face as she appears, glaring at me.

"Was I not clear?"

"See you've got some of your fire back, *Mari.*" I smirk, and she rolls her eyes.

"Oh good for you, you've discovered my name. Why haven't you left?"

I lean against the doorframe, and her body sways like she can't decide to fall into me or run away. The latter would require her to slip out the window, and I doubt she'll take that option.

"Leaving would require you to actually release me. Get out, leave, or fuck off doesn't really do anything other than hurt my feelings. Did you give any thought to my proposal while you were showering?"

She narrows her eyes. "Stop it."

I'm caught in her gaze, realizing her eyes are more grey than blue today. "Stop what?"

"Stop thinking about—never mind. It doesn't matter. My answer is the same as before. We're strangers and we're going to keep it that way. How do I stop you from coming back?"

I shrug, though she doesn't seem satisfied with that. If she doesn't have a summoning circle and she didn't use an ancient spell, I don't know why I'm randomly showing up here. I've gone through all the Hellish options. If it were someone down there, I wouldn't be popping into Mari's house over and over. They'd throw me into a volcano, then drop me into the depths of the ocean. Or they'd find the most crotchety old witch who would curse me—then again, I'm cursed regardless, so I doubt it would matter.

She huffs and I raise an eyebrow. "Well?"

"Well what? I don't have answers. I'm a demon, not a god. I don't have that kind of pull. I could call my sister, but I'm pretty sure she'd either ignore me or make fun of me." I run a hand through my hair. "Besides, you *really* don't want to meet her."

Mari snorts, glancing away. "Demons don't have sisters."

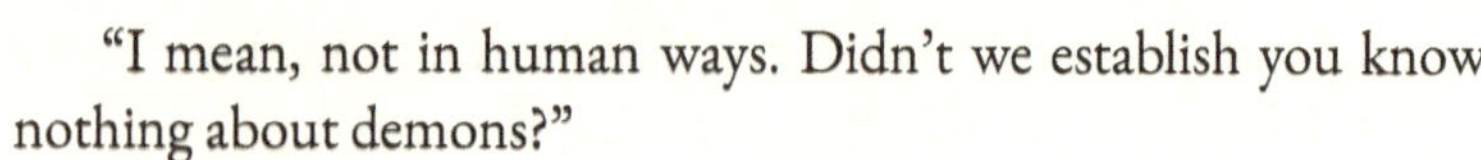

"I mean, not in human ways. Didn't we establish you know nothing about demons?"

"Fine. Who is she, Death or something?" She smirks, though I don't know why.

"Death doesn't have a brother. Or siblings as far as I know. They mostly keep to themselves. Karma, though, she'll get you every time."

Confusion colors her eyes, and she opens her mouth, then snaps it shut. "I'm...why am I even talking to you? Just walk out the front door or something."

I glance over my shoulder. Not that I can see the front door from here. "If I'm bound to you, I won't be able to. Could try it, though. Can I take some soup with me? Human food hits different."

Her brows pull low. "Demons are weird. I don't care if you take the whole damn fridge. Just leave before...just leave."

I jump back just in time to not get squished by the door. "Yeah, I'll get right on that."

As I spin gently, pain stabs into my chest. I double over and stumble into the wall. Electricity crackles across my skin. Squeezing my eyes shut, I focus on slowing my breathing. At this point, I doubt I'll make it to the living room, much less outside. My stomach rolls, and I groan as shadows swirl around me.

And then it's over. The pain evaporates along with the shadows. The nausea subsides and my vision clears. My magic goes silent as if someone flipped a switch inside me. No hum. No crackle. No power. Panic swamps me, and I brace my palms on my knees. In all the centuries I've been alive, I've never felt this before. I've never even *heard* of this before. This isn't a curse or a summoning gone wrong. I need answers, but I won't get them from Mari. As much as I want to pick her brain, she doesn't want me around. No amount of charm will change her mind.

"Seriously?" she mutters behind me.

I glance over my shoulder, and the world vanishes.

CHAPTER SIX
MARI

I toss and turn for most of the night, yet I can't get Dimitri's words out of my head.

He spoke of Death and Karma like they were real people. Maybe not people, per se. Definitely living beings, though. I never really gave much thought to demons beyond what Aunt Star had said. She refused to answer Lark's and my questions, so we figured out pretty quickly not to ask.

Lark never could leave well enough alone, though. She's fascinated with the darker side of things, whether it be demons and Hell or dark spells. It's why I'm sure she got herself into something when she fucked off to gods-knows-where. Should I be saving her? No. But she owes me and I'm not about to let her die with her debts unpaid. Plus, it wouldn't be very sisterly for me to leave her to her fate.

I stare at the shadowy ceiling, too tired to reach over and turn off the lamp. It would probably help me sleep. Then again, every time I close my eyes, I'm plagued with images I don't understand. A dark cage surrounded by even darker stone walls. A closet filled with cleaning supplies. In one there's an iridescent egg, much bigger than I'm used to. Another one has a hooded figure stalking through a misty landscape. I'm sure if I fell asleep right now, I'd be subjected to the images come to life.

The soup may have helped whatever illness is assaulting my

body, but nightmares would send me straight back. My shower earlier did absolutely nothing, mostly because *he* was loitering about. It's like I could feel his presence hanging around. I still don't understand why he keeps showing up. I don't even have any texts to consult. My internet searches came up empty.

I slam my palms on the fluffy comforter. "Ridiculous. Stop thinking about him. He's a demon."

A very sexy demon, my mind whispers. It sounds like my sister's voice, which is annoying as hell.

"Doesn't matter what he looks like."

But he's sweet. He fed you.

I scoff, rolling my eyes. "He didn't feed me. He served me, maybe. I made the damn soup myself, thank you very much."

I don't know why I'm arguing with myself. It's not like it'll change anything. I'll still be stuck in this fucking town, on a fool's errand with a demon trailing me. Unless I never see him again. He did walk right into a purple cloud of smoke and disappear. Maybe magic or the balance or whatever decided I'd suffered enough.

Except he looked like he was suffering too.

A groan escapes me, and I squeeze my eyes shut. "And that's my problem, how?"

The voice doesn't answer. Because of course it doesn't. It's me, not my sister, and I don't have any answers. If I did, I'd love to be able to solve all my problems just by talking to myself. If I could pluck solutions out of thin air, my life would be very different. I sit up and glance around the shadowy room.

It's too early to get up, yet too late to go to sleep. I opt for rising and shining, though I doubt they'll be much shining going on. Once I'm dressed, I drag myself to the kitchen and make a cup of coffee. As the hot liquid slides down my throat, my muscles relax. My head may be pounding and my chest may be tight, but I've got caffeine and that makes all the difference.

For about seventeen seconds.

Then it all crashes down as someone pounds on my front door. If it's an angry mob, I'm going to lose it. I've never cursed someone before, but I'll do it if they try to burn me at the stake. Jeremiah wasn't particularly happy with my threats. I doubt he'd be about to rile up the community, though. It's a small town, yet not enough to back an asshole for no reason.

I shuffle toward the window overlooking the porch. When a crowd doesn't appear, I sigh, then pull open the door. Percy, my only friend in this town, shoves past me with a frustrated growl.

"Come right on in," I mutter as I swing the door closed.

"You're not naked, so…" She flops onto my couch.

"And if I had somewhere to be?" I ask, crossing my arms.

She snorts, peering at me from under her lashes. "You never go anywhere other than the mailbox. You even have your groceries delivered by the little old lady who lives at the end of the lane."

"You sound like you're quoting a nursery rhyme." I collapse into the wingback chair I use when I'm working. "Wait, it's like five in the morning. Why are you here at the ass crack of dawn?"

"Shit's going to hell. Needed to get out of my hovel."

I glance at her and realize there are dark rings under her eyes. She looks as bad as I feel. My nostrils flare when I spot the dark bruises peeking from under her sleeves. Someone grabbed her—hard. I grit my teeth, knowing I can't ask her about them. She'll brush off my questions, then clam up. Waiting for her to reveal what happened isn't ever easy.

I clear my throat. "Gonna tell me what's going on?"

"Lost my job. Date was a bust. Saw my mother. Pipes in my bathroom burst and flooded the entire upstairs. Car broke down, though that one I don't really care about. Oh, and I got scammed out of a bunch of money. So, not much." She lists everything off so flippantly, I wonder if she's making half of it up. I know she's not, though. Percy is honest to a fault.

"Why's it always you?" I mutter.

She shrugs, closing her eyes again. "Karma hates me. Look into my future and destiny will show you doom and gloom. Fate has it out for me. My ancestors must have been bad witches or some shit. I know they cursed a random dude who ended up

being important. Maybe that's the reason I'm being punished in this life."

"So dramatic." My eyes dart to the closet, then back to Percy. "You want advice, to vent, or silence?"

"Advice because I know you're *dying* to give me some." She softens her words with a slight smile.

"Positively perishing over here. Okay, get a new job. Put a hex on the date, then stop dating. Stop going to see your mother. She's toxic personified, and you're better off keeping her at a distance. Hire a plumber." I hold up my hand when she makes a sound of protest. "No, you're not capable of fixing it yourself. Your car isn't broken down. It needs a new battery, which I told you two weeks ago. And how much money are we talking?"

Her nose wrinkles. "I'm not hexing someone. That seems messy."

"Out of everything I said, *that's* what you latch onto? Seriously, Percy. Everything is fixable until it's not."

"It was five hundred," she mumbles as she picks at the fluff on my pillow.

"What was the scam?"

She rolls her eyes, and I know this'll probably be the last answer I get out of her. "A golf cart. It was a great price, said it was an estate sale, then *poof*, he ghosted me. Do you think ghosts are real? I mean, witches are real. *Obviously*. But do you think there are like, ghosts and werewolves and vampires, too?"

"I think it's more likely bigfoot is real rather than vampires."

She shoots upright, wide eyes finding mine. "Have I shown you my cryptid folder? I've been researching them, and I swear some of these stories aren't just stories. They're eyewitness accounts. Can you imagine going camping and suddenly you find bigfoot bumbling around? Honestly, sounds like a dream."

"A dream? To go camping? You're not exactly...outdoorsy."

"I can learn."

"To camp?" I snort, and she bursts out laughing.

She wipes her eyes of nonexistent tears and sighs. "You're

right. There's no way I'm running away to live in the woods. I'd take a nice, wounded werewolf, though. Or a demon."

If she was paying attention, she'd be able to read my face like a book. Thankfully, she's too busy giggling to herself. I clear my throat, forcing my breathing to even out.

"You definitely don't want to meet a demon."

"You're probably right. I'm going to take a shower. Then we can talk about your latest victim."

She pushes off the couch, and I groan. She shoots me a cheeky grin, then flounces off down the hallway, her shawl billowing behind her. I've borrowed that one before when I ran a seance. Not that we were truly communicating with the dead, but they didn't need to know that. They weren't very nice, so I had no problem taking their money.

It's the ones who are truly seeking solace I turn away. Except for the neighbor who brings me groceries. In exchange, I whip up a simple tonic to make her life easier. It's a good exchange and helps my credibility among the townspeople. Have to have a couple wins or people get suspicious. I doubt they really think I'm a witch, though.

I flop onto the vacated couch, and my eyes flutter shut. I need sleep. I won't get any with Percy hanging around or my mind refusing to cooperate. I peek at the closet and bite my lip. After a few minutes, I can't take it anymore and I push to my feet. Percy's singing echoes over the noise from the shower, and my stomach flips.

If Dimitri is hiding in the closet, I'm going to have to explain to my best friend why I'm hanging out with a demon.

"No, I'm not hanging out with him. He just shows up. And he's not in the closet." I suck in a deep breath, then turn the knob and rip open the door.

Nothing jumps out and there's no billowing purple smoke. Just a bunch of candles, a defunct cauldron, and some winter things I don't need anymore. Half of it is my sister's shit. I just don't have the heart to go through any of it. Or the things in her

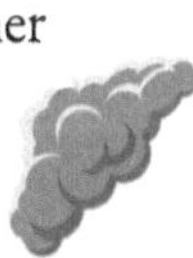

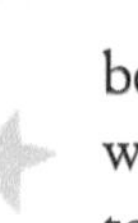

bedroom. I took over the guest room and left hers exactly as it was when she disappeared. It's a relic of a moment in time. I can't bear to mess with it until I know what happened to her.

A soft glow floats in the deep corner, and I lean in to get a better look.

"Searching for something?"

I jump back straight into Percy, then spin around. "What the fuck. Why the hell would you do that?"

She grins, her head tottering from side to side. The towel wrapped around her head unravels, then drops to the floor. She kicks the fabric to the side.

As she makes her way to the kitchen, she calls over her shoulder, "Won't find any answers in there, Mariweather."

I roll my eyes and shut the door. "Not my name."

She knows it's not, but her guesses get more and more ridiculous as the years go by. "If you'd just tell me, then we wouldn't have to go through this all the time."

"Everyone calls me Mari. My aunt, my sister, my professors in uni, my friends—"

"You have friends?" she quips as she pulls pans and food from their respective places.

"Hardee har." I collapse onto the chair and tuck my legs up.

"Pretty sure I'm your *only* friend."

"Way to rub it in. You realize if I told you what my actual name is, I wouldn't have any secrets left?"

She drops a pan onto the stove, obscuring her response. It doesn't matter. We've had this conversation a thousand times before. And it always ends the same way—her saying secrets don't make friends. Then I'll say my friends know the secrets that count, and she'll once again act surprised I have friends. It's a tale as old as time.

Even though my nail beds hurt and my muscles are fraying and my bones are slowly being ground to dust, it's good to have her here. Anything to keep my mind busy. Today I'll focus on just being with my friend. She'll feed me and I'll feel better. We'll sit

on the couch watching campy horror movies while downing an entire tub of ice cream. The usual.

And at no point will I be worried about the closet. The demon has no place in my life. He's vanished and I'm perfectly okay with that. Even if he could help me find my sister, I don't need, nor want, his help. I'll find her on my own like I planned to do all along.

Percy drops a plate in front of me, and the distinct smell of bacon wafts up. My mouth waters at the feast. She takes the chair Dimitri sat in and I shake my head, pushing him from my mind. He's long gone, back to Hell and out of my life for good.

At least I hope he is.

CHAPTER SEVEN
DIMITRI

I emerge from the void groggy and disoriented. It takes me too long to figure out where I am. It's not the cage, thank fuck. As I glance around, I realize I'm at the gauntlet. At least it's quiet—deathly quiet. Triton must be doing something else with the younger demons. Probably showing them how to travel between dimensions. I'm suddenly very grateful I don't have to help this time around.

Most of the time, I like training the new ones. They're all awkward and don't know their ass from their elbow. Running the gauntlet is exhilarating. Plus, it's better than most tasks Ludovic gives me. Part of me wants to oust Triton from his job. Fuck knows there's plenty of demons coming up through the ranks. We could use some more leaders. I doubt Ludovic will approve, and right now, I'm too discombobulated to persuade him.

I do have to talk to Omen, though. Triton's been asking where the hell he is, and I don't really have answers that don't include ratting out my friend. Which means I have to find him soon to warn him.

I gather my magic and skip through the edges of the void to my bedroom. At least it's easier to jump between spaces in Hell, otherwise I would have been dumped off in a pit or something. As I drag myself to the bathroom, my mind keeps wandering back to Mari. I don't think she's as committed to having nothing to do

with me as she seemed. If she hadn't talked herself out of it, I bet she would've taken me up on my offer.

I'm halfway through showering when pain stabs through my head and I press my fists to my skull. The hot spray hits the back of my neck, easing the throbbing slightly. I can't keep going like this. I might have to talk to someone other than Mari about this. Not my sister. I wasn't joking when I said Karma wouldn't truly help. I could ask Providence, Omen's sister. She might have some insight.

As I dry off, the light overhead flickers. I narrow my gaze on the hanging pendant, daring it to go haywire. It's not electricity like they have topside. No, this runs purely on magic, which would be great if I didn't have that shit running through my veins. Other demons don't seem to understand how annoying it is. Not that I complain about it. I keep shit to myself. It's easier than people jumping my shit for being down. The last time I showed the slightest bit of crankiness, Triton thought I was dying.

I rest my forehead against the marble door, letting the cold seep into my skin. Mari wouldn't be able to slam this one in my face. It'd probably be too heavy for her. I wonder if Clara's still in Hell. If she is, Omen's going to have some explaining to do. He can't hide her forever. Humans, especially witches, aren't easy to hide down here. Someone always feels the disturbance in the balance.

After pulling on a pair of jeans and a shirt I swiped from topside, I go searching for Omen. I could jump straight to his door, but I only do that when it's an emergency. Being cursed doesn't really count. I haven't even decided whether I'm going to tell him. Warning him about Triton doesn't count as urgent either.

I take the stairs up to one of the main hallways and immediately veer to the left. Ludovic's familiar horns catch the light as he talks to some other demons. I use a group of them to hide my movements, and I slip through an unknown door. The main passageways may stay put, but the rest take turns disappearing. I should look into who fucks with them. Might lead to some interesting information I could use later.

With a sliver of light filtering through the crack I leave, I catch sight of Omen stalking through the crowd. Others scramble out of his way, though he doesn't notice. He never understood why others were intimidated by him. His resting bitch face is on point. While I'm more likely to grin at someone, he's more likely to scowl. Maybe that's why we're friends—opposites attract or whatever.

As he passes, I step out and he gives me a startled look. I latch onto his arm and yank him into the dark room. I flip on the light, then get a good look at his face. He's clearly not doing well.

"We've gotta stop meeting like this," I say with a grin.

"Get to the point, Dimitri," he snaps.

I glance around as my muscles tense. "You think they actually use any of these cleaning supplies? I mean, it's not like Thursdays are for deep cleaning."

"We don't even have Thursdays in Hell."

I tilt my head and realize he's right. Traveling between dimensions screws with my sense of time. Not that time is linear. None of it ever lines up, which is usually great for my chaotic brain. Right now, it's messing with my head. I contemplate what to talk to him about first and settle on his issues instead of mine.

"Suppose so. Anyway, what exactly did you do with her after I poofed?"

"I took care of her," he growls.

"Well, that isn't ominous," I mutter.

He grits his teeth, and I wonder if I've pushed him too far. He's clearly going through some shit. If he'd just stop fighting his feelings, he wouldn't be in this position. He clearly wants his little witch. I don't see what the big deal is. My thoughts latch onto Mari, and I shake my head. Her and Clara are nothing alike, just like Omen and me. Drawing parallels between our situations will only drive me batty.

"You figure out where you're getting summoned to?" he asks, and I wrinkle my nose, then glance away. "Are you glowing?"

My gaze snaps back to his. "What? No. Why the fuck would I be glowing? It's not like anything happened to make me light up. I haven't been anywhere." I'm babbling, but I can't seem to stop myself even as his brows pull lower the more I talk. "I mean, other than the closet in some random witch's house. At least, I assume they're a witch. I mean, what else could it be?"

"What the fuck is wrong with you?"

I smirk. "Who, me? Nothing. I told you it's nothing."

I'm fucking this up. My magic's going haywire, there's a weird pulsing in my chest, and Omen doesn't look like he's buying a damn word I'm saying. *Doth protest too much* or whatever that human said. Now I really can't tell him about Mari. He'll just tell me to stay away from her, that nothing good comes from consorting with witches. And he certainly won't have any advice on how to deal with this curse.

"Holy shit," he breathes, and I brace myself. "Did you get cursed?"

"What? No." I force out a laugh.

"Then why's your voice all squeaky and high?" He grips the back of his neck and glances at the ceiling. "First Clara, now you. I just can't catch a fucking break."

This is exactly what I wanted to avoid. He doesn't have time to take on my problems. It's not even that big of a deal. So what if I randomly get sucked into the void and randomly get stabbing pains and light up like a freaking constellation exploding? It's nothing I can't handle on my own. And if this is my life for the foreseeable future, it's fine. My mind finally fully registers what he said, and my mouth drops open.

"Wait, Clara's cursed too?" I grimace when he gives me a look. "Fine, I *might* be. What's wrong with Clara? Is she still here?"

I may not be able to figure out my own issues, but concentrating on Omen's might snap me out of this. At the very least,

it'll focus Omen and maybe he'll keep her around. She seemed nice the very few times I met her—exactly what Omen needs.

"I'm not telling you shit. It'll only get both of us in trouble."

I tap my finger on my chin, more to get the nervous energy out than anything, then nod. "Fine, but you know you're going to need my help. Especially if she's cursed."

He doesn't need my help. I'm talking out of my ass, and he probably knows it. Then again, he might be so distracted he won't call me out on my bullshit. I need something to latch onto, though.

He runs his hand through his hair. "She's not cursed. She's spell sick."

A grin splits my face despite a numbness spreading from my fingers and up my arms. "Omen, seriously? You know what to do. She's spell sick and you're her soulbound. Do the freaky and she'll be better."

He doesn't deny they're soulbound, just stares at me with a blank expression. I suspected it a while ago based on how he was acting. Especially when he put me in the wall. What I can't figure out is why he's still fighting his feelings. They're meant to be together—mated despite time and dimensions. They're bound in a way few understand and even fewer find. If *I* had a soulbound, I'd hold on to them as tightly as I could. I wouldn't push them away. Except I've never been in his position, so maybe I would. I doubt I'll ever have the chance to find out.

He scrubs his hands down his face and mumbles, "You did not just call it the freaky."

"Oh ho, I did," I laugh. "How you think she got spell sick?"

"She's got a book."

"A grimoire?" I wouldn't be surprised. A lot of witches had them when the world was younger.

He shakes his head. "Not exactly. I've got an idea where it came from, but that shit is sentient. The fucking thing keeps fucking with reality."

I think about pointing out he used fucking twice in one

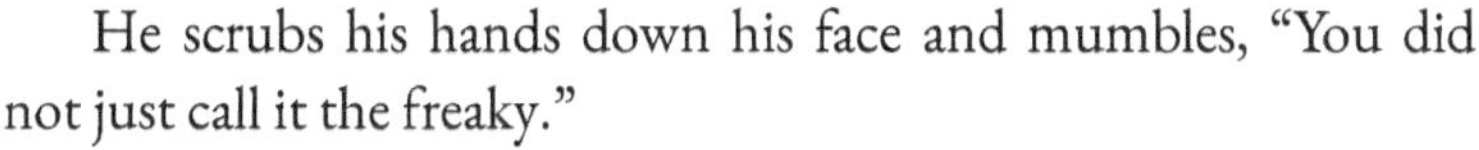

sentence, but I don't think he'd appreciate it. Plus, I have no room to talk. "Yet it got you and her together."

"Won't mean shit if the book keeps showing her spells to make her sick."

I roll my eyes. "Already told you how to help with that. Now, go get your girl."

I push him around, then slap his ass before I shove him out the door. Staying in here while he talks about a sentient book isn't wise. If it's the same tome I'm thinking of, we're in deeper shit than I thought. The thing is supposed to be under lock and key. Not floating around topside with an unsuspecting witch. And now I'm going to have to travel into the depths of Hell. I really don't want to go down there. It's dark and murky and smells.

A low growl forces my attention to the hallway. Ludovic's fist slams into Omen's cheek, and I mutter a curse. I was so focused on hiding my own shit, I forgot to warn him. When the demon rears back again, Omen lifts his arm to deflect it.

"Where the fuck have you been?" Ludo snarls, and I slide around Omen, plastering a grin on my face.

"Ludo! Just the demon I wanted to see. We've got a problem with the gauntlet." We don't. "Triton says the fireballs keep going haywire." He hasn't, but it's a common enough complaint. "Omen's going to help us out." Definitely won't. Ludo won't go searching down there, though. "Hope you don't mind. You can talk to Triton if you do." Here's hoping Triton is very far away with the newbies. "I'm sure he'll tell you to fuck off, but you can try."

I clap him on the back just to piss him off a little more, then grab Omen's arm and march us through the crowd that's gathered. Once we're far enough away, I pull him to a stop.

"You'd better rank up if you don't want Ludo on your ass." It's the only way he's going to get away with keeping his little witch.

"I'm not ranking up. I like where I am," he mumbles.

"Yeah, sure. You just *love* the paperwork and the shit Ludo throws at us, and the portal duties, and the night watches, and—"

He snarls and flames dance along his fingers. "Okay, I get it. I hate my job. Except if I level up, I'll be..."

Alone. He'll be alone. And so will I. Not being on the same rank wouldn't be that big of a deal, except they'd throw Omen somewhere else. Somewhere far away from here. Unless he took over Ludo's job. He'd get to keep his witch, though.

"You know...if you level up, you'd outrank Ludo. Definite perk."

"And I wouldn't be able to go back to the human dimension," he whispers.

There it is. "Yeah, but she's here now. Maybe—"

"I'm not having this conversation," he growls, his face shuttering.

I nod, though I don't fully understand. A shockwave hits me just then, ricocheting around my body, and I curl my hands into fists. I grit my teeth as I try to finish this conversation before I lose it.

"You should definitely have a talk with your witch."

"No. I'm not having this conversation at all. I'm not ranking up. I'm not trapping her here. I'm not keeping her."

He stalks off and I shake my head. "You can't make decisions for her. You don't get to dictate her future, Omen."

He waves, then disappears into the void. Hopefully he's going to talk to Clara instead of ignoring the situation. Another shock hits me and I swallow a grunt. A thread tugs in my gut.

"You've got to be fucking kidding me," I groan as I'm whisked away once more.

CHAPTER EIGHT

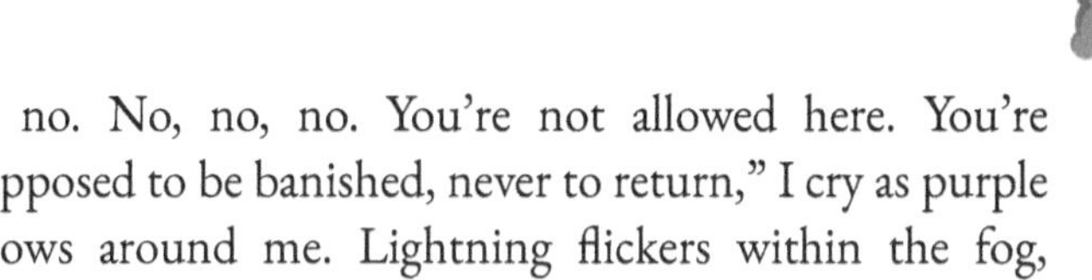

MARI

"Oh, no. No, no, no. You're not allowed here. You're supposed to be banished, never to return," I cry as purple smoke billows around me. Lightning flickers within the fog, revealing a dark form.

Despite the theatrics, I know it's that damn demon. Actually, *because* of the theatrics, I'm certain it's him. There was a gleam in his eyes the first time we met. He's a troublemaker. I can feel it in my bones. My bones that are still trying to figure out whether they want to be solid or liquid, but that's neither here nor there.

"Sorry to disappoint, spitfire," he wheezes as the smoke clears, then drops to his knees.

"Are you bowing or are you hurt?"

A groan is his only response. His forehead almost touches the floor, and I freeze. I don't know how to help a demon. Hell, I barely know how to heal a human, much less someone like him. I'm not equipped for this. It's not like they taught us at school. Even when we had those ridiculous classes, they didn't focus on healing so much as protection.

I rush forward as he tips to his side, unsure if I should touch him or let him fall. When he was here before, I swear I got shocked when he picked me up. He's crackling like a campfire in the middle of summer, burning from the inside out. If he bursts

into flames in the middle of my living room, I'm going to be pissed.

I can imagine the 911 call now. *Yes, there's a demon who detonated in my living room and now the house is on fire. Can you send someone before he burns my sister's house down?*

"Do not combust. Just...stay here," I say as if he could stop himself. Maybe he can. As he so helpfully pointed out, I don't know a lick about demons.

I rush to the kitchen and end up emptying an entire cupboard searching for a plastic pitcher. It's stuffed all the way in the back, of course. Even with the water on full blast, it still takes forever to fill. I bounce from one foot to another, urging it on.

Glancing around the space, I scan for my fire blanket. Percy bought me one for solstice one year after she almost burned down her living room. Apparently her fireplace wasn't a fireplace. I'd say I was surprised, but it's par for the course for her. That year, everyone she knew got a fire blanket. I just can't remember where I stuck it.

Water splashes on my shirt and bare legs. I stutter to a stop, slopping more onto the floor. In the middle of everything, I forgot I'm not wearing pants. Or shorts. And this shirt isn't particularly long. Another groan from the living room has me rushing to Dimitri.

I barely register he's sitting with his back against the couch before I'm throwing the entire pitcher on him. He sputters and flails. I wince, dancing out of his reach. I'd rather not get shocked or smacked. Either seems like an option at this point.

"What the fuck was that?" he roars as he struggles to his feet.

"Water?" I clamp my mouth shut as he slips on the hardwood and crashes onto the couch.

I retreat farther, closer to the front door. I'm not about to stick around if he attacks me. He might not seem like the type, but I've met plenty of good guys who turned out to be nasty pieces of work. They hide behind a smirk and an easy-going nature. Then they turn on you when you've slighted them.

Besides, I don't really know Dimitri. He *is* a demon, after all. I don't know why it matters so much, but my mind keeps reminding me of that fact.

"Where do you think you're going?" he snaps, though he makes no move to get up again. At least he fell onto the couch. In fact, he could close his eyes and take a little nap. It's a good thing I hate that couch or I'd be upset he's soaking the cushions.

"You yelled. Figured I'd give you some space." It's the most neutral response I can come up with.

His dark gaze scans me from head to toe, and a single eyebrow pops up. "Planning on running out the door?"

I grit my teeth as the fear and insecurity slink away. "If I needed to."

"Without pants?" He smirks, and I flip him off. He closes his eyes and flings his arm over his face. "Besides, it's never a good idea to run from a demon."

"Oh? And why's that?" I sneer.

"We like the chase." He peeks at me and smirks. "Unless that's what you're going for. I'm more than willing to partici—"

He groans, his body curling as pain assaults him. I take a step as he almost falls onto the floor, though I doubt I'd be able to catch him. Do I get more water? Flour? He isn't smoking anymore. He *is* crackling again, though. I don't know if I'm supposed to treat this like an electrical fire or not. I really didn't think this through. He lies back once more, panting. Small sparks dance along his skin, and I realize he's not wearing a shirt.

"I really need you to not set my couch on fire. I don't have enough baking soda to put you out, and I'm running low on flour. Plus, the flour would stick to you, and I'd really rather not track it all over. Wet flour is a bitch to clean up."

He gives me a long-suffering look, then shakes his head. "I won't."

Pressing my lips together, I turn back to the kitchen to get towels. "Good to know."

This is the point where things get awkward. He's vacillating

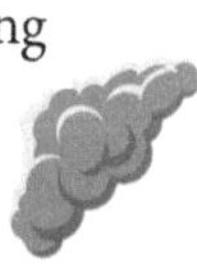

between being pissy and making comments. Inappropriate comments. I'm sure he's not trying to hit on me. Maybe it's part of being a demon—like the chasing. A shiver rolls through me, and I shove the feeling deep. I'll examine it later. When I'm alone.

I spin around as I reach the threshold. "You can't read my thoughts, right?"

His eyebrow pops up once more, much to my dismay. "No. That's more of a dragon thing. Not a demon one. Magic doesn't work like that. Although…"

I gesture for him to continue when he presses his lips together. "Although, what?"

He closes his eyes again. "Not important. Just rambling. Can I have some water? To drink…not thrown in my face. Please."

My mouth drops open, then I snap it shut. I shouldn't be surprised he's polite. I'm still battling the preconceived notions I grew up with. Dimitri is nothing like I was taught.

Despite what I told him earlier, I desperately want to know more. Asking him would require us to get to know each other, though, and I don't have time for that. I lost too much of it while I was sick. I'm still not doing well, but I can't keep putting things off.

When I bring him a glass, I set it on the side table. With his eyes closed and his breathing even, I'm pretty sure he's asleep. He can't be very comfortable. My couch isn't that big, especially for a demon well over six feet. I didn't really notice before since I was distracted by the grey skin and random short circuits. Plus, I was too busy freaking out about the closet, and then I was too sick.

I end up spreading a blanket over him. It doesn't seem like enough. I'm not going to try to move him to my bed, though. I'd rather the claws he's suddenly sporting not slash me to ribbons. Where they came from is just another question I won't be asking. Some of them are too personal, others too weird.

So instead of waking him up and asking him, I curl up in the wingback chair and write them all down. It's the best I can do. Maybe Percy knows something. She's too perceptive, though.

She'll demand to know why I'm suddenly interested in demons when I never was before. Most witches go through a Hell phase. It's not always demons. Sometimes they study the magic, the dimensions, or the void. They pore over ancient texts and seek out elders, all in the thirst for knowledge. Most covens allow them to pick what they want.

I didn't get those choices. I had to research plants, potions, and practices surrounding them. It was boring as fuck and I hated every minute of it. At least Lark got spells, though she was sent to clean out the attic when she was caught looking at the dark ones. They weren't even that bad, but Aunt Star was kind of a bitch. I never did fully figure out what happened in her life to make her so distrustful of...well, everything. Other than the obvious. I suppose I'd hate the world if Lark dove deep into sorcery. Oh right, she probably did.

By the time the sun sets, I've got a list two pages long. My eyes droop, and I vow to get up soon. I need to make myself dinner. And clean the bathroom. And pull everything out of the closet. There must be something in there to find my sister. Maybe she stuck a parchment under a loose floorboard with specific instructions about what the hell she did. If I'm lucky, there'll be a note telling me exactly where she went and how to find her.

Minutes or hours later, I'm jostled awake. It takes me longer than it should to register the strong arms cradling me and the warm chest under my cheek. I should protest or demand he put me down. Except the lack of sleep has rendered me useless.

"Shit," he mutters as he trips over nothing.

"Down," I whine.

"Nah. Least I can do is put you to bed. Gotta get that fire back somehow, and sleeping in a chair ain't gonna do it."

"You talk funny," I mumble.

He lowers me onto my bed and slides his hands from under me. The claws are nowhere to be found, thankfully. I watch him through slits as a range of emotions passes across his face too quickly for me to fully grasp.

"What do you mean?"

It takes me a second to remember what I said. "You speak like a human. Like you've been here a lot."

"Would you prefer I be posh and aristocratic?"

I snicker at his poor attempt at a Cockney accent. "Did you get your training from movies? Is there cable in Hell?"

"No. I've just spent more time than most topside." Indecision dances in his black eyes. "Did you give any more thought to my proposal?"

I swallow hard and suddenly don't know what to do with my hands. "Seems like you're getting the better end of the deal there. All I get is some information. You get a whole curse undone."

He cocks his head to the side and studies me. "Well, I was hoping you'd feed me, too."

"So, I feed you, break your curse that probably doesn't exist, and I get lessons in demons?" The longer he talks to me, the more awake I am, which only leaves room for frustration to creep in.

He shrugs, his grey skin glittering in the moonlight filtering through the window. "You could ask me for just about anything and I'd give it to you. Even if you don't help me, I still probably would."

"Why?" As soon as the question pops out, I wish I could stuff it back in. I don't care why. Maybe a little, but definitely not enough to demand he tell me.

The corner of his mouth tips up. "Dunno. Just something about you. So, what would you like in exchange for your witchy abilities?"

I struggle to sit upright, and he sways closer. I ignore the movement, not entirely sure whether I want him touching me. Every time he has, I get a weird feeling in my chest. It's been a while, but I don't think curses can rub off on someone else. It's not a cold one could catch. Except that only pertains to curses on witches and humans. Demons probably have a whole other set of rules. I swing my legs over the side and face him.

"What if I can't help you?"

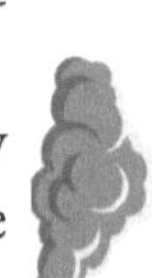

"Helping only requires trying, spitfire. As long as you try, you'll help." He shrugs again, the movement jerky. "At this point I'm desperate, and the only time I feel normal is here or when I'm sleeping in Hell."

"Demons sleep?"

He chuckles breathlessly. "I'll tell you if you agree to break this curse."

I huff, tipping my head back. "Fine. I'll help you, but I want more than knowing shit about demons and Hell."

He steps closer and our knees brush. Tiny shocks skip up my thighs, and heat settles between my legs. This was not part of the deal.

Percy was kind enough to fill me in on what she knew about demons. It wasn't much. I was able to dodge why I wanted to know, and she chalked it up to being bored. Of course, she didn't tell me anything useful, really. All she could talk about was how hot they supposedly were and how amazing they were in bed. She regaled me with stories of past witches having mortal men ruined for them by getting dicked down by a demon.

Staring at Dimitri and the glint in his eyes, I believe the tales.

"What exactly would you like, Mari?" he murmurs, a dark seduction weaving its way through the air. It wraps around my body, and I suppress a shudder of anticipation.

I open my mouth, then snap it shut when his pupil flashes purple. The deep color bleeds into his irises, and he leans back.

"Dimitri?" He doesn't respond, his gaze fixed on a point over my head. "Water. I'll get you some water."

Either he'll poof out of existence again or he'll create a lightning storm in my bedroom. Not exactly the type of lightning I was fantasizing about a minute before. I rush for the bathroom and grab the cup. At least this one fills faster than the last one.

"What else?" I ask as I step back into the now empty room. "What the fuck."

Dimitri, facedown and cockeyed on my bed, must have passed out. At least his back is rising and falling in an even rhythm.

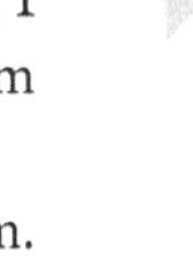

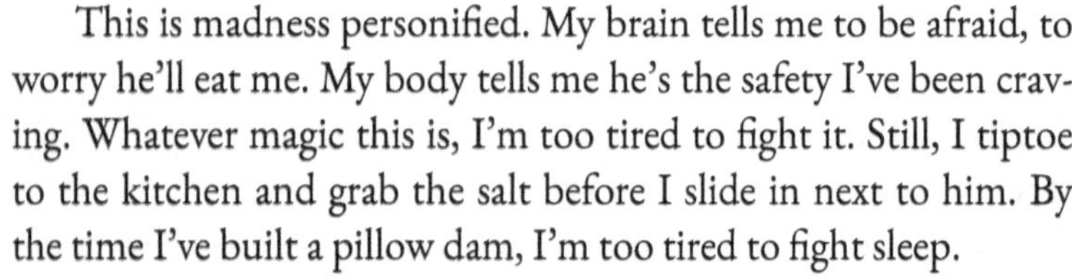

"Thirty seconds, dude. I was gone for thirty seconds, and you take over my bed? This isn't...I should banish you. That's exactly what I should do. Because we've spent a total of maybe an hour together." I shuffle around the room, picking up abandoned clothes and kicking things into the closet. "I don't know you. You don't know me. For all I know, you're a figment of my imagination. Yet here I am, contemplating just saying fuck it and crawling in next to you."

This is madness personified. My brain tells me to be afraid, to worry he'll eat me. My body tells me he's the safety I've been craving. Whatever magic this is, I'm too tired to fight it. Still, I tiptoe to the kitchen and grab the salt before I slide in next to him. By the time I've built a pillow dam, I'm too tired to fight sleep.

CHAPTER NINE
DIMITRI

S oft. My little spitfire is incredibly soft.

I tighten my grip on her and bury my face in—a pillow. My eyes fly open and I jerk back. Instead of holding Mari like I was in my dreams, I'm clutching a fluffy oversized pillow. I can just make out Mari's sleeping face across the wall she's built between us. I'd be offended, except I can't blame her. We've been thrown together. Add in my status as a demon and I'm not winning any points with her.

She sighs, turning onto her side to face me. Her long dark lashes flutter across her cheeks, and her plum-colored hair curls around her neck. My fingers twitch, and I fight the urge to brush the strands back. Or twist them around my fist and kiss the shit out of her.

Strangers, Dimitri. You're strangers.

I'm surprised she didn't banish me back to Hell. I doubt I would have been able to leave, though. Every time I pop back here, I ping-pong between feeling like shit and feeling better than I ever have in my existence. I'm loath to attribute the latter to her presence. I'm already dancing a fine line. It's more likely that as my bones settle in the dimension, I'm good. Then the curse finds me and attacks my magic once more. It leaves me wobbly, and before long I pass out.

I wish I wouldn't have gone comatose in her bed. She prob-

ably cussed me out. I wonder if she tried to move me. She's tall enough, but with all my hours running the gauntlet, I've got more than a few pounds of muscle on me.

When I can't take it anymore, I slip my arm from under the pillows. Lightly, I brush her forehead with my thumb. She mumbles in her sleep, and I freeze, then pull my hand away, tucking it back under my head. I clutch the pillow against my chest with my other arm. When her fingers latch onto my wrist, I hold my breath. She's got a good grip.

Mari mumbles again and tugs my hand closer until my fist is curled under her chin. She clings to me like a lifeline, and I wonder what she's dreaming. Part of me wishes I could see into her head. It would help me figure out what she's hiding.

She doesn't want lessons on demons. She may be curious, but this is something else. I haven't been well enough to do any research and part of me doesn't want to. Finding information about humans is easy, witches are a little harder. Still, I'd be invading her privacy. When I looked up Clara, I found only the most basic of things. Mari's situation would require me to dig deep.

I don't know how long I lie there, watching her while she clutches my wrist. By the time her lids flutter again, the arm under my head is numb and my stomach grumbles.

She blinks at me and, for once, I have nothing to say. My thoughts are quiet instead of running a million miles a minute. It's as if her touch calms me in a way I've never experienced in the centuries I've been around. I keep expecting her mind to catch up to her actions and for her to shove me away.

"Hi," she breathes, then yawns, ducking her face under the edge of the comforter.

"Morning."

"Is it morning? I've been waking up at two. And four. And five, for weeks."

"In the afternoon?"

She gives me a look, her lips twitching. "In the morning, demon. This is the first full night's sleep I've had in a week."

"Since you got sick?" My heart clenches, but I don't know why. I'm not the reason she got ill. I didn't even know she was sick. And I got her soup.

"Yeah. Right after you showed up, actually. Migraine mostly." She rolls her eyes when I press my lips into a thin line. "You're not the reason. I've been getting them since...for quite a few months."

There it is. That shadow in her eyes every time she's about to reveal her secret. She had it when I mentioned ancient texts. And when I offered to teach her about demons. She needs something, yet she won't ask for it. I wonder if that's just the way she is.

"I'm just surprised it's been a week since I showed up."

Her brows pull low. "What do you mean?"

I sigh, fighting a smile. "That will cost you. One possibility for a cure for my curse."

She scowls and her nose scrunches up. "Fine. Have you really been so sick you didn't realize a whole week had passed?"

"I thought it was less. Time works differently in Hell. Or maybe it's different here. I don't entirely know. An hour here could be two minutes or two years down there. Or vice versa. Antidote, please."

"Did you get bit by a supernatural creature recently...or a bunny?"

I frown as I sift through my memories. "I got bit a lot when I was younger. Omen called me reckless. Recently, I don't think so."

She closes her eyes and squeezes my arm. I don't think she realizes she's been holding onto me the entire time. She ducks her head and yawns, using the back of my hand as a shield. My lips twitch, and it takes everything in me not to wiggle my fingers.

"Suppose it's not that, then. What else do I get for tracking this down?"

"You certainly have a one-track mind, huh?"

She shrugs, though the movement is awkward. "I don't like not knowing things. Obviously." She flops onto her back and narrows her gaze as she stares at the ceiling. My chest tightens when she drops my hand. I tuck it under the pillow, trying not to draw attention to it.

She huffs. "You're not going to eat me, right?"

My mouth waters and I smirk. "Not unless you ask nicely."

She makes a noise in the back of her throat. It only makes me wonder what types of sounds she'd make if she were underneath me. If she'd let me, I'd pay her in orgasms. As soon as I get this curse under control, I might just try to convince her. If her blushing is any indication, she'd be down. Right now, I doubt she'd take me up on the offer. She's still too wary of me. Then again, she did crawl into bed with me. Maybe she's closer than I think.

"So Percy was right," she mutters.

I don't think she meant to say it out loud. Regardless, an ugly emotion curls in my gut. The gears are still turning in her mind while I grit my teeth. Asking who the fuck Percy is won't win her over. It could be a client. A sibling or a friend.

Or a lover.

If they are lovers, then why the fuck am I in bed with her instead of them? Unless they have an arrangement. Maybe it's common for witches to have more than one partner. It's not like I have any room to judge. I haven't exactly been celibate over the centuries. There's absolutely no reason for me to be jealous of a faceless person who has the pleasure of hearing her passion. I just don't know if I could share her. Not that it matters since she definitely isn't going to sleep with me.

I clear my throat. "About what, exactly?"

"Oh, my best friend said demons know their way around—" She tenses, pressing her lips together.

"More secrets, huh?" I roll off the bed and to my feet, instantly regretting it. I end up back on the bed as my head swims and my stomach rolls. Pain lances up my neck and to the base of

my brain. I swear I can feel the organ swelling as my magic short-circuits.

Mari's voice drones in the background as if one of us is under water. My hearing clears when her soft hand lands on my shoulder. I'm teetering on the edge of unconsciousness, yet her touch grounds me to reality.

"Are you okay? Do you need more water?"

I shake my head. She shuffles around and slides off the bed. My fingers twitch when she stops in front of me. Gripping her waist, her thighs, her ass, would ground me even more. Except for *Percy*, the best friend. Who she may or may not be fucking. And the fact I might keel over and take her out with me. Instead, I dig my nails into my legs and hope the feeling goes away.

"This is really bad. Okay, no big deal. I'm just going to...Stay here, okay?"

I protest as she rushes out of the room, purple hair streaming behind her. I swear I catch a glimpse of black underwear peeking from underneath the hem of her oversized shirt. Groaning, I fall back onto the mattress as my cock gets impossibly hard. Even while cursed, I want her. With every new revelation, I fall under her spell a little more. It's too soon. Too fast. Too reckless.

Nothing good would come from my pursuing her in this state. She clearly has other things she's dealing with. If she trusts me enough to open up, I'll keep my pants on. No more flirting. No more off-hand comments. And no more sleeping in her bed.

Grunting, I push my body upright. My joints creak and my claws shoot from my fingertips. I hold up my hands, keeping them far away from her bedsheets. The last thing I need is to wreck her things. Standing without using my hands should be easy. In my current state, though, it takes me much longer than I'm willing to admit.

Mari paces back into the room, a phone pressed to her ear. "No Percy, I just need any books you have on curses. Not for me. For...a friend." She pauses as she gazes at me with concern. "Yeah, yeah, didn't know I had friends. Joke's getting old, hon. Do you

have some or not? Because all I have is the basic spellbook Lark had stuffed in the closet. There's other things in there she jotted in the margins, but it's not exactly what I need."

When she focuses on me, I shake my head. I don't want her to bring anyone else into this, much less Percy. If some rando waltzes in here with a gleam in their eye and a potion in hand, I'll fritz out. Already my magic sparks in my veins, throwing electrical shocks places it definitely shouldn't.

My skin pulls tight against my muscles, and I will the feeling away. It doesn't work. If my flesh cracks and I transform in the middle of her bedroom, she'll definitely run away screaming. Perhaps she'll stab me. A blade won't kill unless it was blessed by Providence and I'm pretty sure she doesn't do that anymore. It will hurt like hell, though.

"Of course I'm not harboring demons in my basement," Mari says with an unconvincing laugh. "Why ever would you think that?"

I raise a single eyebrow, and she gives me a look. I'm pretty sure it means shut up, but I didn't say anything. She wanders closer, and I swallow hard while trying to act nonchalant—like I didn't just almost break her bed from falling on it. Her nearness does wonders for my symptoms, though. Maybe a witch cursed me and my only reprieve is another witch's presence. Now *that* would definitely be Karma's doing. She's petty like that.

"Do you have the books or not?" She licks her lips, drawing my gaze to her mouth. "No, don't come over here." Pause. "Because I'm naked."

Laughter peals from the other end, and I realize Percy is a woman. Doesn't mean much since Mari could be sleeping with a woman just as much as with a man. I'm more inclined to think she has a preference for other witches rather than humans. The knot in my chest doesn't loosen, and I struggle to keep my nonchalant demeanor. From the look on her face, she isn't buying it.

She steps closer as she listens to whatever Percy is saying. By

the time she stops, she's practically standing between my legs. I'm not going to be able to keep the promises I made to myself if she keeps doing these things.

"Okay, so if a demon were to, I don't know, burst into flames or something? What do I do?" She purses her lips as she waits for a reply.

I glance at her legs, then squeeze my eyes shut. She's temptation come to life. At least for me. Controlling my breathing is no longer an option. Hopefully she's too engrossed in figuring out my curse to notice. When I open them again, it's just in time to see her reaching for me. She tucks her knuckle under my chin and tips my head up.

Our gazes collide, hers full of concern and mine, I'm sure, full of desire. I attempt to wipe my face of emotion.

"I have to go," she whispers, and her thumb swipes at the screen without taking her eyes off me. She drops the phone, and it tumbles across the carpet.

My jaw tics and I make a conscious effort to relax. "Get any answers?"

"Yes," she breathes. "I believe I have."

CHAPTER TEN
MARI

I shouldn't have touched him.

Now I'm caught in his gaze and my skin is fused to his. I couldn't walk away if I wanted to. Which I don't. I knew I should have slept on the couch or banished him back to Hell. Now I'm in the middle of this and I don't know how to stop.

Percy wasn't any help with the curse, and I don't want to take advantage of Dimitri's vulnerable state. Then again, he doesn't look sick anymore. If anything, he looks like he wants to jump my bones. I'm inclined to let him, though I have no idea why.

Just days ago, I thought demons were fairy tales—based on true beings but largely exaggerated. Yet here I am touching him and wondering if his lips are really as pillowy soft as they look.

His nostrils flare and I wonder if he can smell my arousal. That would be embarrassing unless we were together. Then it'd be hot, I suppose.

I lick my lips, then ask, "Are you..."

"Yeah."

I don't think he knows what I'm asking. He probably doesn't care. Part of me wants to tell him I figured out what I want in exchange for breaking his curse. The other part is screaming at me to remember he's a demon. Why that matters, I can't quite figure out. Because my aunt said so? Because witches and demons have a fraught history I know nothing about?

I wish my sister were here. She'd know what to do. Whether she'd tell me to go for it or run far away, I don't know. Which is the problem.

He clears his throat, a bolt of lightning flashing in his dark eyes. "Did your...friend have anything?"

I slowly shake my head, then drop my hand to my side. My skin cools and my fingers tingle at the loss of contact. It takes a minute, but his question finally sinks in fully. The thread between us frays, and I narrow my gaze.

"Why did you hesitate?"

His eyes widen. "What?"

"Don't pretend like you don't know what I'm talking about. Why did you hesitate when you called her my friend?"

He snorts and chokes at the same time, and I fully expect him to cough up a hairball. "I don't know what you're talking about, Mari. I just wanted to know how to break this curse. If I can figure out what kind it is, I'll probably be able to find out who put it on me and deal with them accordingly."

"Kill them?"

Shock floods his face. "What? No. I mean, maybe. Depends on why they cursed me. Or how bad it's supposed to get. If this is all it is, then I suppose...don't give me that look. Not everyone is sunshine and rainbows, spitfire. There are bad demons in Hell just like humans in your world."

"But killing them—" I don't know how to finish the sentence. It's not something I ever thought about, but I've never been in a situation where I'd have to make that decision.

He holds up a hand. "Killing them in Hell isn't the same as here. You know that, right?"

"Uh, no. Killing is killing."

He smiles, his entire demeanor transforming. Gone is the broody demon, replaced with the charming one who doesn't look like he'd hurt a fly. Which is laughable, considering we're talking about him doling out irreversible justice.

"If I stab someone here and they die, they'll go to Hell. Or one of the other dimensions aligning with their soul. They'll suffer or celebrate in accordance with their fate. For eternity."

"Aligning with their soul?" The concept sounds painful.

He waves, his hand brushing my arm and sending goosebumps along my flesh. He doesn't seem to notice. "We don't have time to get into all of that. It's...complicated, and I'm not well-versed in that particular study. Different things happen if I killed someone in Hell. A demon could be sent to a sulfur pit or the dragon plains. Depends on what they did, honestly. A deity or some other entity might be banished to another dimension. Humans are a bit tricky. Half the time they don't feel anything. Like poking a tomato, really. If they fucked up, then they could get a worse assignment or dimension. Now, if I stabbed them for ridiculous reasons or was wrong, then I'd suffer their fate instead."

"And a witch?"

"I'm not about to stab a witch, Mari. I don't have a death wish." He smirks, shooting me a roguish look.

"Because of the implications?"

"Yup. But mostly because if you stab a witch in Hell, you get the Council on your ass. The red tape is fucking terrible. Don't even get me started on the paperwork. A witch wrongs you in Hell? Let it the fuck go. By the time you fill out all the proper forms to retaliate, it doesn't matter anymore."

I'm pretty sure my brain breaks at that. Forget the demon showing up in my closet. Or my sister disappearing from this plane. Different dimensions and humans being poked like fruit... or vegetables. I can never remember which a tomato is. Either way, it doesn't matter. What's truly stopped me in my tracks is paperwork.

"I...paperwork? There's paperwork in Hell?"

"Way too much, honestly. I swear that's half the reason Omen keeps disappearing. He says it's because Clara keeps summoning him, but he sticks around for way too long. Pretty sure it's to avoid the paperwork Ludo keeps giving him."

"You have a lot of paperwork waiting for you then?"

"I've been helping at the gauntlet. Until I got cursed, that is. So, yeah, I've got a bit waiting for me."

I could point out he missed my point, but it's not worth it. Explaining a joke instantly makes it not funny. I don't even know if it was a joke in the first place. Maybe I just wanted him to tell me he stayed because of me instead of avoiding something else. Which is ridiculous. Logically, I know that. Doesn't make the rejection hurt less.

I press my lips together and glance away. "I'm going to make coffee. I have some books around here. I'll see what I can find."

He opens his mouth like he'll protest. Turning and walking away is easier. Cowardly, yet easier. Telling him whether to stay or go isn't my call. He doesn't have to stick around for me to research. It's not until I'm in the kitchen I realize he never answered my question about Percy. Maybe he thinks she's human.

"Doesn't make sense why she'd have spellbooks," I mutter as I go through the motions of making coffee. "Fuck, I could use a donut."

After a good night's sleep, my headache is completely gone. Now I'm in that post-migraine stage where my thoughts don't quite sit right in my brain. Like the pain from before drowns them, and now they're a bit waterlogged until they dry out. It's a strange feeling where time doesn't line up with reality.

"This isn't going to work," he mutters from behind me, and I tense.

"Well, you're free to leave, then." I plan on saying more, except my throat closes and my eyes burn.

Ridiculous, Mari. Get your shit together. He doesn't have to be here. You don't want him here. It's been a fucking week, not years. You're not even dating.

My little pep talk does nothing. It's as if logic has no place in my life anymore. Actually, it probably fled when my sister disappeared, I moved into her house and assumed her life. I swear I hear her whispers in the dead of night, urging me onward.

I shake my head and inhale deeply. He hasn't left. His presence fills the room without even trying. Maybe it's a demon thing. Lark seemed to exude the type of energy he does. Could be she was part demon which is a ridiculous notion. My heart clenches, adding to the moroseness I've fallen into. With her gone, I'm left adrift. My one goal is to find her. If she left on purpose and hates that I found her...well, I'll deal with that when I find her.

"Mari..." he sighs.

"It's fine. If you can stay in Hell, you'll probably get better. And I'm sure I can find a book to help me find what I'm looking for."

His silence says it all—he agrees. I don't know a lot about curses, but I do know recharging your magic helps. Demons probably aren't much different from witches in that regard.

"What is it you're looking for, spitfire?" he murmurs, his breath ghosting across the shell of my ear.

A shudder runs through me. His fingertips brush my leg, right beneath the hem of my shirt. Fire ripples from the spot, heating me from the inside out. One touch shouldn't do such things. My body sways, whether toward him or away, I'm not sure.

And then he's gone. His touch. His breath. His presence.

I glance over my shoulder to confirm what I already know. I'm greeted with an empty kitchen. Bitterness tinged with disappointment washes over me. The coffee machine beeps. I don't have the stomach for it anymore, yet I pour some into a mug. Reluctantly, I slide the second cup back into the cupboard. If this was my house, I'd get rid of them all. I'd have one of everything, maybe two so I wouldn't have to do dishes every night. If only there were a spell to do all the chores. Maybe there is and I just haven't found it yet.

Sighing, I leave my steaming cup on the counter and go to search the closet. I haven't felt well enough to dig through it all. There has to be something that'll point me in the right direction. If Lark left anything, she'd hide it away. Somewhere only I could find. I have no idea where, though.

We used to do all the normal sisterly things when we shared a room. Hidden messages on the mirrors that only showed when they fogged up. Coded notes stuffed in random places like the inside of the toilet roll. Crystals arranged in a specific order only we understood. We even learned Morse code one summer so Aunt Star couldn't eavesdrop as she was wont to do. We were closer than typical siblings—united under the banner of trauma.

I doubt I'll find a set of instructions laid out perfectly for me taped behind the faux-fur coats. Still, I end up tossing them behind me. Before I know it, the living room looks like a tiny tornado took up residence. Only the pertinent items lie on the table I use to read cards for unsuspecting patrons. It takes me another ten minutes to clear everything off.

"Won't be needing this anytime soon," I mutter as I move the fake crystal ball.

Spreading out the contents, I stare at the mishmash of witchy paraphernalia. At first glance, I doubt any of this was used recently. Lark always did have a problem with throwing anything away. Nice box? Have to keep it, just in case she moved. Journal with three pages of notes? Better save it for when the mood strikes again. Faux-fur coats a friend off-loaded? Might move to a colder climate someday and will definitely need them.

Despite the ridiculousness of it all, I'm not about to get rid of anything. Not only are these Lark's possessions, but she might come back for them someday. If I clean out her house, she'll throw a godsdamn fit. We'll fight, she'll give me the silent treatment, and we'll start this whole fucking thing over again.

Except it's never been like this before. She's never disappeared without a trace.

"Shut up," I growl at the voice in my head that still sounds suspiciously like my sister's.

I sift through the rubbish, tossing old feathers and used candles aside until I get to the books. The standard spellbook Aunt Star gave us both isn't useful. I have my own copy packed away in a storage locker. Summoning spells or dimensional travel definitely isn't in here. The other books are smaller and covered in soft leather.

As I flip open one titled *Necromancy*, a chill walks down my spine. This is not standard. And nothing like what we studied when we were younger. I don't even understand why Lark would want to know about necromancy. Reanimating dead bodies? No thank you. Unless she was planning on killing me, then reviving me just to do it all over again.

I grit my teeth, not sure whether to laugh, cry, or throw the book when I spot Lark's perfect script on a note tucked inside.

Mari-

Stop digging through my things. I'm not about to make an army of zombies. This is about plants. Not that you'd care. Go back to your slimy clay.

It's not dated, but it's from a few years ago when I went through a sculpting phase. Finding a hobby isn't as easy as it looks. I've tried a whole host of them, never fully settling on one. I shoot a guilty glance at the forgotten knitting project lying in a basket next to the couch. It's a mess of yarn with random knots I made somehow. I still don't know how to knit, but I also found out I can't count.

I toss the book aside, not caring whether it survives the trip, then wince. I don't have it in me to be angry with her. She knew I'd snoop with a cover like that. Frustration takes over, and I swipe my arm across the top of the table. A strangled cry leaves me, and I sink to my knees.

"Where are you?" I choke out, then gasp for breath between sobs.

I let Dimitri distract me, but no more. As my forehead sinks to the floor, I vow not to let a demon derail me from doing what I need to do.

I have to find her.

CHAPTER ELEVEN
DIMITRI

"Dimitri!"

Omen's voice ricochets around my head, leaving my ears ringing. I mask my confusion with a grin when I spot Clara. The last thing I want to do is scare her. Being a witch in Hell isn't exactly the easiest thing in the world. Throw in she's shacking up with Omen and I feel for her. Omen was my roommate way back when, and I almost threw him off a cliff. She doesn't seem any worse for wear. Her spell sickness appears to have resolved itself, though there are still dark rings under her eyes.

"Hey, Clara. Nice to see you're still in Hell." I turn to Omen and my eyes widen. "Uh, why do you have a dragon egg? And how the fuck did you get it away from the horde?"

"It was just sitting in the coals. I just grabbed it. She needs eggs." He gestures to Clara, and I take in the dough covering her hands. "Not this egg. Like, squawking eggs."

"Chicken," Clara says in amusement.

"I know, but they squawk. Funny little fuckers."

I press my lips together. I'm not about to bring up the time a flock of chickens attacked him when we were sent on assignment to another dimension. He had pinpricks all over his arms for a week afterward. From the hardness in his eyes when he glances at me, I should keep my mouth shut.

"Perhaps you should take the dragons back their egg. I'll keep

Clara company." I lean against the counter. Twin flames flare to life in his dark eyes, and I suppress a chuckle. It's so easy to rile him up.

"The fuck you will. Get your own witch," Omen snarls, shoving the egg into my chest. "Take this back and get us the right egg."

His words send a chill down my spine. An image of Mari pops into my head before I can stop it. She's not my witch and I doubt she will be anytime soon, if at all. I thought we were getting somewhere in the kitchen. At least, I was trying to get somewhere. Instead, I got thrown into the void. The more it happens, the more it's like being sucked through a straw. My body can't take much more. Eventually, my magic will bottom out and I'll be defenseless—useless.

"Please and thank you, Dimitri," Clara says softly, not quite a reprimand for Omen, but close enough.

He doesn't care if he snaps at me because I don't give a shit. Her? Yeah, he'll think twice then. We've lived together for so long I don't take him too seriously, and he puts up with my erratic ways. It works for us most of the time. If he starts in on Clara despite his better nature, we might have problems. It has nothing to do with another witch I've recently met either.

Pain shoots through my temples at the thought of Mari, and my magic rears up. I turn to Clara. "Fine. But I'm doing this for *you* because you're actually nice to me. And you have manners."

I snatch up the egg I dropped on the counter and step into the void, leaving thunder in my wake. I don't have time to take the dragon spawn back. Getting the chicken egg is more important. No use interrupting Omen and Clara when they inevitably make up. I'll deliver the iridescent one back to the horde after. I tuck it into my pocket for safekeeping. With a little magic, the egg fits perfectly. The tough exterior should keep it from being smashed. Hopefully.

It doesn't take me long to step into the dimension Omen got attacked in. It's on the same plane as Hell and doesn't expel enough energy to send my magic into a tailspin. If I get yanked topside again, though, it'll be one helluva storm. I've never been so lopsided in my travels.

I drop right into Omen's kitchen, declaring, "Got it."

Omen grabs at Clara as if I'll whisk her away to the netherland or something. I roll my eyes as she hops down and takes the eggs with a thanks. I open my mouth to say something to cut the tension when Omen latches onto my arm and yanks me from the room.

"Hey, hands off the merchandise. This shirt cost me a kidney," I grumble as he pulls me into his tiny-ass backyard. I kept telling him he should have a greenhouse back here. It's close enough to the lava geysers to be the perfect environment for pota-toes. Then he could make me fries. Not that he knows how to cook, but that's neither here nor there. Now that Clara's here, maybe she'll make me more.

"What in the fuck is going on with you?" he demands, crossing his arms as fire licks up his arms and sets his hair ablaze.

"Projection much? *I'm* perfectly fine. *You,* on the other hand, had better get your shit together."

He sighs, glancing away. "We've known each other a long time, Dimitri. You think I didn't notice your little display when you left? It's either incredibly childish or completely uninten-tional. Explain. Now."

I hold up my hands in surrender. "Told you I was cursed. Nothing to do with nothing. It's fine. I'm getting it sorted."

"How, exactly? Because the last time I checked, it's been a long time since a demon was cursed. It's more likely you're getting punished for...something. What'd you do? Did you rig Ludo's room to play bagpipes again? Or fuck with the Fates down in Underworld? You know how they hate that." He huffs as he runs his fingers through his hair. "Fuck, you didn't link dimensions again so they'd all have electrical storms every thirteen minutes, did you?"

I sigh with a grin. "Ah, those were good times. But no. Sadly, I

haven't done anything other than help Triton with the newbies, run interference for you with Ludo, and be sent topside every other hour. Other than that, I ain't done nothin', I swear."

He doesn't buy my act. He gives me a stern look and his nostrils flare. I brace myself for the lecture or the yelling. I'm never quite sure what I'll get with Omen. He's got a short fuse, and his patience lasts about seven minutes before he's done. Instead, his brows pull low.

"As someone who just went through the pain of hopping dimensions with no recharge in between, I know you've got to be running on empty. If you keep going—"

"*I'm* not going anyway. It's not like I have a choice. Hell, half the time I was up there was spent in a godsdamn closet, Omen. This isn't a case of summoning. The universe is just knocking me around. Something'll give soon, and I'll be fine. You just worry about what you're going to do with your little witch. Now, if you'll excuse me, I have a—"

My stomach lurches, but I'm already in the void. I crumple to the floor in front of Mari and groan. She screams a curse at me, and my hearing goes out. There's a slight hum, yet nothing else. I stare up at her from my back, unable to move my limbs. It takes me a minute to realize she's on her knees, tears streaming down her blotchy face.

I croak out what I think is a question, but I'm pretty sure it's just grunts. Whatever happened between now and when Omen called, it wasn't good. I roll my eyes around the room and take in the destruction.

Was she robbed? Attacked? Punished because of my presence?

Storm clouds gather on the ceiling, and I inhale deeply through my nose. I still can't move, but my magic can. Flickers of lightning dance within the shrouded darkness. When rain splatters across my face, I squeeze my eyes shut. I couldn't stop this if I wanted to. And I desperately want to. Flooding Mari's house will only add more bullshit to her plate.

A crack of thunder has her flinching. She throws her body

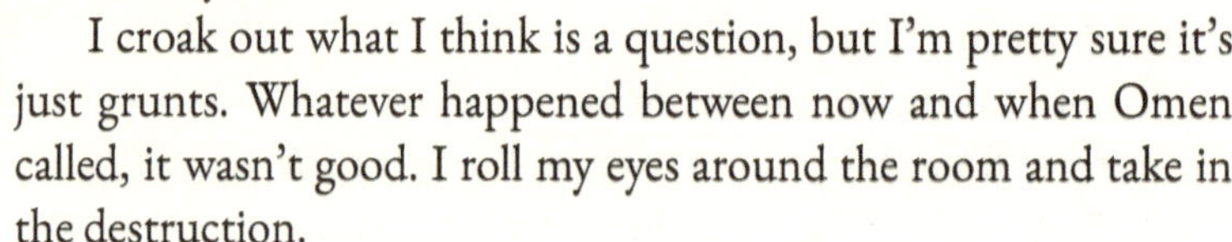

over mine, though I don't know why. I forget how much she doesn't know about demons. Clearly, she has no idea this is all me. The storm can't hurt me. I could swim through an electrified pond with no repercussions. She, on the other hand, could die.

My fingertips prickle, the sensation traveling slowly up my arms. Wind whips around the room, sending her hair flying. Her scent washes over me, and I groan internally. I need to break this curse if only to keep her away from me. She's temptation wrapped in a prickly exterior. If I keep getting thrown in her path, I don't know where things will lead. While I don't have the same reservations as Omen about witches, Mari doesn't want to even associate with me, much less do anything else.

Bitterness crashes into me, and the rain stops, the wind dies away, and the lightning fizzles out. Black clouds laced with purple roil overhead. The thunder rumbles constantly. I can't turn everything off at once. I don't really know if I want to. It's comforting in a way little else is. Too often my mind takes off, never allowing me a moment's peace. The calming presence of a storm gives my thoughts breathing room. It allows me to *think*—to just be.

Mari's nails dig into my side. The small bite of pain allows logic to sneak back in. I can't leave her to be hurt merely because I find the circumstances calming.

I pull in a deep breath and focus on the strand of magic careening inside me. Seizing it with my mind isn't easy, and I lose my grip on the rain. Mari's voice filters through the low hum, and I can finally make out her muttered curse. Or maybe it's a spell. Either way, there's a lot of fucks thrown in.

She sits back and stares at the ceiling. Somehow she's created a shield between us and the wetness. At least her house won't flood now. An ache blooms in my chest, but I can finally move my arms. I press the heels of my hands into my eyes and concentrate on pulling the magic back. Loud pops echo through the space, but I refuse to look until every last piece is contained within me.

Silence blankets the room. Not even my harsh breath can be heard. I don't know if Mari fled. She should if she hasn't. I open

my mouth to tell her to go, yet nothing comes out. Electricity coalesces within my gut, forming a ball of magic that spits and sparks. I won't be able to hold it back for long before I need to expel some.

"Mari," I croak as pins and needles shoot up my legs.

I drop my hands to peek at the damage I caused, and I'm met with total blackness. No moon. No sun. No lights. We must be in the deepest part of the night. Exhaling gently, I loosen the tiniest bit of magic and let it illuminate the room. It takes me longer than it should to sit up.

If I thought the place looked destroyed before, it's nothing like it is now. I wince, both at the tightness of my muscles and the mess I caused.

"Fuck. I'm sorry," I say, then glance toward where I last saw her.

My heart stops.

Sprawled across the floor with purple strands covering her face is Mari. And she isn't moving. I thought she ran. It would've been the smart thing to do. I shake off the shock and rush to her side. Gently, I roll her over and breathe a sigh of relief when her chest rises and falls shallowly. Humans have pulses, but I have no idea how to check them.

"Fuck," I snarl.

Her skin shimmers as a web of electricity covers her. I don't know how to help her. Now would be a great time for my curse to work in my favor. I could whisk her off to Hell and find someone to wake her up.

Clara. She's a witch. She'd know what to do. Except I can't leave this plane without a path through the void. My hands hover over her, indecision rendering me useless.

"Come on, spitfire," I whisper, my fingers brushing hers.

Her eyes fly open with a gasp. I jolt away as her back arches, a strangled cry leaving her. Her gaze snaps to mine, rage flaring to life, and I hold up my hands in surrender.

"Bastard," she spits out. "Fucking demons."

"I didn't—"

"I don't give a fuck." She struggles upright and shoves her hair from her face.

"It wasn't—"

"It never is!" Sparks fly from her fingers as she waves them around, though she doesn't seem to notice. "You keep popping up at the most inconvenient times. As if I don't have enough going on."

I wince, realizing how much I've disrupted her life. "You could—"

"Oh no," she snaps and pushes to her feet. She sways and I reach out to steady her. She slaps my hand away, and a shockwave skitters down my veins.

"Spitfire," I plead from my knees.

"No. I refuse to do anything else for you. I was perfectly content cleaning out the closet. You made it *rain*. Do you know how sca—fuck." She picks up a small green book and brushes off the cover.

I swallow hard and take in the space again. Everything I thought was destruction is merely some spring cleaning. Not that it's spring. I'm pretty sure it's summer right now. Or maybe autumn. I can never keep track of the seasons up here.

"Are you even paying attention? For fuck's sake. The least you can do is get up and help me clean." She plants her hands on her hips in front of me. When I nod, she holds up a hand. "Wait."

Her mouth twitches, and I brace myself for more yelling. I'm surprised she's so riled after practically dying. I'm pretty sure I sucked all the magic from her soul. It'll be a minute before she's replenished enough to even light a candle, much less throw up another shield.

"What are we waiting for?"

Her eyes darken and she smirks. "I kind of like you on your knees."

CHAPTER TWELVE
MARI

I can't believe I just said that.

From the roguish grin he's aiming at me, he's not complaining. Of course he isn't. It sounded like I was flirting with him.

You were flirting with him.

Was I? Or was I trying to throw him off? Except he's been docile since I woke up. Is this shock? Is that why I'm so discombobulated? Ever since Percy told me demons are amazing in bed, it's all I've been thinking about. Dimitri is the only demon I know so it stands to reason he's starring in every fantasy my mind can conjure up. Doesn't mean I actually want to sleep with him.

Except you do. You really, really do.

No, I don't. This isn't like me. I'm logical and even. Steady and volatile all at once. I'm the shitty yet reliable sister. When our aunt took a turn health-wise, I was the one the coven leaders called. Dependable. When my sister needed to get rid of an ex, I was the one who ran him off. Brutally honest. Lark always said I wielded my pain, my cruelty for the good of others. I didn't know what she meant then. I still don't.

Waffling between wanting to fuck Dimitri or banishing him to the ether isn't unusual. Along with all my stunning qualities came a wicked case of indecisiveness. Decision paralysis, my aunt

called it, though how she knew that term, I don't know. She was practically a shut-in by the end.

I shake my head and focus on Dimitri. He licks his lips, pulling my gaze down. My eyes widen when I notice his horns growing from the top of his head, longer than the first time I noticed them.

He brushes a hand over them and chuckles. "Handlebars?"

I scoff, though I don't have a quippy comeback. Slowly, as if he expects me to give more commands, he pushes to his feet. It takes everything in me not to stumble back.

"Now, spitfire, I'm only going to say this once, so listen closely." He leans close, his lips brushing my cheek, and he whispers in my ear. "I don't get on my knees for just anyone, but I'll do it for you anytime."

"You're incorrigible."

"Why yes, yes I am. Something tells me you like that." He pulls back slightly. "As much as I'd love to keep up this dance, I'm pretty sure you're in shock. And I won't take advantage of that. Let's get you in the shower. Then we can—"

"Can't," I mutter, and he raises an eyebrow. "I'm still...sparking. I'd rather not get electrocuted."

He's shaking his head before I've finished. "You won't. Promise. If you didn't get shocked to shit when my magic went haywire, you won't now. See?"

He reaches out and laces our fingers together. Heat gathers between our palms. He's right. I've been bouncing from one thing to the next, completely unhinged at my sister's disappearance, I haven't thought things through. I don't know him or what his true intentions are. He showed up randomly, and I never questioned it. Not really. Without information about demons, I'm woefully out of my depth here.

"Okay," I breathe, then untangle us. "This isn't...I don't know what to..."

I can't get my thoughts in order enough to even tell him what I'm thinking. He doesn't rush me or try to finish my sentences. As much as I love Percy, she'd be throwing out suggestions about what I'm feeling. Lark wouldn't even bother letting me work through things on my own. She'd hand me the answer since she knows me so well. Then again, if she did, she wouldn't have disappeared without a trace. She'd know what it would do to me. Unless I was a necessary casualty in her quest for knowledge.

I wouldn't be surprised if she fell so deeply into magical lore she forgot what the consequences would be. If she just would have called me, I could have warned her. I'm sure my insistence all these years to leave well enough alone made her second-guess talking to me. I don't blame her. It's exactly what I would have done.

"I need something," I whisper, throwing caution to the wind. I'll loosen the reins just enough—trust him just a little.

"What kind of something?" He glances around the room at the many items strewn about.

"Not something witches usually have."

His eyes narrow, and I swear recognition flares in his eyes, though he can't possibly know I'm looking for a book. His nostrils flare, and a curse forms on his lips. Then he disappears.

"Of fucking course."

"Percy, we're going out. Don't care where. Don't care what we do. I just need out of this house."

I shouldn't be taking out my piss-poor attitude on her. She's not to blame for the mess in the living room. Or the fact I still don't have any leads on my sister. It's not her fault that every time I stop moving, Dimitri pops into my head.

I imagine he poofed off to Hell. Again.

The problem is, he hasn't really left. The longer he's gone, the more worried I become. I fucking hate it. I don't pine. It's not in my nature. Yet as spring bursts into summer, I'm still wondering

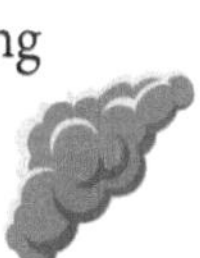

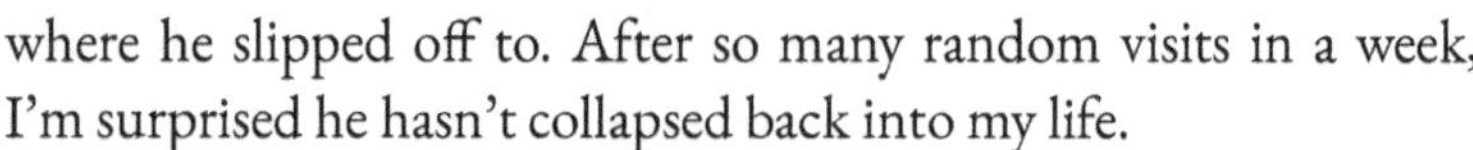

where he slipped off to. After so many random visits in a week, I'm surprised he hasn't collapsed back into my life.

Maybe he found a cure and doesn't need you anymore.

The voice in my head has morphed into my aunt's. She always was a pessimist. Nothing good ever came from anything in her eyes. Most people would think we make our own happiness. Not Aunt Star. She just assumed everything would eventually go to shit regardless of what she did. Maybe some of her cynicism rubbed off on me.

"We looking for low-key and calming? Because there's a goat yoga class tonight—"

"Not goat yoga," I say quickly as I flip through the necromancer book again. For some reason, I keep coming back to it. Not that there's anything in here I can use to fix the summoning circle. There isn't even a scrying recipe in here.

"Sorry, forgot you're scared of them." She laughs, and I roll my eyes.

"I'm not afraid of them. They chew on your shit, and I don't exactly have a lot of clothes left." I've thought about borrowing some of Lark's, but I can't bring myself to do it. It'd probably make her appear just to yell at me for taking her shit, though.

"Sure you're not. Except last year there was that petting zoo, and you practically bowled over that five-year-old to get away from them."

"They should have a warning so people don't get too close," I cry, slamming the book shut.

Her peals of laughter ring down the line. "They did. In big bold letters," she says between gasps.

"Whatever. We're not doing goat yoga. Let's go clubbing."

Her giggles cut off abruptly. "For real? Do you even have clothes for clubbing? When was the last time you went to a club? Do you have a push-up bra? You realize you'll have to wear a dress, right? An oversized shirt and no pants won't cut it. Plus, we'll have to drive at least an hour. Unless you're thinking of going to a dive bar and just randomly calling it clubbing."

"You fucking sound like Dimi—" I wince, then rush, "I'm aware of what it takes to go clubbing. I'll just channel my sister. What time should we go? Five?"

"Five?" she chokes out. "Girl, they won't even be open then."

"Well, if we leave at five—"

"No. I'm saying, they won't be open until like nine. Maybe ten. Are you sure you want to go clubbing?"

"Yes. I need to not be me for a little while. It'll take my mind off everything, and then I can focus on what needs to be done."

She doesn't respond, and the silence stretches on so long I'm afraid she hung up. If she doesn't go with me, I doubt I'll go myself. I need to get out of here, though. Out of this house, this town, this life. Just for a bit. I'll get rip-roaring drunk, flirt with those willing, maybe hook up with someone...well, that's pushing it. I can pretend, though. I'll cleanse my mind of a certain demon. Who knows? I might find what I'm looking for when I stop looking. Isn't that how it always works? Lose your keys, search for days, give up, then six months later they show up in the most obvious of places. It's science or something.

"Percy?"

"Yeah, I'm here. Who's Dean?"

"I...I have no idea what you're talking about." I started to say Dimitri, but it doesn't sound a lick like Dean.

"Mmmkay. Listen, you know I'm here for you, right? Whatever you need, I'll be there."

I freeze, running over our conversation. "Uh, yeah?"

"So whatever you're planning, just talk it through with me first, okay?"

"Perce, I'm not going to do anything reckless. No dark magic or running off into the woods to find bigfoot. I promise. I can't stop searching for Lark, though. I've put it off long enough, and I have a feeling it's not going to be easy or pretty."

"Are you sure she even wants to be found?" she whispers as if saying it too loudly will invite the ghouls in.

"She wouldn't have just left. It's not like she went up in a puff

of smoke, Percy. You know her well enough to figure that out. We've exhausted all our other options. I can't keep waiting for her to show up. I know I probably should, but—"

"No, I get it. I'd want to know what happened, too. Not that I have siblings so I can't really relate. I can't imagine, though. Not fully, obviously. But—"

"I get it, Percy. Just know I'm not going to go off the rails. Even if it does run in the family. So, clubbing. What time should I be at your house?"

She huffs. "Fine. I'll take you clubbing. But if you meet someone and decide to go home with them, I'm dragging your ass out of there so damn fast. We're not fucking randos tonight. It's just not in the cards."

I power walk to my bedroom, then stop. "Wait, the actual cards or the turn of phrase?"

"Wouldn't you like to know, weather boy?"

She hangs up before I can call her out for perpetually being online. Half the time she's speaking in memes I haven't seen. I haven't exactly had room in my head for anything other than keeping myself afloat. I resist the urge to check my bank account. There's enough in there for me to take a couple days off.

At least I haven't had any other clients like Jeremiah. With what I threatened him with, maybe he told his friends. A cautionary tale or whatever. The weird witch will wither your willy. I could get that printed on a business card—hand them out at the grocery store. I'm sure I'd get a few scorned exes that way.

I flip through all the clothes in my closet five times before giving up. Calling Percy and admitting I don't have anything to wear isn't an option. She'd lend me whatever I need. Except she's a lot shorter than me. A dress to her knees would barely cover my hooha. Plus, her hips aren't as big as mine. Nor are her boobs. She'd never be able to wear it again.

Which is why I'm standing outside my sister's bedroom door. The knob heats under my palm the longer I stand here. I told myself I wouldn't go in here—not to raid her closet or search for clues. I wanted to figure it out without invading her space. She was always protective of her peace. I suppose it didn't help we were forced to share a room when we were growing up. She just wanted a place that was entirely hers. And then I moved into her house and used all her things. The least I could do was vow to stay away from her bedroom.

Yet here I am, breaking that promise. I don't have to go through her things. If she was into the dark side of magic, she'd take pains to hide it.

I turn the knob and swing the door open. "Or not. What the fuck did you do, Lark?"

Black. Every single surface is black. From the walls to the ceiling to the bedspread—complete darkness. Even the light from the hallway doesn't penetrate the deep void she's created. I flip the switch and yelp, jumping back.

"What in the holy goddess did you do?"

Somehow she's magicked her room to become a kaleidoscope of color. Gone is the blackness, replaced with something I can't begin to explain. The room cycles through each color—blood red, forest green, sky blue. The bulb above her bed loops faster, adding more and more hues. Plum to gold to magenta permeates everything. I shut my eyes when my stomach rolls and nausea bubbles up my throat.

When I peek at it again, the color has settled on the exact shade as my hair. It's a lot more welcoming than the desolate gothic void from before. I hurry to her closet and rifle through the dresses. I pick a black one at random and yank it from the hanger. The irony isn't lost on me, but my hair wouldn't go with half the pieces in here.

I rush from the room, slamming the door behind me as my heart hammers in my chest. I'll deal with *that* conundrum later. Right now, I need to forget I'm a witch for a few hours.

CHAPTER THIRTEEN
DIMITRI

The last thing I want to be doing is paying a visit to Providence. Yet here I am, standing in front of her while she plays with a ball of yarn. I'm sure it's something very important. I don't fucking care. I have better things to do than sit around waiting for her to acknowledge me. Especially since she's the one who brought me here in the first place.

"Magic's a fickle thing, isn't she?" Providence murmurs.

"Never really thought of magic as a woman."

She smirks, her silver eyes finding mine. "Whatever else would she be?"

I roll my eyes. "Fine. Magic's a woman. Karma's a woman. Fate's a woman."

She nods her head as if I'm finally understanding. "All the best things in life are women, don't you agree?"

"If I disagree, are you going to fill my veins with vinegar like you did three decades ago?" I ask with a raised eyebrow, and she shrugs.

Sighing, she finally drops the ball, and I swear a tiny scream emanates from the thing. A shudder rolls down my spine. If I had a grave, someone would be walking over it right about now.

She sits back, a throne appearing out of seemingly nowhere. She stuck us in a blank space, only revealing items as necessary. It always freaks me out to be standing yet not actually be standing. I

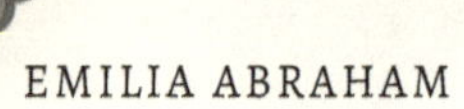

give her a pointed look, and she waves. Another chair appears, though obviously not as ornate. She always was a bitch. Lovingly, of course.

"Do we have a reason for meeting today?" I ask when her stare becomes too much.

She steeples her hands and taps her fingers against her mouth. "I'm concerned for Omen."

I roll my eyes. "You've never been concerned a day in your life, Providence. What's the real reason?"

"Fuck you, Dimitri. I care about my brother. I just show it in different ways."

"Good of you to drop the mystical act. Now what's the real reason?"

"Ack, fiiinnne." She claps her hands, and we're in a lush garden, complete with a gurgling fountain—her home. "I *am* worried about Omen. Though I might have been alerted to his...delicate condition from the strands. They're pulling and tightening in the wrong places."

She twirls her hands around, and the glowing ball of yarn reappears. She studies the thing like it contains the secrets of the universe. Maybe it does. I wouldn't know. I don't fuck with things like destiny and threads.

She huffs and the ball vanishes. "Listen, he's fucking with my job. But also, I did a little peeking—"

"Spying."

"*Peeking*. He's...morose." She spits out the word like a curse. "He's drained his magic, which means..."

"How the fuck would I know what that means? He can't die in Hell." Should I be arguing with her? Probably not. Do I want to help Omen? Of course. I just don't know how much I have left in me. Getting back to Mari is my top priority.

She shakes her head, giving me a disapproving look. "Such wasted talent. Anyway, his magic is tied to the Empyrean. He's literally sucking souls into his house. They'd end up there regard-

less because of his...whatever. It doesn't matter. He just needs to get his shit together so everything can right itself."

I squirm in my chair, unwilling to admit I have no idea why he's upset or drained of magic. He looked fine the last time I saw him. Sure, there was tension between him and Clara, but that's nothing new from what he's told me.

"What exactly am I supposed to do about this? I can't *make* him better." If I could, I'd uncurse myself.

Realization dawns on her face and she grins. "Would you look at that. The great and mighty Dimitrius doesn't know what's happening with his best friend, and I do. Oh, this is good. Wait, I want to remember what this feels like."

Scowling, I cross my arms. "Get on with it, Prov."

"Oh fine. Party pooper. He sent his witch topside. No idea why. And yes, I did know he was harboring a witch in Hell. I took care of the paperwork. I also may have sent a few well-deserved threats so he wouldn't have any issues with his soulbound staying, should she choose to."

"He sent her back? What the fuck." I run a hand through my hair and jab my finger into my horn.

"Why don't you just pop over there and tell him I'm going to pay his witch a little visit. That'll get his ass in gear. I have a theory I want to check out, anyway." She waves her hand as if to dismiss me.

Instead, I give her a deadpan look. If I give in without something in return, even if I want to, things will get sticky. I'll get a scolding, first of all, and I hate that. Lecturing a demon doesn't go well in the best of times. When they're the same rank as you, it goes even worse. Also, I could really use some help.

"What's in it for me?" I ask when she merely stares at me.

"How bold of me to assume you'd do it to help your friend. When was the last time you saw him?"

I shrug, glancing away. I have no idea how much time has passed in Hell while I was topside. Based on how it's been

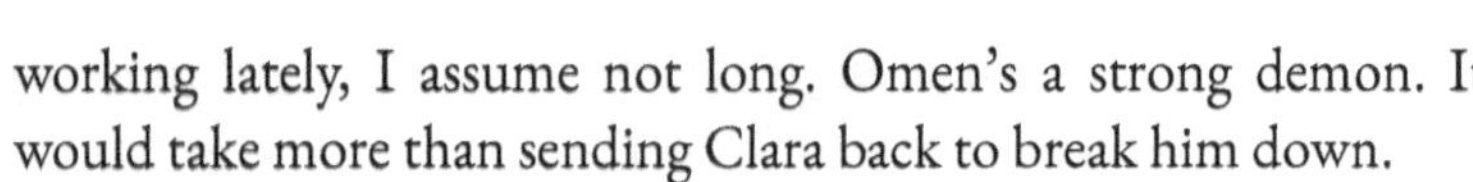

working lately, I assume not long. Omen's a strong demon. It would take more than sending Clara back to break him down.

"Inconvenient," she mutters. "Are they soulbound?"

I shrug again, keeping my face as neutral as possible. "You'd have to ask him. Doubt it, though."

Her nostrils flare, her black skin flickering like lightning encased within dark storm clouds. "This right here is why you're annoying. I hope you understand that."

"Well aware, Prov. Are you going to answer my question?"

She exhales heavily and narrows her eyes. "Fine. What do you want?"

"Don't know yet."

Her mouth drops open and she scoffs. "You want me to give you an open-ended promise? Are you for fucking real? You remember who I am, right?"

I brush my palms across my thighs as magic swirls around us. "You think I'd forget?"

"Well, sometimes familiarity makes one forget pertinent information," she snaps.

"Didn't forget you're fate, Providence. Which is why I want the vow."

"Oh, a vow. Nothing big, then." Her eyes narrow, pinning me in place. "You're still going to go check on Omen. You're a softie like that. So, why would I—"

"Because I know all your embarrassing secrets." I smirk as the realization crashes into her.

"You fucking bastard. Fine. But you know the rules. If you want a love or binding spell, go visit a witch. If you want to find your soulbound, no you don't. And consent is always top billing, so don't—oh, what am I saying. You're a stickler for that shit."

"Not shit to have a willing participant in whatever I'm engaged in," I slap my hands on my legs, then push to my feet. "I'd say it's been a pleasure, but you're a bitch and if you ever yank me around the dimensions again, I'll fill your bathtub with squids."

Outrage flashes across her face, then dissolves as a full-body shudder takes over. "You wouldn't."

"Try me," I spin, intent on stepping into the void to get to Omen when I glance over my shoulder. "What about curses?"

She gives me a look. "What about them? Wait, is this your—"

I hold up my hand. "I don't need you for an education on curses, Prov. I'm asking if you can break them."

She shakes her head. "Only one I know who can is Karma. Somehow, I think you're better off doing the research yourself. Unless you made up with your darling sister?"

I roll my eyes and disappear into the void, not bothering to answer. Instead of Omen's room, though, I'm dropped into a dingy alley topside. I glance around, taking in the bright lights piercing the night. Thick bass rumbles from the building to my right, though the one on the other side sits silent. It's not that I've never been to a city up here before. It's been a long time, though. At least, I think it has.

As soon as I learned how to travel through the void, I would sneak up here to explore. Sometimes Omen tagged along. He was always more of a stickler for the rules—thought he had something to prove to our demon handlers. We were young and reckless and full of false bravado. Back then, this world wasn't so busy. There weren't as many humans, and technology hadn't burst from its bubble yet. Omen enjoyed the solitude more than me.

All that to say, I've been to a club before. It's been a while, though. Human emotions ran rampant, and they didn't always act in their best interests. Sometimes I wish it didn't take so much for demons to get a buzz. Not much up here does the trick. It might help ease the pain of the curse.

At least I'm not passed out in this dirty alley. Other than a strange tugging in my gut, it's as if it never afflicted me. I'm wary of believing I'm suddenly cured. They don't typically work like that. The music cuts out, and I freeze at the sudden silence. Three inhales later, the beat drops and the crowd inside screams. I tense, then remember—joy. They're not being tortured or whipped into

a frenzy like other situations I've been in. They're, dare I say, happy.

"Wouldn't it be nice," I mumble. The thought stops my brain from skipping to the next thing.

I'm happy. Always jovial. Always joking. Always jesting.

Except most of the time I'm faking it. Or playing at the emotion. Omen may be able to play off surly like a positive trait. I'm not capable. Being able to bury my emotions is my best asset, honestly. Otherwise, my friends would be constantly worried about me.

Curiosity more than anything has my feet moving toward the entrance. Just before I step into the bright neon street, I stop. Groups of humans filter past, unaware of the presence of a demon a mere few feet away. I close my eyes, hoping I have enough energy to mask my natural form. It's less scary than my true form, but I doubt the humans would appreciate a grey-skinned demon with black eyes prancing around them.

I step onto the sidewalk and wait for the screams of terror. A woman barely gives me a glance as she passes by with her friends, and I breathe a sigh of relief. When she looks over her shoulder, hunger heavy in her gaze, I duck my head. I can't do anything about my height. Slouching will have to do. I doubt it will deter anyone ravenous enough. I'm not here to hook up with some unsuspecting human.

For some reason, an image of a certain purple-haired witch pops into my mind. I should seek her out, find out what she was so close to telling me. Do I think she was about to reveal all her deepest, darkest secrets? Probably not. There was something, though. Something I could help with. And I desperately want to help her. I'll figure out why one little witch has such an impact on me later.

"Line's back there, buddy," a surly man six inches shorter than me grunts when I approach the front.

I glance down the block and purse my lips. More than a couple of people are watching our exchange. No, watching *me*. I glance down, taking in my leather-covered arms and simple white t-shirt. The jeans are a little tight, but nothing to alert the harpies about.

I lean closer and the man, *bouncer*, bares his teeth. "I'm with the band."

Flashing him my most charming smile doesn't do anything. I sigh, then snap my fingers in his face. His eyes take on a glazed appearance, and I wait for a beat, then push past him.

"Have fun, man!" he calls after me.

Hallways jut off to each side before the space opens up. Tall ceilings with the guts of the building exposed sit high above my head. It's less crowded than I expected. I wonder why the bouncer isn't letting more people in. It's not until I reach the railing in front of me that it clicks. A huge dance floor sits a story below. Hundreds of humans writhe to the music. They sway in time, merging with each other to create a cacophony of limbs tangled together.

A different kind of magic swirls around, infusing the very air with a rapturous energy. My blood and magic thrum through my veins and I spin, intent on joining them.

Half a step and my brain catches up with what I spotted in the crowd. Purple. Bright yet deep purple. It couldn't be Mari. I swing around and search the sea of people for her distinctive hair. It takes me a minute to find the woman, and my shoulders drop as relief floods me. Definitely not her.

Except...yes. Yes, it fucking is.

Before I can fully think things through, I snap my fingers and manipulate the shadows created by the lights to vanish. Wings burst from my back, and I vault over the railing.

This is a bad idea. A very bad idea.

CHAPTER FOURTEEN
MARI

I needed this. More than I thought I did. Taking my mind off everything was the right move. As my hips sway to the music, my head empties. I ignore the sweat-soaked bodies brushing against me and let go. In my head, I'm an incredible dancer. My arms sway in a fluid motion, and my ass—oh my ass is on fire.

A giggle escapes me, and I clamp a hand over my mouth. "No giggling," I whisper to myself and catch Percy's eye.

"What are you doing?" she mouths. Or maybe she's shouting and I just can't hear her over the bass and people singing.

I shake my head, then drop my hand. Giggling isn't my thing. I do not giggle. Except apparently when I've had more than a few drinks.

Now that I've stopped moving, I cringe at the sweat streaking down my neck and between my boobs. I lift my glass, then pout when I find it empty.

I grab Percy's arm and haul her closer to shout in her ear. "Going to get another."

She nods, and I snake my way through the crowd. I end up bumping into every single person as I make my way off through the sea of people. I forgot how crowded clubs get. Especially on a Saturday night. When I reach the edge of the dance floor, I pause to catch my breath.

I close my eyes as I inhale, trying to get my bearings. The floor

sways beneath my feet, and I wonder if I'm at my limit yet. Will one more drink put me over the edge from happy buzz to blubbering mess?

One more. You deserve it.

For once, I don't argue with the voice. "You have a good point. One more is an excellent idea."

I glance around, wondering if anyone caught me talking to myself. Sometimes I forget how to act in public. I've been so focused on everything else, I usually opt to stay inside. What if my sister came home? What if she sent a distress signal and I wasn't there? The guilt would eat me alive. This is the first time I've gone out since I moved to Lark's place.

When I turn to plot my course to the bar, I freeze. A man stands several feet away, staring at me. He's chiseled angles and dark mysteriousness. I snort at the thought. Is mysteriousness even a word? Another giggle threatens to escape, and I swallow it down, focusing on the man again. There's something familiar yet enigmatic about him. I'd remember meeting a man like this.

I smooth my sweaty palms down my thighs, using the move to try to tug down the skin-tight dress. Lark must have shrunk since the last time I saw her. If she was wearing this, she wouldn't be able to bend over without showing her whole ass. Much like me. Then again, I didn't care after the fourth drink.

His brows pull low and his nostrils flare. I glance over my shoulder, hoping there's someone behind me. When I swing back around, I stumble to the side. He takes a step as if he'll somehow catch me, but I'm able to right myself. I wiggle my fingers at him with my bottom lip between my teeth.

Not sexy. Stop it.

Immediately, I drop my hand as my cheeks heat. He probably won't be able to tell. I get red as a tomato when I dance. And when I exercise. And when I fuck. Another giggle escapes me, and I press my lips together in chagrin. I really need another drink to stop this weird phenomenon.

"He probably isn't even looking at me," I mutter, wobbling forward.

I shouldn't have worn the heels. Percy convinced me, saying they'd be a good weapon should we get into trouble. It was a ridiculous argument. If someone were to attack us, we're fucking witches. We could kick ass with our witchy selves. I snort, knowing the only thing I'll be kicking is every piece of furniture in the house later.

The man steps into my path, and I move to the side. We're in a strange dance I'm not entirely prepared for. Finally, he's right in front of me. His dark hair flutters in what I assume is the air conditioning, though I'm still overheated.

"Excuse me," I say sharper than I intended.

He shakes his head, and I huff. If he's just going to stand there and stare, my buzz will flee faster than Jeremiah when threatened with shriveled balls. Then again, I did say I was open to having a good time. I scan him from his head to his toes, and his form wavers. Maybe I shouldn't have another drink.

I paste on my best smile, intent on at least trying to flirt. "You come here often?"

Inwardly, I cringe. Outwardly, I show too many teeth and bobble my head. This is not fucking working. I'm too tipsy to flirt. He's basically glaring at me like I stole his dog, anyway. I feel like a fool, and it doesn't even make me feel good. This whole interaction is awkward and weird.

"Listen, I don't know what your deal is, but I'm taken," I shout when the bass drops. Dimitri's face pops into my head, and a genuine smile pulls at my lips. No, that bastard abandoned me for Hell. He might not have had a choice, but I didn't even get a note, or a call, or a carrier pigeon. The least he could've done was let me know he's okay.

The ball of fear I've been studiously ignoring pulses in my gut. He could be dead. Do demons die? I can't remember what he said about that. Ever since he left, I've been on a rollercoaster of

emotions. Which doesn't make a lick of sense. He was a blip in my life, and I have bigger things to worry about. Yet I can't stop my brain from conjuring him at the most random of times. Like when I'm awake. Or when I can't sleep. Or when he invades my dreams.

"Are you going to move?" I ask, and he lifts an eyebrow in question.

"What? Want me to gush about my amazing boyfriend? Fine. I will. He's tall. Probably taller than you. Muscles for days, yet light on his feet, like he could take flight at a moment's notice if I was in danger. Am I in danger, mister?" I give him an expectant look, and he smirks.

I rear back and swallow hard. The expression is exactly like the one Dimitri kept throwing at me when I would snap at him. As if my annoyance was cute and he couldn't help himself. No, Dimitri has grey skin. And pure black eyes with purple irises. And his skin cracks sometimes. He's electrifying and possessive and caring. Besides, he's cursed and constantly collapsing. This man hasn't even spoken.

"Name?" he asks, his tone low and gravelly, yet his voice carries over the music.

"Dimitri, if you must know. And he's waiting for me, so…" I shoo him away.

He doesn't move. Instead, he leans close, and I tense. Maybe my heels *are* going to get a workout. I wonder if blood will come out of the fabric. Percy will forgive me. If I stain the dress, though, Lark will kill me. Then she'll use her handy necromancer book, resurrect me, then kill me all over again. She's very protective of her clothes. It's part of the reason I stayed out of her room.

His lips touch the lobe of my ear, and I freeze. "I *have* been waiting for you."

The man's words filter slowly through my alcohol-soaked brain. When they finally do, I rear back. I'm pretty sure he's being a dick. Or a creep. Either way, I'd rather not entertain this charade anymore. Those warm fuzzy feelings I had vanish in a puff of smoke. Much like Dimitri does when he fucks off to Hell.

"I don't know who you think you are, but..." My mind blanks as he stares at me expectantly. I completely forgot what I was going to say. It was going to be really fucking good too. Like the kind you brag to friends about. Frustration builds in me, though it's muted by the blanket of liquor seeping into my bloodstream.

When I don't continue, he smirks. "Nice to know you think I'm *so* amazing, spitfire. Would have been nice to know we're dating. I'll let it slide, though. Oh, and to answer your question, I may *be* a danger, but I'm not a danger *to you*. Thought you'd have figured that out by now."

Realization slams into me and I scowl. He crosses his arms and waits for my reaction. Well, he's not going to get one. I'm going to turn around and march away. Bastard thinks he can trick me? Waltz into my girl's night and crash it? Does he think I'll just fall into his arms and swoon? I shall do none of those things.

I lean away and my head suddenly feels too heavy for my neck. I'm going down and I doubt I'll be able to save myself. Shock spreads across his face, and I close my eyes. I don't need to add to my embarrassment. After this, I'm definitely getting that drink to numb the pain—physical and emotional.

His strong arm snakes around my waist, and he picks me clean off my feet. All my resolve disappears and my body dissolves into him. At least, that's what it feels like. It isn't often I'm dangling in the air, yet here we are.

"How much did you have to drink, Mari?"

I glance up at him and blink slowly. I trace a finger between his brows, smoothing out the deep grooves etched into his flesh. He scowls and his eyes flash purple, revealing the demon hiding underneath his human disguise.

"So serious," I murmur, fascinated by how soft he is despite the chiseled cheekbones and hard jaw. I bite my lip as something rigid presses into my stomach. His jaw isn't the only thing that's hard.

"Answer the damn question, Mari."

"I dunno. But I was having a perfectly fine time before you showed up."

He rolls his eyes, then drops me onto my feet. It's more like a slow slide along his body. My ankle ruins the whole thing by forgetting its main function. A yelp leaves me, and yet again he catches me around the waist.

"You're done," he growls.

"What? No," I plead. "I promise I'll be good. It's just these damn shoes."

He narrows his gaze, studying my face, and I attempt to put on the most sober smile I can muster. I have no idea if it's working. Probably not, seeing as he's still holding me upright.

"Fine. One more, then I'm taking you home." He scowls again. "Don't give me that look."

"What look?" I ask, wiggling until he finally puts me down again.

"That wicked little grin like you just came up with a plan I'm going to hate. It's...disconcerting."

He flexes his fingers on my hips, then drops his hands. My bottom lip pushes out before I remember I should be pissed at him. He's tricked me, manhandled me, and ordered me about. Not to mention he abandoned me right when I was going to ask him for help. I'd finally decided to trust him, and he just disappeared.

I fix my face into what I hope is a haughty and aloof expression. "I'm going to get another drink. Why don't you stay here and watch me walk away."

Before he can respond, I step around him. It takes all my remaining active brain cells to stay upright and not stumble my way to the bar. I don't glance back at him. His eyes are fixed on my ass, though. The heat from his gaze warms me more than I already am. Hell, he could be trailing right behind me and I wouldn't know. Hopefully he listened since it was really fucking hard to stay upright all the way over here.

It takes a minute to catch the bartender's attention and

another five before he's finally in front of me. I give him my order, then tack on another two—one for Percy and a water for Dimitri. I don't know if alcohol affects demons like it does witches, but hopefully the insult will land. If not, at least he'll be hydrated.

"Thanks," I yell as I dig in my cleavage for cash and drop it into the tip jar. It's probably sweaty and I cringe. No helping it, though, without pockets.

I spin around to search for Dimitri, almost tipping into the person next to me. A large hand shoots out and steadies me, and I blink up at the man. It takes a minute for my mind to conjure a name for him. My arm tingles, almost burns. 

"Dusty. What are you doing here?" I yelp a little too loud. He isn't exactly blocking my way, but he's too close for my liking.

I hate to admit it, but I understand why Lark was smitten with him with his floppy blond hair and dazzling smile. She was enamored with him for two years, though I only met him once. She kept him to herself, and I suspect it was because she knew I'd mention the multiple red flags she was collecting. I suppose we didn't really have any good role models for healthy relationships growing up. Perpetually single or gone too soon, those are our legacies.

"Enjoying the night." He steps closer when a group pushes past behind him. "You?"

"Same. Percy's here," I blurt out. I am definitely not sober enough to deal with this man.

"Oh yeah?" He smirks. He never did like Percy. She was too loud, too brash, too flighty for him. Personally, I think he knew Percy told Lark to dump his narcissistic ass.

I nod, sending my head swimming. "Yup. Girl's night."

"Without your sister?"

The comment sobers me more than anything else could. He knows she went missing. Actually, he was the second person I confronted when she stopped answering my calls, after Percy, of course. At the time he seemed sincere in his concern, but don't

they always? He might not be the one who made her vanish, but there's something he knows.

"It was something to see you, Dusty. I gotta get these to Percy and...my boyfriend." I may have used Dimitri as an excuse to fend off a would-be suitor, yet a boyfriend is coming in handy. I might just use this lie more often.

"Boyfriend, huh? Always thought you were—"

"Were what?" I snap.

"Oh, nothing. Good to see you, Mari." He smirks again, then brushes my arm as he turns away.

My skin burns, and I juggle the drinks while trying to rub the spot. Dimitri appears in front of me and snatches the glasses. He eyes me as I press my hand against my arm. I don't like Dusty touching me, even accidentally.

"Who was that," Dimitri growls, more of a demand than an inquiry.

"An ex. Not my ex. My sister's," I mutter as I lose track of Dusty in the crowd.

Dimitri's head turns, probably still able to see the man. "I didn't like how close he was."

"If you were so worried about him, then perhaps you should have come over sooner," I snap, grabbing Percy's and my glasses. "Have fun with your water."

After all the commotion, my buzz has taken a sharp nosedive. When I get to the edge of the dance floor, I throw back my drink. I down half of it in one go, then sigh as the alcohol works its way through my system. My one more might need to be three if I keep losing that good feeling I had while dancing.

This is supposed to be *my* night. So why do I feel so guilty? I shake my head, focusing on the fuzziness creeping along the edges of my brain. I won't let anyone ruin my one chance to be free from what my life has become.

CHAPTER FIFTEEN
DIMITRI

This is not how I thought tonight would go.

In fact, ever since I crashed into Mari's world, things have been wonky. The contentment I once felt with my life has fled along with most of my sanity. I used to be confident in my decisions, fulfilled in my role in Hell. The moment I blasted out of her closet, the stability I once felt dissolved with the clouds I created.

I should go—leave her to her night. She has her friend, who might be her lover, to take care of her. Checking on Omen should be my first priority—my *only* priority. There's no logical reason for me to stay. Except I can't walk away. It could be because I'm worried about her or that I want her to get home safely. I'd be lying to myself.

I still remember the feel of her in my arms. Her touch has imprinted itself into my very being. Walking away means never experiencing her skin against mine again. It means leaving her to fate. I was never very good at trusting Providence at the best of times. Believing her to take care of one little spitfire of a witch? Yeah, no.

Shaking my head, I trail after Mari. She's frozen on the edge of the dance floor. She throws back her head, finishing her drink. When I asked her how many she had, it wasn't to shame her, though she seemed to take it that way. I've had drunken revelries

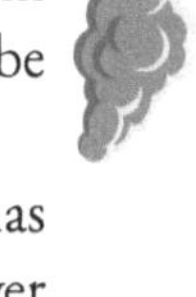

with witches before, and they go from having a nice little buzz to puking extremely quickly.

Mari's hips sway to the beat of the music. When she lifts her friend's drink to her lips, I push past the group of people streaming toward the stairs. Even if she isn't close to the edge, I need to be there just in case.

A server stops next to her, and Mari beams at him while she sets her empty glasses onto the tray. The man says something and Mari laughs, then shakes her head. Jealousy curls in my gut and cements my feet to the floor. Mari isn't mine. She's free to do whatever she wants. Since I can't force myself to leave, I should hang back. Keeping myself at a distance while making sure she's safe is better than acting like a possessive lover.

Instead of listening to my better sense, I stomp forward. Humans scatter from my path as my magic snakes through their legs. I'm going to have so much paperwork if I get back to Hell. Ludovic will have my ass for interfering with humanity. This may be small, but he's a stickler for the rules. Maybe I can hide behind Triton. He's been noticeably absent, though.

I reach for Mari as she attempts to slip into the crowd. She squawks yet doesn't push me away. She glares at me over her shoulder.

"What are you doing?" she demands.

"You want to dance? Fine. We'll dance."

She rolls her eyes, and her fingers circle my wrist. "You're infuriating."

"I've been called many things before but never infuriating." I lean down and whisper in her ear. "Won't you feel safer grinding that perfect little ass on me instead of some asshole who thinks his dick is the greatest gift to women?"

"I'm not admitting that, but I won't stop you if you come with me," she says stubbornly.

"Good girl," I murmur, and she shivers. I tuck away that little piece of information for later. While witches and demons don't usually hook up, I'm done resisting her. Not that I tried very hard before. She's too perfect, too enticing. If I'm not careful, she'll be my downfall. I'm not sure I particularly care, though. For now, I'm going to enjoy being with her while I don't feel like shit. I'll deal with Omen and Providence and my curse tomorrow. Or the next time I'm in Hell.

I bury my face in her neck and spear my magic out to create a path. If I'm not careful, someone will spot my mask slipping and we'll be in trouble. I'm not ready to make a mad dash for the exit just yet.

She strains against me, and I lead us toward the middle of the crowd. I spot another witch among the humans, her skin glittering in the party lights flashing over the throng. This must be the infamous Percy. Witches aren't hard to spot when you know what to look for, and Percy isn't any different.

The gap closes behind us, leaving us with a bubble of space and I force us to stop. Percy's eyebrows climbs higher, disappearing under her swooping bangs. Her gaze snaps to Mari and she presses her lips together. Mari does a weird flopping thing with her hand, and I can feel her roll her eyes. Mostly because her entire body tries to roll with them. A grin splits my face.

Mari tips her head back and gestures me down. I duck closer and her lips brush my ear. If she feels my cock hardening against her back, she doesn't give any indication.

"Percy's my best friend. Be nice."

I turn my head, our mouths almost touching, and her eyes grow wide. "Are you fucking her?"

I meant to be more tactful when I asked. Subtly isn't in my repertoire tonight. Besides, she probably wouldn't pick up on it in her tipsy state. She shakes her head, her brows pulling low. Realization dawns and she grins.

"Are you jealous?"

"Nope. Just wondering," I mutter, though I don't think she hears me over the music.

The lie sits on my tongue as she turns back to Percy. I press a light kiss to her neck, then straighten. I don't know why I did it,

but the taste of her washes away the falsehood. It takes all my focus to empty my mind and not whisk her away.

Percy scowls at me, though that's not surprising. To her, I look like some random man Mari picked from the crowd. With my arm around her waist and her relaxed state, I'm sure this doesn't look good.

Unless she knows I'm a demon.

That would complicate things. Most witches know more than Mari does about us, but they also don't like us very much. There's a fraught history between our kinds. If Percy's been taught any of the saga, she's sure to attack me. I don't know how Mari will react to that. Being put between her best friend and me, she's sure to pick her friend. I'd expect no less.

"We should dance," I murmur into her ear.

Her hips are already swaying, keeping time with the music swirling around us. A man comes up behind Percy and lightly touches her arm. They exchange a few words, and her hands end up behind his neck while his hands fall to her hips.

As Mari moves, her ass grinds into my cock. Maybe this wasn't a good idea. I'm going to end up throwing her over my shoulder and taking her someplace more secluded. The alley didn't seem too dirty. I doubt she'd appreciate fucking there, though. Like hell would I take her in the bathroom. Only assholes and degenerates fuck women in a public toilet. Then again, I've probably had dirtier experiences.

Mari doesn't deserve something quick and dirty. She's worth more than that. She deserves candlelight and flower petals and wooing. So much fucking wooing. Except I don't know how to woo a witch.

Mari turns and presses her palms to my chest. I wish she was gazing at my actual form instead of this skinsuit I hastily threw on. She raises an eyebrow as her body slithers against me. Her tits brush against me, and my cock hardens even more, though I didn't think it'd be possible.

She says something, but it's too quiet—too slurred—for me

to understand. Those drinks are finally hitting her. My main job won't be dancing, it'll be keeping her upright. With her flushed cheeks and pert nose, I don't think I've seen a sight more adorable. She scowls, only endearing her to me more. If I'm not careful, I'll fall hard for her.

It wouldn't be so bad. Until she rejected me. Or I was called to Hell once more. If I can't break this curse, I'll end up bouncing around dimensions, leaving her for days, weeks, months. No one should live like that. Always waiting for someone to come home. I don't know if I'll be able to resist her. Especially with the way she's moving against me.

I get lost in the music, in the thrumming of bass within my blood, in her glittering gaze. It's not until Percy's waving her toward the edge of the dance floor I let her go. Trailing behind, I stand just out of earshot while the friend sends me dirty looks. When she leaves with the guy she was dancing with, I'm surprised.

Mari smiles lazily at me. "You'll take me home, right?"

I nod, then lead her outside into the cool night air. She fans her face and lets out a deep sigh. When she wobbles, I wrap an arm around her waist and guide her into the alley. I have no idea if I'll be able to transport her through the void. It might reject us, throw us out into some desolate wasteland. Or we could end up right where we're supposed to be.

"I don't know how my curse—"

She sways in my hold, her eyes already shut. "Don't care. Home, please."

I exhale heavily, then scoop her up. The last thing I want is to lose her *in* the darkness. Especially while she's drunk. With a whispered prayer to whichever deity's turn it is to watch over the void, I step into the shadows.

My muscles sag when we're dropped into her living room. Mari mumbles, cuddling closer to my chest. I make my way toward her bedroom in the dark. Tonight didn't go the way I'd expected. I got what I wanted, though.

For a moment, I captured joy in my hands. I don't know what

true happiness feels like, but dancing with Mari came pretty fucking close. Ending the night tucking her into bed feels appropriate. At least I didn't get called to some random corner of Hell.

I spend a bit too long staring at her while she sleeps. When I turn to go, her hand catches mine and I glance back.

"Are you leaving?" she mumbles. I'd planned on it. Omen needs help, and Clara probably isn't doing much better. Triton's been missing for a minute, and Ludovic is acting weird. Add in the issues I need to sort out with my sister and my plate is full.

She huffs when I don't answer and peeks at me from beneath heavy lids. "Stay. I don't want to be alone."

I lean over her and whisper, "I'll take the couch."

When I try to leave, though, she tugs once more. "With me."

I can't deny her, especially when she slowly blinks at me, anticipation and vulnerability resting in her eyes. She expects me to tell her no. She's probably used to not getting what she wants. Pretty sure she said she never goes clubbing and she missed going out. The words were slurred, though, so I can't be sure.

"I'll stay until you fall asleep."

I swallow hard as I glance around for a place to sit. She tugs, her nails digging into my palm, and my resolve crumbles. When I crawl in next to her, she whines, yanking on the comforter under me.

"You're going to be my downfall, spitfire," I mutter, and she snorts.

"Just get under the covers. We'll pretend this never happened tomorrow."

She curls up next to me, pressing her ass into my hip. This is going to be a very long night. After another ten minutes of her wiggling and me staring at the ceiling, I let out a low growl. She freezes, then glances over her shoulder.

"Did you just growl at me?"

"If you keep moving, neither of us will get any sleep," I snap.

Her lips curve into a sly grin, and I brace myself. "Maybe I don't *want* sleep."

"You're drunk. Not just drunk—witch drunk. Which is arguably worse than regular drunk. Good decisions are never made while fueled by alcohol."

She pouts, whether to guilt me or because she's genuinely hurt, I don't know. The way she's acting doesn't seem like her. She's sassy and fights me at every turn. She doesn't pout when she doesn't get her way.

"Fine. But if I wake up in the morning and you're gone, don't bother coming back."

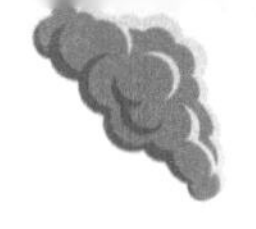

CHAPTER SIXTEEN
MARI

"No, Percy, I didn't puke. Yes, I have taken pain meds. No, I haven't made the tonic yet because it smells like feet and tastes like an old man's jockstrap after sixteen rounds of sports," I mumble toward the phone sitting on the counter. I dig my thumbs into my temples.

My head's been pounding since I woke up twenty minutes ago. Hopefully, the meds kick in soon or I'm going to bash my head into the wall. Percy's call didn't help either. Apparently, I had the bright idea to put my volume all the way up, and the shrill, tinny music blasting from the device sent a shockwave through my body I might never recover from.

"So, did you sleep with him?" she asks quietly. She must be feeling the effects of last night, too.

"With who?" My memories are blurry, but I know who she's talking about. I was hoping she would have forgotten.

"Mr. Tall-dark-and-handsome who looked like he wanted to devour you." She snorts, then groans.

"He did not," I mutter as I make a cup of coffee, my mind wandering to the demon currently sleeping in my bed. "I ran into Dusty at the bar, by the way."

Something clatters on her end. "What the fuck was he doing there? I thought he moved to...Nantucket? San Antonio? I can't

remember, but I *do* remember lighting a candle for the residents to protect them."

"No, he never moved. I think he said he was, but then Lark disappeared and he stuck around. He said some weird shit I can't really remember. I still think he had something to do with—"

"We've been over this, Mare. He didn't even know she was a witch. How would he have done anything? And you'd know if she was dead. Like, not just visiting a foreign dimension, but actually truly, soul in Hell, dead."

"I know, but still. He's hiding something, and I hate that I can't figure it out. It might not have anything to do with Lark."

"Speaking of...why were you asking about demons? Do you think she was kidnapped by them?"

It takes me a minute to process what she's saying. "Kidnapped? She drew the circle, Percy. She had instructions to do that. Unless they somehow learned how to bust out of...I gotta go."

I hang up before she can protest. Could Lark have been taken? I didn't think demons did that, but as we've established, I don't know shit about them. I need to ask Dimitri, accept his help. If I didn't make an absolute fool of myself last night. Once I downed Percy's drink, the rest of the night was a blur. I remember dancing, feeling weightless, then his warm body against mine. A memory scratches at my brain—maybe yelling at him to take off the creepy mask? I don't particularly recall.

When I woke up, he looked like his usual self, though a bit rundown, I suppose. Black smudges circled his eyes, and his skin was cracking at his fingertips. I didn't stick around long enough to examine him more. Every time I see him, he seems to be collapsing under his own weight. He needed to rest and waking him up wouldn't help.

At least, that's what I'm telling myself. It has nothing to do with embarrassment or avoiding awkwardness. I'd just be delaying the inevitable. Eventually, he'll get up. He'll come in here with that lazy grin of his and I'll melt a little inside. Then I'll deflect my

feelings with some snappish comeback. It is the way. I've been doing this for years every time I get a tiny hint of a crush. I never let anyone get close enough to woo me.

Not that a demon is wooing me.

If I push him away enough—keep him at arm's length—I'll be able to pick his brain without losing my heart. Not that my heart is in danger. A crush doesn't equate to love. Those fairy-tale endings don't happen to prickly women like me.

The thought has me wrinkling my nose. My aunt called me that often—prickly, waspish, cruel. She had a litany of descriptions for me while praising my sister for her levity and lightheartedness. Lark was always the lifeblood of the house, keeping our aunt in line and off my back.

I shake my head and sigh heavily. As soon as Dimitri's up, I'm going to need to ask for help. No more pussyfooting around the issue. I don't particularly like the idea of him knowing about Lark, but I don't have a choice. Telling him to keep the information to himself will be my first order of business.

Another heavy sigh leaves me when I spot the pile of books I left on the small dining table. I need to go through them again. I thought they were merely references for her. Maybe she was trying to be a better witch or something. Yet I keep coming back to them. I swear the necromancy book is following me around. It showed up on my nightstand the other morning when I was sure I'd left it in here.

"Morning," Dimitri grunts as he steps into the kitchen.

I croak out some semblance of a greeting, but he doesn't even look at me when he makes a beeline for the coffeepot. I flip open the standard spellbook from when I was a kid, pretending to read it instead of tracking his movements. He doesn't even ask, just opens the fridge and starts rummaging around.

The way he moves through the space is familiar. As if he's spent many a morning in my house.

Lark's house. Not mine, I remind myself. I may have been living here for the past four months, yet it doesn't make it mine.

As soon as I start thinking like that, I'll have to accept Lark isn't coming back. And I refuse to do that.

"What are you doing?" I finally ask when he pulls a pan from the bottom cupboard.

"Making breakfast. Why don't you go take a shower? I'm sure your head doesn't like your body right now," he murmurs.

"You don't—"

He holds up a hand. "Do we really have to go through all that when we both know we'll just end up right where we started? Go."

I grit my teeth, holding back the verbal lashing I want to unleash on him. I mutter incoherently as I stomp from the space.

"Bossing me around like he's the boss of me." I cringe at my own grumblings. "I'm only going because I planned on showering before he got up." I kick the bathroom door shut and nod to myself in the mirror. "Fuck, I look like shit."

Suddenly, I'm incredibly grateful he avoided my gaze. He would have poofed right out of here if he got a look at my splotchy face and smeared mascara. At least it looks like I had a fun time.

The light overhead becomes too much, and I slide the dimmer until it's at a more respectable level. A groan leaves me when I'm under the hot spray, and I forget all about Dimitri commanding me. I doubt I'll be able to choke down any of the food he's making. Unless I want to throw up on him.

By the time I'm done, the distinct smell of bacon fills the air. I peek out the door before tiptoeing across the hall to my bedroom. I grab the first shirt I can find. Dimitri must have tossed his own clothes on top of mine since it smells like him. I tug on shorts, then shuffle toward the kitchen.

I peer around the wall and find him facing the stove, his back to me. He's humming, though I can't place which song. Maybe it's one from Hell. Do they have music in Hell? Do they have cities? Houses? Electricity? There's so much I don't know. If it's anything like here, then maybe Lark isn't suffering. If it's like the movies depict, she's fucked. Even if it's like Aunt Star told us, she's probably screwed.

You won't find out until you ask. I roll my eyes at my sister's voice. She can shut the fuck up. All she had to do was send me a text and she couldn't even do that. Like hell am I going to listen to her now. Regardless if she's right.

"You going to hover in the living room or join me?" he calls, and I huff, slinking into the room.

He sets a platter on the table, and I stare at the deliciously greasy mess. When he plops down a milkshake next to my plate, I give him a questioning look.

"Sugar'll help."

"How exactly?"

"Maybe it'll sweeten you up." He smirks, then turns back to the stove to get more food.

When he settles in the chair across from me, I sink into my seat. We dish everything up in silence. Suffocating silence. I open my mouth more than once to break it, always thinking better of it before I make a sound. He doesn't notice he's so focused on his plate.

His fork is halfway to his mouth with a heaping pile of hash-browns when he lets out a growl. I freeze, glancing around. Nothing moves. Maybe it's a Hell thing.

"Fuck off, Providence," he snarls, never taking his eyes from his plate.

"Um..."

A woman materializes next to me. I yelp as my chair tips back and I fall in slow motion. And then the world stops. Or rather, I stop my sluggish descent. Dimitri's foot tugs on the bottom of my seat, righting me. My hands slap the table, and the silverware rattles against my mug.

"What a way to greet me," the woman, *Providence*, says with a sniff. "You forgot this."

She drops an iridescent object on the table, narrowly missing the eggs.

How did he know I like my eggs over easy and not scrambled?

I shake my head, focusing on Providence. She might be a demon, but she seems more like a goddess with her straight silver hair cascading down her back and her eyes flashing from silver to gold before finally settling on solid black. I press my lips together, unable to rip my gaze from her.

"Knock it off, Prov."

She tilts her head as she stares at me. "Or what?"

"Squids."

Her nostrils flare and her sharp cheekbones become plumper. I blink several times, trying to figure out what the fuck just happened.

"No need for that," she snaps, then turns her attention to my demon. *The* demon.

"Then you can leave."

I clear my throat, and Providence's gaze flicks to me. I point to the object. "Sorry, what is that?"

She rolls her eyes to Dimitri. "Another little witch? Are you two collecting them or something? Next thing you know, Triton's going to be hiding one in his attic or something. I swear, you demons get bolder with each passing cycle."

"Would you shut the fuck up?" Dimitri growls. "I've got enough problems without you piling on more?"

She holds up her hands and steps back gracefully. Actually, I think she's floating. I glance at her feet, but white clouds obscure her from the knees down. She bends, forcing me to focus on her face. I swallow hard. She's not particularly scary. For some reason, her presence unsettles me. Especially when she tilts her head and stares into my eyes. It's as if she's searching for my soul to snatch it up and eat it.

Her lips twitch, and I wonder if she can read my mind. I repeat one word over and over in my head. If she wants to decipher my thoughts, she's going to have to try harder than...before? What the fuck am I doing?

"Petrichor? The smell after a good rain?" she murmurs, and I gag on my own spit.

"What are you babbling about?" Dimitri interjects, but neither of us pays him any mind.

"No, witch. I can't read your mind."

"Then how—"

"You were mouthing the word." She grins, and it transforms her face into something not as terrifying. "Welp, I better get going. Lives to destroy, couples to devastate. You know how it is."

Dimitri sighs heavily and grabs the object she dropped on the table. He tucks it away in a pocket I can't see. From the way he's acting, I doubt he'll tell me what it is. Honestly, it looked like an egg. Not one I've ever seen before, though.

"Get on with it then," he growls, still staring at his plate. He hasn't looked at me once since he stumbled into the kitchen.

"Nice to meet you," I whisper.

She narrows her eyes, that smile still playing on her lips. "Little piece of advice, dear. Don't wait. Good things never happen to those who do."

She gives a pointed look at Dimitri before wiggling her fingers at me, then vanishing as quickly as she appeared. A barrage of questions sits on my tongue, and I open my mouth to unleash them. They die on the tip when he holds up his hand. His shoulders slump and he slowly shakes his head.

Then he disappears.

CHAPTER SEVENTEEN
DIMITRI

"Fuck me," I groan, rubbing the bump on the top of my head.

"Dimitri?" Triton's voice floats from the dark, and I grit my teeth. I may have been avoiding Mari as best I could in that small-ass kitchen, but that didn't mean I wanted to leave. I'd rather see her than Triton anytime.

"What the fuck, Triton." It's not a question.

"Uh, I was trying to do something else."

I glance around the dark landscape. He steps in front of me, blocking my view of what I'm pretty sure is a ring of candles. Why the fuck would Triton need a summoning circle? He's a demon, not a witch. As far as I know, they're the only ones who use them. Other humans have tried, and a few even got them right. They fell out of fashion a long time ago, though. Then there were the stakes and the burning and most of it stopped.

"Well, can you send me back?" I snarl.

With time being wonky between the worlds, I can't guarantee I haven't abandoned Mari for months. At least time never gets the chance to run on either plane. Otherwise one of us would be hundreds of years in the future while the other lagged behind. It'd be a constant race to see who could get to the end of the world first.

"Oh, yeah. Sure."

He trips over his feet and mutters a curse. The flame from one of the candles wicks out, and I'm shoved into the void once more. Did he summon me? Or was this Providence fucking with me? That's not exactly her style. More my sister's. Karma's a bitch, but I love her. Even if she is being ridiculous right now.

My stomach flips when I drop back in my seat in Mari's kitchen. She's nowhere to be seen, but I can sure hear her. I lean to the left and spy her in the living room. The space looks like it did when she unpacked the closet—destroyed, decimated, tornado-like. In the middle of the mess is Mari. She throws things around, bellowing and cursing. Whether she's pissed off at me or someone else, I don't know. I'm slightly terrified to find out.

I clear my throat, and she whips around to glare at me. I press my lips together when she narrows her gaze. Guess that answers my question.

She stabs her finger in my direction and growls, "You."

"Good to see you're feeling better," I say, fighting a grin. I can't help myself. From the blush on her cheeks to the wisps of hair flying about her head, I'm entranced. I much prefer this version of her to the one last night.

"Oh, I'm feeling *much* better. And you forgot this." She chucks something round and hard at my face.

Either she has a lot of faith in my abilities or didn't care whether it whacked me in the face. I am a demon, though. My hand snaps up and I clutch the dragon egg. I wonder how long it's been gone from Hell. If the horde notices this little one is gone, they'll come after Omen. And he'll deserve it. He never did pay attention when we learned about the dragons residing in the adjacent dimension.

"Are you...upset about the egg?" It has to be more than that.

She straightens, her face clear of the rage. "Egg? That's what —no. You're not going to distract me. That's all that happens with you. I have plans, and you're constantly muddling them up."

I lean back in my chair and cross my arms. "What exactly have

I muddled up for you? Truthfully, I don't think I'm why you're upset."

Am I goading her? Yes. Is it just so I can watch her keep being a spitfire? Maybe. Either way, I might finally get some answers. My curse hasn't flared up the last couple trips here. I could choose to believe it's well and truly gone. Walking away from her would be easier. I'm in this now, though. I'll spend the next century wondering what she was hiding and how I could have helped.

"Upset? You think *this* is upset?" She stomps closer, then plants her fists on her hips. "Oh, buddy, I can be *so* much more upset if I want to be."

"I'd love to see it." I smirk, counting down from three.

"Fuck you," she seethes. "Fuck demons. Fuck being a witch. I want *human* problems. I want to worry about the weather and what I'm going to make for dinner and whether I should have another cup of coffee. Instead, I'm stuck in this fucking house with a demon who can't figure out how to *be* a demon or at least stay in one goddamn place for longer than a couple hours. I just need the book. A spell. A sign. *Something* to tell me I'm on the right path."

She's panting by the time she's done. Tears drip down her face as she stares over my head. This wasn't the spitfire I wanted to goad. When she's ranting about me, that's one thing. This...this is something more. I imagined her secrets to be something mundane I could fix. Not being a witch? I can't do anything for her there. I don't have the ability to strip them of their power. Few do in Hell.

"Which book?" I murmur, and she blinks slowly at me as if she's forgotten I'm here.

"Doesn't matter," she whispers.

She swipes at her face and makes a noise in the back of her throat before turning around. When she starts cleaning, I know I've lost her. Or at least, sharing time is over.

I push to my feet, and the lightheadedness is back. Catching the edge of the table, I close my eyes and wait for it to pass. Sleeping most of the night helped, but not for long apparently.

When the dizziness passes, I make my way into the living room and watch her for a bit.

"It's a dragon egg," I murmur, and she tenses.

"I can't hear you when you mumble. If you've got something to say, have the balls to say it with your full chest."

I snort, glancing away. "It's a dragon egg. Omen's soulbound needed an egg. He just swiped the wrong one."

"What's a soulbound?" She turns to me with confusion on her face and a small green book in her hands. "Wait. A dragon? You brought a fucking dragon into my house?"

"Uh, no. It's not a dragon...yet. And technically, Providence brought it here. It must have fallen out of my pocket when I was in the void and she picked it up. Thought I had hold of it when I got pulled away."

Her mouth tightens as if she's holding back what she really wants to ask. "Do you still have it?"

I really don't want to answer her. "A soulbound is basically soulmates. Though it's a bit more intense than humans make it."

"Yeah, yeah, yeah. One soul is bound to another. Can I see it?"

Sighing, I pull it from my pocket and hold it out. She scrambles over, her bad mood vanishing in the wake of something new and exciting. I glance over my shoulder and note her clean plate, filing away the information for later. If there *is* a later for us.

She hesitates, her hand hovering over the egg. "Is it hot?"

"Why don't you just take it and see? It's not about to hatch so you're fine."

Her eyes snap to mine. "How do you know?"

I shrug, then grab her wrist, turn over her hand, and drop it in her palm. "Worked with them for a bit."

"You worked with dragons? Didn't they want to eat you?"

I smirk, raising an eyebrow. "You thought *I* wanted to eat you when we first met, spitfire. Which I'm still willing to—"

"Stop talking," she growls, but there's a hint of a smile on her

lips. "It's glowing. And not as hot as I thought it'd be. Wait, is that because it's dying?"

"For someone who was concerned with dragons eating demons, you're pretty cut up about a baby dragon not making it."

Her mouth drops open. "It's a *baby*."

I hold my hands up with a chuckle. "Okay, no jokes about the baby. Got it."

"Don't you need to take it back?" she asks as she cradles it to her chest. I start to reply when her nose scrunches. "Who's Providence. I mean, what's Providence? And who's Omen? And Clara?"

"You realize by asking me about my life, you're going to have to tell me about yours, right?"

She tips her chin up. "If you don't want to tell me anything, just say that."

I hold my hands up and gesture her into the living room. If I don't sit down soon, my knees are going to give out. Not that she needs to know that. There's nothing she can do for me other than find a cure, which I'm not entirely sure she can. I don't even know if she would help me. Our relationship thus far hasn't exactly been stable. Asking again feels like a fool's errand.

Once we're settled on the couch, I take a deep breath, trying to figure out where to start. "Omen's another demon. We're best friends. Providence is his sister, though it's not like siblings up here. It's hard to explain. You just met her, but I doubt you'll see her again. She keeps to herself most of the time. Um...Clara is the witch Omen is soulbound to. She summoned him, and they're kind of in the middle of some bullshit. I don't know. I try to stay out of the nitty gritty—only give advice when it's necessary."

Her eyebrows climb up her forehead the longer I speak. "Clara's a witch? Why didn't you just ask her about your curse?"

"Did you miss the part about them being in the middle of bullshit? I barely touched her arm a while back and Omen almost flamed out on me. Put me into a fucking wall."

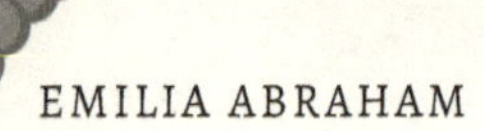

Alarm flashes across her face. "Why are you laughing about that?"

"Mari, I'm a demon. It's how we deal."

"Putting each other into walls and turning into balls of fire? Because I'm assuming when you say 'flamed out' he literally turned into flames."

I nod, realizing how observant she's been. I thought most of the time she was merely tolerating my presence. Now I'm not so sure.

"So?" I prompt, hoping she'll open up.

"So what? Oh, is this the part where I spill all my deepest, darkest secrets? Maybe throw in a couple childhood traumas and a good generational prophecy or two?"

I sigh, wondering how far I should press this. "Why do you do that—push me away? Do you do it to everyone or am I just special?"

She clamps her lips together, her fingers stroking the egg absently. "Clearly, I don't make friends well. Didn't realize that was a fatal flaw."

"You're doing it again," I murmur, and she huffs.

"Fine. You want me to open up? I have Percy. And my sister. My parents are dead and so is the aunt who raised us."

I swallow hard. "I wasn't asking—you know what? I'll take it. What about your coven?"

Her face screws up and her gaze meets mine. "What coven? I didn't grow up in one. Figured that was for, like, *witches*."

"Covens are pretty universal. I mean, not all witches are in one, obviously, but it's a common enough thing. You realize you're an actual witch, right?"

She snorts, fixing her gaze on the egg once more. "There are definitely different types of witches. You've got your extreme witches who make it their entire identity. Then there's the earthy witches and the dark witches and the—"

"Okay, I get it. But covens are universal."

"Then you've got the foolish witches. The ones who dive so

deep into the lore, so far into their delusions, they're no longer able to function. They forget about the world around them and all the responsibilities they have. Unless it's to admonish those around them about the dangers of being a witch. How it would be better to cut that part out of themselves rather than suffer a fate worse than death."

She's so blasé I almost think she's reciting something she read once. In actuality, I think this was her life. With her parents dead, I'm guessing her aunt was the one who suffered. And heaped that suffering onto her nieces with no thought of how it would impact them when she was gone.

She drops the egg in my lap and sighs. "I need a book. One that has darker magic in it. Like a scrying spell that can span dimensions."

She's still holding something back. It rests in the tightening of her eyes and the twitch of her lips. She *wants* to tell me more, but something holds her back.

"I don't have spells."

"Then how do you keep vanishing? Where do you go?"

I smile ruefully. "Oh, spitfire. I'm a demon. I walk through worlds."

CHAPTER EIGHTEEN
MARI

I don't know where to look. I didn't mean to reveal all *that* to him. He's too observant, too easy to talk to, too personable. He's the type to get others to open up without even trying, and I fucking hate it. Or at least, I hate feeling exposed. I refuse to meet his gaze, though it's burning a hole in me. I've gotten enough pitying looks over the years. I don't need another one.

Walking through worlds. He walks through worlds probably as easily as I walk to the mailbox. He possesses magic I could never dream of. Hell, most witches have stronger powers than I do. I can feel it, the magic, sluggishly moving through my veins. Accessing it is another challenge I don't have time for. Envy bubbles within me at his abilities, and I shove it deep. It's not his fault he can do a bazillion things I can't. Doesn't stop me from wondering all he's seen—of wanting him to take me with him.

"Any particular worlds you want to visit?" Dimitri finally asks, breaking the silence. It's as if he's plucked the very thoughts from my brain and handed me the opportunity I've craved all my life. To visit other dimensions? To experience all the places a witch has never been? To live out a dream I've fantasized about since I was a child?

"I wouldn't know anything about other dimensions. I barely know anything about demons, clearly."

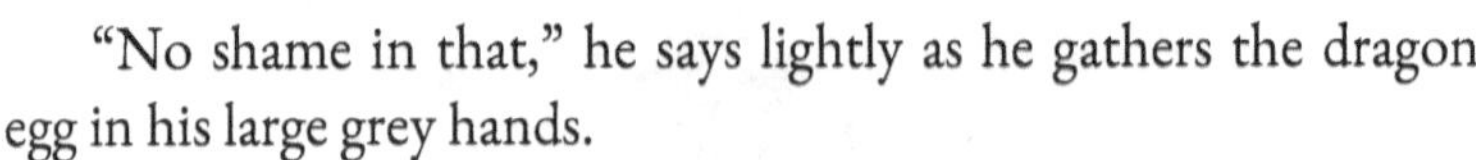

"No shame in that," he says lightly as he gathers the dragon egg in his large grey hands.

"Sure. Um, don't you have to take that back now? It's getting cold."

He nods as he gazes at it, pressing his lips together. "Want to go with me?"

My head snaps up and my chest tightens. It takes everything in me not to tackle him. Or scream. Or demand we leave right now. I try to keep my face passive and my voice nonchalant.

"If you need me to."

He leans closer, forcing my eyes to his. "Oh, I definitely need you."

He grabs my hand, and we're plunged into darkness. A scream sticks in my throat, then dissolves as his arm loops around my waist. I press my face into his chest, focusing on his scent rather than the void of nothingness we're hurtling through. Wind whips my hair around us, catching on something before whipping away again. It's going to be a bitch to get the tangles out.

"You can open your eyes, spitfire," he murmurs in my ear.

I lift my head hesitantly, blinking at the strange landscape he's brought us to. Glittering specks interrupt the dark night sky overhead along with a small purple moon. Dimitri tucks a strand of hair behind my ear, and I realize I match the moon. Or sun. Whatever it is. Black, craggy mountains rise, blocking the horizon. The breadth of the place is incomprehensible to my witchy mind.

"Is this…"

"The dragon realm. They used to be more spread out. Then—"

"Let me guess, humans tried to hunt them all, and they retreated for their safety?"

He chuckles, and I swear he drops a kiss to the top of my head. When I glance up, though, he's gazing out at the landscape.

"Actually, they're in their nesting period. Lasts a couple hundred human years. They'll go out more again once the hatchlings are born and able to fly."

He drops his hold on me and grabs my hand. He tugs me toward a large obsidian wall, and I dig my heels in.

"Problem, spitfire? Thought you wanted to meet the dragons?"

"I said no such thing. In fact, this is kidnapping, sir."

He grins back at me. "If you'd like me to fake kidnap you to get your feet moving, I can certainly do that."

I narrow my gaze. "I'd like to see you try."

In a blink, he tips me over his shoulder and takes off for the wall. I shriek and he shushes me. That more than anything pisses me off. I hate being shushed. I dig my knuckle into his back, then wince. I always thought love handles were supposed to be soft and squishy. Like a little gift to hang on to. His are pure muscle along with his back. I swear they're all rippling in front of my face.

"Keep it up, spitfire. I like your sass. Gets me—"

"Do not finish that sentence," I growl, wiggling. The last thing I need is to be in a foreign land while horny. He chuckles softly, and I crane my neck to take in the area once more.

"Where are we going?" I whisper. I'd rather not attract the dragons' attention. I wonder if they barbeque their meals before they eat them. Do they just go whole hog? One bite and they're done?

"Into the horde. Careful or I might feed you to one of them."

I huff, though I'm not entirely sure he's joking. I prop my elbow onto his shoulder blade and rest my chin in my hand. It's not the most comfortable, but at least the blood isn't rushing to my head. My gut begins to hurt long before we're close to the wall.

"Don't freak out," he mumbles.

I shriek again as wings sprout from his back and batter me in the face. They dissolve, then reappear, somehow accommodating my body over his shoulder. My arms end up around his waist, and I scream into his lower back as we lift into the air. Time warps and my mind shuts off, though my voice doesn't. I kick my legs and he grunts, the noise disappearing into the wind.

His feet slam into the rocky terrain, sending shards scattering across the ground like ice skittering across a frozen pond. He flips me over his shoulder, making my stomach roll. I won't feel even a little bit sorry if I puke on him now. He drops me to my feet, and my body sways. I swear I feel drunk. It reminds me of last night and the horrid hangover I had this morning.

"Well, at least you didn't freak out," he says with a grin.

"A little warning would have helped," I rasp, planting my hands on my knees. I concentrate on breathing deeply. In through the nose, out through the mouth. I can't remember what it's supposed to help with, but I do it anyway.

He rubs my back, still chuckling lightly. "Look at all these firsts for you."

"If you say 'I'm proud of you' or 'good job' or any other platitude, I'll aim toward you when I throw up."

His fingers slide against my cheeks, forcing me to meet his gaze. He's warm. Warmer than he should be after flying through the cold bite of wind. I wonder if that's the electricity in him. Or the heat radiating from the wall. Down here, I can't tell if it's too hot or too cold. It's like the perfect day. All I'd need is a light jacket to keep me comfortable. Up there, though, is another story.

Yet I'm not really thinking about flying. Or the weather. Or anything other than his skin against mine and the way he's looking at me. Like I'm something special. Something to be cherished. I wrap the feeling around my heart, letting it heat me from the inside out. For just a moment, I allow myself to imagine what it'd be like to be loved by someone. Loved by him.

It's glorious. Oh, it's glorious. To be seen as my true self? To be seen completely? It's a gift few in the world experience. And here he is, handing me this present as if it's nothing. As if he doesn't even realize how monumental it is.

"You look deliciously ruffled," he says with a smile.

"I look like I'm about to puke." Because of course I say the most unhinged thing to push him away.

"You'll do better next time. Ready?" He strides off toward the wall.

It takes a moment for his words to filter through my muddled brain. "Next time? Dimitri!"

I scramble after him, my toe catching on a particularly large black rock. I'm able to right myself before I faceplant, then freeze, staring at my feet.

"Dimitri," I call, and he turns. "Where the hell did these boots come from?"

"You realize I've got magic, right? Come on, spitfire. They get antsy when you hang around outside."

My mouth drops open when I spot the opening he's headed for. Shimmering silver strands cover a large section of the wall. They dance along the nonexistent wind, and I swear I hear bells. Tiny tinkling bells ringing softly through the air. I tip my head back, trying to spot the top. It's lost in a dense fog filled with lightning flashing silently within the clouds. When I glance down again, my clothes have changed. At least, I think they have.

"Leather? Really?" I snort. I don't even know the names for half the things encasing my body. The pants are tight, molding to my legs yet still giving me room to move. "A corset? Seriously?"

Dimitri appears in front of me, a grin plastered on his face. He's more energetic—healthy—than I've ever seen him before. Maybe staying in Hell, or a dimension close to it, helps. Maybe he's not even cursed. Could he just be allergic to Earth? Is it technically Earth if my world is just another dimension? I crinkle my nose. Thinking about this stuff always gives me a headache. I like what I can feel, what I can see. Which is especially hard when one is a witch. So much of my magic doesn't have a rhyme or reason to it. We do things that don't make sense to create something that does. It's probably the reason I've shied away from my roots for so long. Plus, growing up with an aunt who thought the entire universe and every creature within every dimension was after her didn't help.

"Would this make you feel better?" He snaps his fingers, and

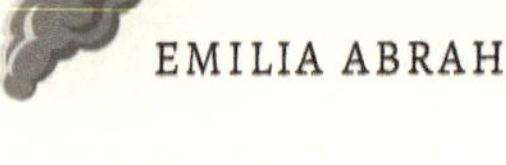

he's dressed in a masculine version of my own clothes—complete with corset.

"I—yeah. Sure." My mouth waters, and a wave of heat washes over me. A man in a corset never crossed my radar. A demon in a corset even less so. Dimitri in a corset? Yeah, I could definitely get used to this.

I ogle him until my eyes alight on something hanging from his belt. "Is that a dagger? Why do you get a dagger and I don't?"

He winces, then gives me a sheepish grin. "I wasn't sure if you'd hurt yourself. Or accidentally stab someone, thinking they were a threat."

I open my mouth, then snap it shut. He's right, as much as it pains me to admit. I'm in a foreign place about to see things I've only dreamt about witnessing, with a demon who thinks it's cute to not communicate fully, probably to catch my reaction. Normally, I'd be pissed. Right now, I'm too enamored with the demon standing in front of me to care.

"Fine, but if one of them eats me and I don't have a weapon to defend myself, it'll be on your head, mister." I march past him as if I know where I'm going. Most of the time, if I act like I know what I'm doing, shit works out. I tip my chin up, bury my fear under a blanket of false confidence, and keep going.

"Hey spitfire? I admire your gall, but you can't just walk through. There's a process."

I wave my hand over my shoulder. I'm sure I'll be fine. With confidence and a side of audacity, I'm sure I'll get through. I'll show him what happens when you bring a witch along. For good measure, I wrap a shield around myself. It's easier now that I've used the spell recently.

When I reach the barrier, I force my steps to be even. Energy radiates off the strands, and I have a strong urge to turn around. Just when I'm about to touch the thick threads, my feet leave the ground and I'm thrown backward. Time slows and my throat closes as I fly through the air. With my luck, a sharp rock will impale the back of my head and I'll die instantly. In a dragon

realm. Accompanied by a demon. Silently, I apologize to my sister for failing her.

Strong arms fold around me, tucking me against a hard chest. Dimitri's shuddering as if my life flashed before *his* eyes, too. I suppose bringing a witch to a hellish dimension and then inadvertently killing them wouldn't look good. And there'd be a shit ton of paperwork.

It's not until my feet are planted firmly on the ground again that I realize he's not shaking from fear or worry. Nope, the bastard is laughing. At me. I scowl up at him. His arms tighten around me, though I'm pretty sure he's using me to hold himself up. If he says one word...

"So, you need to go through the other door," he wheezes.

"You could have warned me," I grumble.

"Told you there was a process. Not my fault you didn't listen. If you wanna blame me, though, go right ahead."

"Oh, how kind of you."

He drops a kiss to my temple, then lets me go. It's so quick I barely have time to savor it. Obviously, he's made comments—flirted, even. Now I'm wondering if he meant them. Maybe he's this familiar with everyone. The only other being I've seen him interact with is Providence, and he was pissy. Percy doesn't count since they didn't say two words to each other. I've almost convinced myself he's just a playful demon when he grabs my hand and pulls me forward into the unknown.

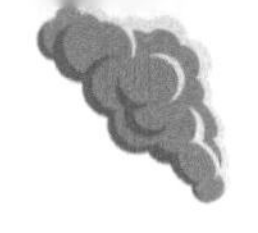

CHAPTER NINETEEN
DIMITRI

Messing with Mari is quickly becoming a favorite pastime. Could I have been clearer about things? Sure, but what's the fun in that? Besides, I followed behind her, caught her before she hurt herself. Not that she can die here. It's one of the few dimensions one can visit without truly perishing. She'd be sore for a few days, that's all.

I probably should tell her.

"Hand here," I say, pointing to an inconspicuous spot on the wall. She narrows her gaze, then hesitantly does what I said.

A doorway shimmers to life, large enough to accommodate most beings, including dragons. Her gasp is delayed, though I wonder if it's more for dramatic effect than genuine surprise. I gesture for her to go first, and she raises a single eyebrow.

"You think I'm walking in there after the stunt you pulled? Nuh-uh. You go first." She crosses her arms.

I grab her hand and yank her through. This time her gasp is real. I suppose I don't know what it's like to go through a magical doorway as a witch. The dragons have magic nothing else does. They protect their own with a fierceness I've rarely seen before.

"Why?" she whispers harshly. "That was fucking cold."

"No one with ill intent can pass through either doorway, including other dragons. A millennium ago there was a rogue dragon who fancied himself king of them all. When he met resis-

tance, he gained access to this world. Destroyed an entire clutch of eggs. It took a long time for them to regain what they lost."

She's quiet for a long time as we travel through the dark. There's just enough light for us not to trip into the cavern on either side of us. I'd bet all the magic in my veins she hasn't noticed yet. Maybe her witch eyes can't see. Or the dragons put in place a hallucination to make other beings feel better walking this narrow path.

"I doubt they'd agree," she finally murmurs.

"What do you mean?"

"They wouldn't be able to get back what was destroyed. The babies are forever lost to the rage of one. I would imagine the dragons who remember, if they're still around, will always feel the sting of grief when thinking about what could have been."

"I suppose so. Every dimension has tragedy. I imagine it's much the same everywhere."

She falls silent again, and I glance back at her. When her eyes meet mine, she pulls in a tight breath. "I don't mean this to sound insensitive, but...demons have tragedies?"

I laugh, though there's no humor in the sound. "Yeah, we do. A long line of them. Mostly, we just get angry when confronted with it. Some, like the dragons, mourn. Some fight. Others wallow and hide. Demons? We get pissed. We go to war. We deci- mate and demolish without a second thought. Being around a demon when they've been wronged, or worse, someone they care for has? Yeah, you don't want to get in our way."

"Protective assholes, got it," she mutters, and I squeeze her hand.

Even if I get nowhere with her, at least she'll know what she's getting into the next time she encounters a demon. The thought has the possessive beast within me rising. I shove it down, not wanting to scare her. Because if she saw my true form, snarling and foaming at the mouth, she'd run screaming toward the drag- ons. She'd welcome Death through them regardless of their indif- ference to her. Hell, I wouldn't put it past her to force their hand

—paw? I have no idea how to label their body parts. I probably should have learned that when I was stationed here during my demon training.

"How much farther?" she asks, a slight whine to her tone.

"We could fly if you'd like to get there faster."

"No, thank you. I'd rather not fly in pitch black. It was bad enough being thrown over your shoulder."

I slow to a stop, still clutching her hand. "Wait. You can't see anything? No lights at all?"

"Um, no? Am I supposed to?"

I hum, glancing around. The longer we walk, the brighter it's become for me. The crevices bracketing our path aren't as deep, the mountains beyond moving closer.

"Don't know. I'm not sure a witch has ever been here."

"Is that going to be a problem?" She attempts to pull away from me, and I grip her tighter.

"Dragons aren't like what the humans think. They might look like some of the depictions, but they don't really act like that."

"Are we talking Dragonheart or Puff the Magic Dragon? Or like—"

"I don't know what any of those are, Mari. They have a strict code of ethics." I tug her along once more. "Oh, and they communicate through your mind."

She makes a sound in the back of her throat. "They can read minds?"

"Didn't say that. I say they communicate by...speaking into your head. It's awkward at first, but you get used to it. You just have to think about what you want to say. They won't be privy to your secrets. They're respectful like that." I don't tell her they *could* read her mind if they want to. They could break her completely. Dragons would never do that, though, but she doesn't need another thing to worry about.

I turn sideways as a narrow passageway appears in front of us from the fog. I wonder if she can see it. She'll be perfectly fine with her smaller frame. Some light must have filtered in for her

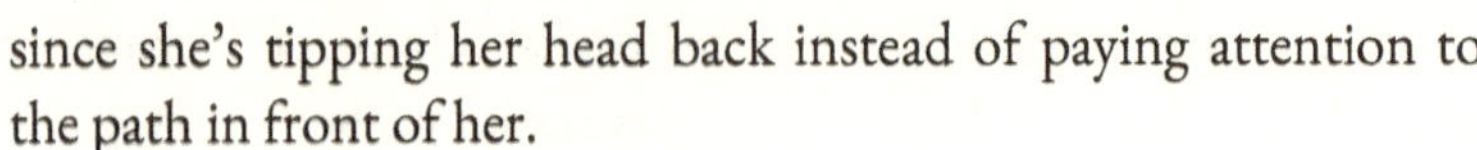

since she's tipping her head back instead of paying attention to the path in front of her.

"Mind your elbows," I mutter.

She scowls, then holds her breath as we go through. When we step out into a field of bright red flowers, she gasps, her hand flying to cover her mouth. I try to remember what it was like the first time I saw this sight. It was so long ago, I can't quite grasp the feeling. Elation? Wonder? Awe? Probably all of those. They're reflected on her face.

"How did...why...what are..."

"They're lava flowers. You don't have them topside, but they're a lot like poppies, I suppose. Except they grow when lava flows under them. This area's been like this for a long time." I want to give her as much time as I can to admire the view. Except I don't know how time is passing up there. I probably should have had her text Percy just in case, but I didn't want her to change her mind.

All I could think of was bringing her someplace she'd never been before. Throughout this whole journey, she's trusted me. Sure, she freaked out when we flew. And she's snapped at me several times. I'm beginning to understand it's a defense for her. She'll push me away before I can do it to her. If I keep showing up —if I just stay—eventually she'll accept I'm not leaving.

Until I do.

The thought hits me in the gut, and I drop her hand. She doesn't notice. She's too busy trying to figure out if the flowers will burn her. I could do this again and again if I get the same reaction from her. There are so many places I've been, things I've seen and experienced, while she's been barely anywhere. I could show her.

I cross my arms as my magic crackles across my skin. My emotions are a rollercoaster, rising and falling with each thought. Half-assing things with her won't go over well. Plus, she has issues she's dealing with. She needs help, not someone to fuck her. No matter how much I want to.

Swallowing hard, I reach for her. Even if I'm not going to actively pursue her, doesn't mean I can't touch her, hold her, flirt with her. If she gives any indication she wants me to back off, I can do that too.

"Mari, we have to get going. Time's of the essence and all that," I murmur softly.

She swings around, wonder still hanging in her eyes. "Huh? I thought...Sorry."

"Don't apologize. I wish I could let you stay here as long as you want, but time works differently in your world. I don't want you to go missing."

Her face screws up, and she glances away. I open my mouth to ask her what I said, to ask her what's wrong. I snap it shut when she gazes out once more at the field of flowers.

"Okay, let's go." She marches along the perimeter in the wrong direction, then freezes. "Can we take a picture? Where's my phone?"

She pats along her hips, and my mouth waters. When she gazes over her shoulder, my eyes snap up. No reason she needs to know I'm ogling her. Then again...No. Flirting, fine. Touching when necessary. Or when I get the urge. Ogling is off the table.

"I don't have any pockets," she snaps.

"Um, okay? I don't think I do either. Do you really need pockets?"

"Always. A girl *always* needs pockets. We have so few joys in life, at least let us have that."

I narrow my gaze. "Why do I get the feeling you're fucking with me?"

She gives me a deadpan stare. "I never joke about pockets, sir."

A shiver rolls down my spine. Nope. Not going to say anything about her calling me sir. I snap my fingers, adding pockets to her outfit. She huffs as the fabric puffs from her hips. I wince, then snap again. At least she doesn't look like she's wearing clouds around her waist.

"Better. Thank you."

"You shouldn't thank a demon, spitfire."

"Why's that?"

"They'll get the wrong idea. Also, you're going the wrong way. It's over the next hill."

After walking a few minutes, she clears her throat. "You haven't told me what to expect."

"Can't really explain it. Not in ways you'd understand," I say, wishing I could just fly there, though I doubt she'd appreciate that. She makes a face. "Wasn't meant to be insulting, spitfire. You just haven't been to the dimensions I have."

"Like where?"

I launch into the harrowing tale of Omen battling chickens with her interjecting questions the entire time. It's nice not to bicker with her for once. The longer she's here, the more relaxed she becomes. Maybe it's the scent in the air. The lava flowers don't smell like anything else I've encountered. Sweet, yet calming. It's part of the reason the dragons chose this particular world to nest. It could be impacting Mari's mood, which I'm not going to complain about. As much as I enjoy her fire, having a calm conversation with her is...nice. Plus, she hasn't told me to get to the point once, despite my rambling with inconsequential details.

"How many other worlds are there?" she asks softly just as we crest the hill.

"Millions, I suppose. I doubt anyone's counted. When I was younger, I had the grand plan of visiting every single one of them. Like a fucked-up bucket list." I laugh lightly as I gaze at the fortress laid out at the bottom of the hill. "Gave up on that pretty quickly."

"You talk like a human. Or maybe just a demon who's spent a lot of time in my world."

"Well, the food's excellent there. Kept bringing me back. Plus, there's only a few other beings so contradictory, yet resilient. Humans as a whole are a lot like phoenixes. Only difference is they're the ones burning shit down. Yet they always rise from the ashes, mostly stronger and wiser than before. Still got some shitheads running around, but then they come to Hell and we have a grand old time making them suffer." I grin and her eyes widen.

"What type of shitheads?"

"Oh, you know, the real bad ones. Not really the time to talk about them. Dragons don't particularly like them. Sometimes we send the dragons a little gift, let them play around with the dictators and murderers. Triton thought we could have demons come and watch for sport. Dragons nixed that one pretty quickly. Said we'd get queasy. And if a dragon's telling you a *demon* will get sick? Yeah, you don't argue with them."

Her mouth parts, then closes as she works through everything. I probably shouldn't throw random information at her. I'm sure it's disconcerting. Shutting it off would be like turning off my brain, though. And Mari hasn't complained.

"Who's Triton?"

"A demon. I work with him sometimes, training new demons coming up in the ranks. He's the one who pulled me away last time. Actually, I should figure out what the fuck he was doing, because if I didn't know any better, I'd say he was using a summoning circle."

"You know what a summoning circle looks like?" There's an edge to her voice like she's trying to sound nonchalant.

"Sure do. Been summoned a time or two in my day. It's why I was so sure you had one."

She leans closer and whispers, "Are we waiting for something?"

I tug the dragon egg from my pocket, then pass it to her. "More likely to get in if you're returning that."

She turns it over in her palms. "If the dragons are so protective over their eggs, how did Omen get it? Also, not to be a bitch about your friends, but that's kind of a dick move with the drag-on's past, don't you think?"

"Well, I didn't get the full story. He said he just popped in and then out again. He shouldn't have been able to, but weirder things have happened. Also, I don't think he knew it was a dragon's egg.

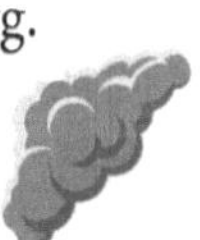

Not everyone knows their history like I do. Omen spent his practicum in Waterworld studying...sea monsters? I think that's what you'd call them."

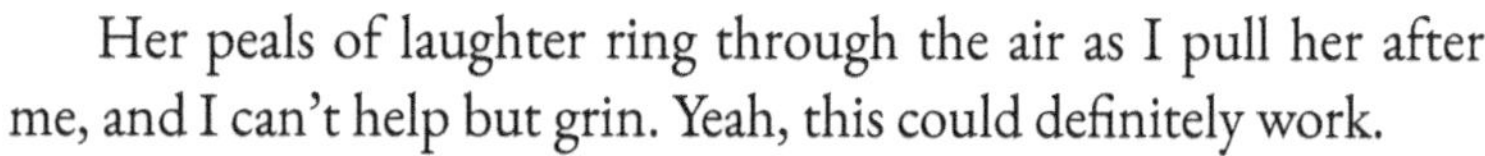

"You had practicums?" She waves the question away. "You have sea monsters?!"

I shake my head and lace our fingers together before leading her down the hill toward a small door set in the side of the large castle. With my curse fading and Mari finally opening up, we just might be on the right path. Maybe I'll take her to the sea monsters next.

Her peals of laughter ring through the air as I pull her after me, and I can't help but grin. Yeah, this could definitely work.

CHAPTER TWENTY

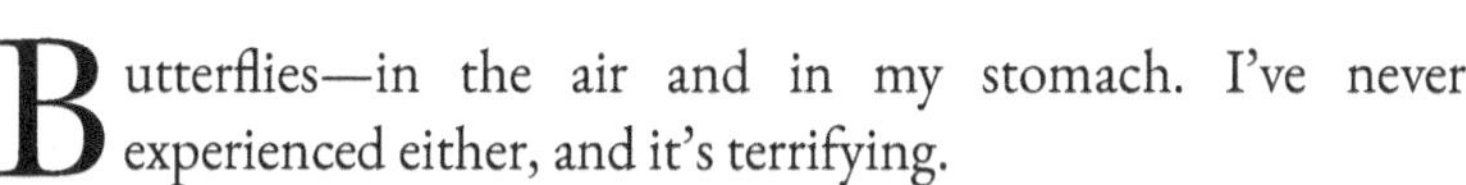

B utterflies—in the air and in my stomach. I've never experienced either, and it's terrifying.

I've spent most of my life trying to stay grounded. Only now do I realize what I've been missing. The butterflies fluttering around us are bright blue, almost electrified. With every brush of their wings, a spark alights across my skin. It reminds me of Dimitri's magic, and I wonder if they come from the same source.

I never gave much thought about where magic comes from—my own included. It was just something I was born with. My aunt made it seem like it was a disease that needed to be eradicated. Yet she still used her own magic whenever it fit her needs. It wasn't until Lark and I got out of the house and away from her that we truly learned anything. Without a mentor, it was slow going. Lark was always better at finding answers.

Most of the time, I waited until she knew things and she'd teach me. It must have been annoying for her. When we got a little older, I honed the skills I needed and left the rest. When she disappeared, I had to deep-dive into a lot of magic I wasn't used to. Maybe I did summon Dimitri and didn't know it. I never claimed to be a competent witch.

"Why does this whole world feel like seven different dimensions mishmashed together?"

He shrugs as another butterfly lands on his shoulder. He's

covered in them, little blue lightning strikes illuminating his rugged face. His wings pop from his back and he winces. Whether that's from the butterflies taking flight or his wings coming out, I don't know. And I'm too afraid to ask. I'd lie and say it's because I don't want to pry into his life, but it's more than that. I'm already getting attached.

The rollercoaster my emotions have been on ever since he tumbled into my life doesn't help. One minute I want him, the next I want to kick him in the shin, after that I want him to vanish. Except there's this need sitting right below the surface, desperate to know more about him.

"Okay, now we really need to go," he mutters, checking an invisible watch on his wrist.

"Where do your wings go?" I blurt out as we walk through the forest. It's not quite the question I want to ask, but it'll have to do.

"Where does your magic go when you're not using it?" He raises an eyebrow and smirks.

"Okay, but...never mind."

"Saw the scars, huh?"

I clamp my mouth shut and stare straight ahead at the path carving its way through the trees. I knew I should have shut the fuck up.

"Sorry," I mutter. "How much farther? My feet are starting to hurt."

I pick up my pace, though why I think I can outrun a demon is beyond me. In two steps he's snared my wrist and yanked me to his side. I don't try to pull away. Mostly because I like the feel of his skin on mine. I could definitely blame it on basically being a recluse since I moved into my sister's house. I'd be lying.

"I used to have actual wings. Now I have to settle for ones formed from storm clouds—my magic, basically." He doesn't elaborate how he lost them, and I'm not going to demand he tell me.

"How did they carry both of us to the wall?"

He laces our fingers together and presses our palms together. "I can fly for a bit before they either disappear or give out. That was easy, especially since I haven't used them in a while. Also, I haven't been as fatigued since I slept at your house."

"You don't look like you're about to pass out, at least." I give him a half-hearted smile, and he grins.

"Keep it up, spitfire, and I just might think you want to keep me around."

I glance around as we step from the trees. Dense fog blocks any view I might have had. I wonder if he can see something I can't. Apparently being a witch puts me at a disadvantage.

"Pretty sure I'm stuck with you until you get me back home. Doubt I'd be able to find my way back alone."

We would not keep you here, young one.

Dimitri's grin stretches wider as he watches my shocked face. He leans closer and whispers, "Be rude not to answer, Mari."

"Um, that's not what I was saying?"

Dimitri's shoulders shake, and he tucks his chin to his chest. Bastard.

You do not need to speak out loud, though if you're more comfortable doing so, proceed.

"Dimitri, stop," I hiss.

He gestures toward me, but I have no idea what the fuck he's trying to get me to do. I can't see a dragon, and I certainly don't know how to address them. He really gave me nothing. I totally wanted to come, I just wish I had more information.

"I'm sorry. The demon didn't tell me what—that is, I have something that belongs to you." I hold out the dragon egg, and it glows from within. The dragon makes a humming sound I feel in my soul.

The fog clears just enough to reveal a huge dragon. I don't know what Dimitri was talking about. It looks like every other dragon I've seen in movies, though it's glowing a soft orange. Not under their scales, more like their entire body shimmers when it moves, much like the egg I'm clutching. I didn't realize how large

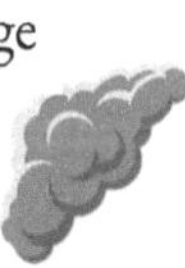

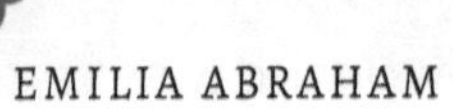

they'd be. This one has to be as tall as two of my sister's houses stacked on top of each other. Maybe more. I was never good at dimensions.

I'd wondered where they got to. Thank you for returning them to our domain. Their giver will be grateful.

"I don't believe the p-person who took it understood."

A booming laugh echoes inside my head, and I wince. *I can guarantee the demon had no clue. The whelp you're holding did, though. I imagine they thought it was a grand adventure. They'll hatch soon and regale us with their tales of other dimensions.*

"Okay, well, where do I..." How the fuck do I ask a dragon to hold out his hand? Is it a paw? A claw? Dropping it on the ground and nudging it over with my toe seems uncouth, and I doubt they'd appreciate that.

I pull from Dimitri's grasp and elbow him in the side. He glances at me from the corner of his eye, humor still twinkling in them. I swear if he makes me figure this out alone, I'm going to steal his dagger and poke him with it.

Dimitri cocks his head, his eyes turning glassy, then presses his lips together. "I'd rather keep all my organs on the inside, so why don't you just go put it in the nest, hmm?"

He points to a spot within the fog I can't see. A whimper leaves me, and the thought seriously crosses my mind to stomp my foot. Then the smoke clears and an entire landscape of dragons appears. Lava flowers grow everywhere, including on top of what looks to be large caves. They sway softly in the warm breeze, infusing their song into the air. Some dragons lounge outside the caves while others fly overhead.

It stretches on for miles. We could stay here for years and probably never see all of it. A peace settles around me as I watch a dragon poke their nose directly into a bonfire. Ringing the flames are stones. They're the same dark rocks that make up the wall— obsidian, I'm pretty sure. Unless they're some type we don't have in my world. I suppose it doesn't matter, but I have the need to know everything.

I swallow hard, then shuffle closer to the surprisingly small nest made of grey coal. I nestle in the dragon egg between two others, and it pulses, setting off the rest. Crouching next to them, I stare as they surge in a pattern only they can understand. It's as if they're saying hello. Or perhaps asking what happened, where they went, and what of the other worlds they visited. It's mesmerizing.

I don't know how long I stay there, but my legs have gone numb and my neck has a cramp. Dimitri's warm hand lands on the sore spot and I moan, tipping my head forward. As he massages my muscles, my knees hit the rocky ground, digging into the leather. He chuckles, yet instead of annoyance rising within me, warmth gathers in my chest.

The middle of a dragon realm isn't the place to get enamored with a demon. After today and what he's shown me, I don't know if I'll be able to resist him. I can't even remember why I wanted to in the first place.

"Time to go, spitfire," he murmurs, the deep rumble of his voice echoing through my body.

I glance up and find the fog firmly back in place. "I should have said goodbye. And thank them."

"Having you be mesmerized enough not to know they were walking away is enough. They know. Besides, I can bring you back whenever you'd like."

With that promise, I struggle to my feet. He grips me under my arms and lifts me. Heat filters through my veins and settles on my cheeks. I was so caught up in the dragon eggs I forgot Dimitri was here. I'm sure he would have just handed it over and left. Instead, he was stuck here watching me cry over them.

When I'm upright, I let out a heavy sigh. My worries have disappeared, or at least quieted while I was here. They stay in the corners of my mind, allowing me this small moment.

"Okay. I'm ready."

He smiles softly, and I turn to go back the way we came. He wraps his arm around my waist, his fingers splaying across my hip.

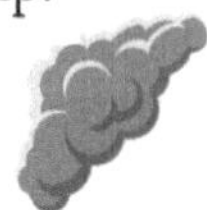

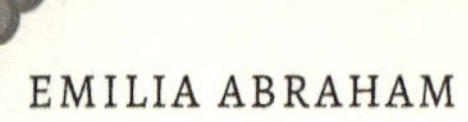

Within seconds, the world goes dark and my ears pop, then we're...right back at the lava flower field.

"Whoops," he mutters. "Was shooting for your living room."

He drops his hold on me, stepping back, and I mourn the loss of his touch, his warmth. When I face him, he's looking at everything *but* me. Then I realize he's naked. Very fucking naked. When I glance down, I notice I am too. My first instinct usually would be to cover up—ask where my clothes went. Unless I sew some flowers together, I'm going naked and, I don't know how to sew. At least I don't have to tell him to avert his eyes.

I can't pull my gaze away from his body—his very chiseled, perfectly proportioned body. It's as if he were formed as an aphrodisiac for the human gaze. From the dips near his hips to his defined collarbones, every inch seems to send my heart into an apoplectic rhythm. And I haven't even really looked at his cock. My gaze shies away from that area in a belated sense of chivalry.

When his eyes finally meet mine, I realize I'm not much better than the assholes in the club leering at women showing a bit of shoulder. I tip my head up and fixate on the glittering sky. I should apologize, but I'm afraid I'll drool if I open my mouth.

He chuckles, and I can feel him shaking his head. "Didn't realize the clothes would disappear in the void this time around."

"It's fine. I...uh..." I swallow hard, grasping at my words. Telling him I want to climb him like a tree...no, he's not a tree. He's a mountain. Climb him like a mountain doesn't have the same ring to it, though. Either way, I probably shouldn't confess all the dirty thoughts running through my mind.

He snaps his fingers, and I glance down. Nothing happens and he cringes. Apparently we're just going to do this whole thing naked. I don't know what *this whole thing* is, but that's fine.

I clear my throat. "Thank you for bringing me here."

His face comes into view, and he grips my chin to tip my head down. "Want to try that again?"

Gazing into his eyes where twin purple flames dance, my mind blanks. I stutter out something unintelligible, and his grin widens.

I scowl, digging deep for something other than the want to melt into him. It doesn't come. I've spent a good while fighting against my feelings, pretending they don't exist. Pushing him away meant I could focus on what I needed to do. At least, that's what I thought. I'm not so convinced this whole thing wasn't inevitable.

"Thank you for bringing me. It was one of the best things that's ever happened to me."

He raises an eyebrow. "The *best*?"

I press my lips together and nod, though he's still gripping my chin. "Well, you did show me dragons. That's pretty spectacular. Although…"

I pull from his grip and step back. I don't really know what the hell I'm doing. Is this how people flirt? Maybe this is totally normal for demons—having conversations while buck naked. He could be messing with me, laughing at how far I'll go to gain his attention.

Yet when I meet his gaze, he has the same look in his eyes after we flew—like I hung the moon and hold all his dreams in my hands. As if I'm someone to cherish. Like I was worthy enough to be brought to the world of dragons.

"Gonna finish that sentence, spitfire, or keep me in suspense?"

"Would have been better if we saw some baby dragons."

CHAPTER TWENTY-ONE
DIMITRI

I scowl, though she's avoiding my gaze. She has to be messing with me. The entire time we've been here, she's been in a daze, completely captivated by everything I showed her. Now she's demanding more?

"Baby dragons," I growl, and she shrugs.

It's taking everything in me to keep my eyes on her face instead of any lower. The void must have eaten our clothes. They were formed by magic. I just assumed we'd get our original things back without any extra steps. That's how it usually works. Between this and not showing up where I meant, I wonder if this is my curse. Maybe it morphed. Can a curse have stages? I have no idea.

She clears her throat, and I focus on the present. Sparks flick from my fingertips when I realize I'm staring at her tits. Her perfectly formed tits, with beautiful nipples that make my mouth water. I shake my head and spin around with a muttered curse.

"When are they hatching?"

"Any time now, though that could mean years or seco—"

A small roar cuts through my words, and my head snaps up to search the bed of flowers. Mari squeals and I whip toward her. She's dancing from one foot to the other on the edge. I have no idea if they'll burn her, and I stalk closer. Shit will go south if she

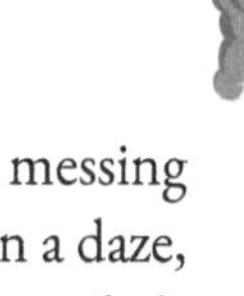

accidentally tramples one. The whole lot will rise up to defend themselves.

"Mari," I snap, and she turns, delight stamped on her face.

She squeals again as a small tuft of flames erupts from several hundred feet away. Pure joy radiates from her. She's forgotten all about being naked. Forgotten she's in a foreign land. Forgotten the worries plaguing her. It's transformed her. No, this side of her was always there. It lurked beneath the surface, behind her snappy responses, and underneath the pain. She hides it well, but I saw it.

"Thank you," she whispers and launches herself at me.

A grunt leaves me as I grab her. She winds her legs around my waist. Her warm hands cup my cheeks, and I catch the wild look in her eyes a half a second before she's kissing the shit out of me. I freeze for the next second, and she starts to pull away. She doesn't get far.

Gripping the back of her neck, I meld her body to mine. When she moans, I take full advantage and lick her bottom lip. It doesn't take long for my skin to crack, revealing deep purple lines underneath. I drink in her whimpers like a demon dying of thirst. I'd gladly subsist on only her and the delicious noises she's making.

She pulls away, panting as she rests her forehead against mine. Galaxies sparkle in her eyes, a whole host of worlds I've never explored. I desperately want to fall into them.

"You're sparkling," she whispers.

"So are you," I whisper back.

"Can we..." She pulls in a shaky breath. "Can we not talk about it? Can we just...I'm sick of analyzing—"

I cover her mouth with mine, cutting off her words. If she needs something to occupy her mind so she doesn't overthink this, I'm more than happy to oblige. She wiggles in my hold, and I groan. With my cock trapped between us, the friction is delicious but not enough.

I slide my palm down her body, then grip her ass with both hands. A needy whine leaves her, and I lift her higher. Her heels dig into my lower back as she tries to impale herself on my cock. I should slow this down, make sure she's not going to regret this.

When I rip my mouth away from hers, though, she lines herself up and sinks onto my length. A deep groan leaves me instead, and I tip my head back.

"Perfect," I wheeze as her pussy flutters around me.

Her back arches as she attempts to move. There's no way I'll be able to fuck her properly like this. If we had a wall, I'd slam her against it. With a table, I could lay her down and...I cut off my fantasies. There will be time for all that later, hopefully.

"Hold on, spitfire," I say through gritted teeth, and she whines, yet wraps her arms around my shoulders and buries her face in my neck.

I close my eyes and reach for my magic. If it doesn't work, I might cry. It's hard enough with her clenching around my length. Slowly, too slowly, dark clouds gather around us, then settle into what I hope is a cushy bed. When I shuffle forward, I trip over a rock and send us tumbling.

She clings to me as we sink onto the makeshift bed. Somehow, I don't squish her, and she bites my neck while her shoulders shake. This is not the way I thought things would go. In fact, this is the last place I imagined taking her for the first time. Maybe the third, but definitely not the first.

She flings her arms out, letting the fluffy clouds cushion her. I push to my knees, hoping I don't sink into anything other than her. She arches her back and my cock hardens, though I don't know how that's possible. She moans, clenching around me, and I grunt.

"Keep that up and we're not going to get very far," I mutter, then roll my hips and she spasms again.

When she peeks at me from slitted eyes, I know I'm a goner. She's pulled me completely under her spell. No one else has captivated me as completely as she has. I shake my head, shying away from complete dedication. This isn't the time or place to have an epiphany. Especially while I'm deep inside her.

"And if you don't start moving, I'm going to take care of things myself." She smirks, and something primitive rises within me.

I drop my hands on either side of her head and thrust lightly into her. She gasps, tipping her chin up, and I take full advantage of her exposed neck. I brush my lips across her soft skin, then sink my teeth into her neck. Licking the spot, I relish the taste. One day soon I'll bury my face between her thighs and drink up every drop of her pleasure. I pull back until only the tip remains inside her, and she whimpers.

"Dimitri," she whines, digging her heels into my lower back as she tries to force me deeper.

It isn't easy teasing her like this when all I want to do is claim her completely. I wrap my lips around her nipple and flick the hard bud to distract myself. It doesn't work, but still I worship her tits. She lets out a cry filled with frustration, longing, and desire, and I grin. When I nip at her other nipple, she gasps again.

When her hand slips between us, I grab her wrist and force her arm over her head. "You're distracting me, spitfire. Do you know how long I've been craving this? Craving *you*? Now, let me play."

I suck her nipple back into my mouth, pulling another moan from her. It's as if words have failed her. As long as she remembers how to scream my name when she comes, we'll be just fine.

She trembles under me, constantly wiggling as I memorize each dip of her skin. When she whispers out a plea, begging me to fuck her, I give in. This has been a torturous rapture, and I don't want it to end.

I plunge into her once more, earning another moan. The sound mixes with my own groans as her heat envelops my cock. I glance down, watching as I disappear into her over and over. Magic swirls through the air, the clouds forming a canopy over us. I push to my knees and grip her hips. Her fingers wrap around my wrists, and her nails dig into my skin. Lightning flickers through the fog, raining glittery sparks across her body. She meets me thrust for thrust, and already my gut tightens.

Fighting off my release is the hardest thing I've done to date. As she writhes underneath me, a vision of my future flashes before my eyes. I swallow hard, focusing on Mari. She's my present. I don't care what happens later. Not right now. The future can keep its secrets as long as I get to be in this moment with her.

She shudders and her back arches. I slide my hand between us and find her clit. One touch of my fingers is all it takes. She explodes. She may not scream my name, but every inch of her is blanketed with ecstasy. From her disheveled purple hair swirling around her to her toes curling into my back. 

I never slow, drawing out her orgasm as long as possible. I want more—more of her rapturous pleasure, more of her desperate moans, more of her desire-filled eyes finding mine. Her hands fall to the side, and I slow to a stop. She blinks at me, her swollen lips parted as she gazes at me.

"That was—"

"Oh, I'm not finished, spitfire." I slide my hand around her neck and tug her toward me.

She whimpers, and I kiss her hard and fast before slipping out of her. My cock weeps, mourning the loss of her heat. No amount of reassurance will help.

"Where do you want me?" she breathes, then grins. I release  her as she scrambles onto her hands and knees.

"Fuck me," I whisper as she pops her ass in the air.

"No, fuck *me*," she says, then buries her face into the makeshift bed.

She wiggles her hips, and I grab them, willing my claws back in. I doubt she'd appreciate pain right now. Then again, maybe she's into that sort of thing. I shake my head, shoving the thought away for later. We'll be having many discussions about what she wants, what she needs, what she craves. I'll give it all to her.

"Need some help, sir?" she asks with laughter tingeing her tone, and I growl.

I bury my cock in her, gritting my teeth to stop myself from recklessly pounding into her. She pushes back with every thrust, not noticing my hesitancy. When she begs me to go harder, faster, my breath stutters in my chest and I oblige. Bolts of lightning crack across my skin as I hurtle closer to the edge of oblivion.

When her fingers curl into the dark clouds by her head, I know she's close. Without slowing, I slide my hand around to play with her clit. Instead, I find her own fingers there. I place mine on top of hers, giving the extra pressure she's craving. I sink my teeth into her ribs, wishing she was facing me. I want to watch her eyes roll back in her head again, knowing I brought her to new heights.

"Come for me," I command through gritted teeth.

She spasms around my cock, her body tensing under me while she soaks our thighs with her pleasure. Her hand goes limp along with the rest of her, and I wonder if I've pushed her too far. Mist fills our little bubble, cooling her skin, and she sighs. I grip her hips once more and tip my head back as I relish the feeling of her pussy clinging to me as I surge into her again and again.

"Dimitri," she says, her voice barely a whisper on the wind. "Please."

I don't know what she's asking for. I wrap an arm around her waist and my hand around her throat before hauling her upright. I hold her lightly, and her pussy quivers around me.

"Touch yourself," I growl, and immediately her hand drops between her legs. I drive into her, mesmerized by the sight of her.

A choked sob leaves her, and she stops. "I can't."

I press a kiss to her jaw, right above my fingers. "You can and you will."

"Demanding," she gasps as I take over, brushing my thumb over her clit.

Within seconds sparks fly around us, and she grabs my wrist. I expect her to pull my hand away from her throat, yet she squeezes and keeps me in place. I flex my fingers and press harder into her sensitive bud. I grunt as she spasms around me one more time, and I follow her into oblivion. Thunder cracks and lightning crashes around us. My magic's never been this out of control while being with someone. It's her. It has to be. I'll accept nothing less.

She slumps in my grip, and I lower her to the fluffy magical bed. The clouds dissipate around us, and the song of the lava flowers fills the air. I collapse next to her and haul her closer until she's wrapped around me. She hums as I skim my palm up and down her back. Whatever secrets we hold between us, at least we got this right. Something primitive wakes up inside me, and I bury my nose in her hair.

I could definitely get used to this.

CHAPTER TWENTY-TWO
MARI

If someone had told me a year ago I'd be snuggled up to a demon in my bed while staring at the glow-in-the-dark stars Lark stuck on the ceiling, I would have laughed.

Then the guilt crashes down on me. While I was off meeting dragons and having a salacious time with Dimitri, my sister's still missing. She could be in trouble, kidnapped, hurt, or worse. I'd know if she was dead, but that's a small consolation when I think about it. Which I try not to.

As soon as Dimitri showed up, I sloughed off all my responsibilities. I let him distract me with his erratic magic and curse and body. If I was a good sister, I would have been laser-focused on finding her. It wouldn't matter if I was at a dead end. In fact, I should have been using Dimitri to find answers. The thought leaves an icky taste in my mouth.

I don't want to *use* him, per se. But when fate drops a demon in your lap, you probably shouldn't ignore their usefulness. Still, it probably wouldn't be a good idea to wake him up to demand he help me. His proposal all those moons ago isn't looking too bad right now. I should have taken him up on it then.

Too stubborn.

"Fuck you," I breathe, and Dimitri stirs underneath my hand. I'm half-draped over his body and acutely aware how naked we both are. Which I shouldn't be. This shouldn't be awkward at all. We had sex in

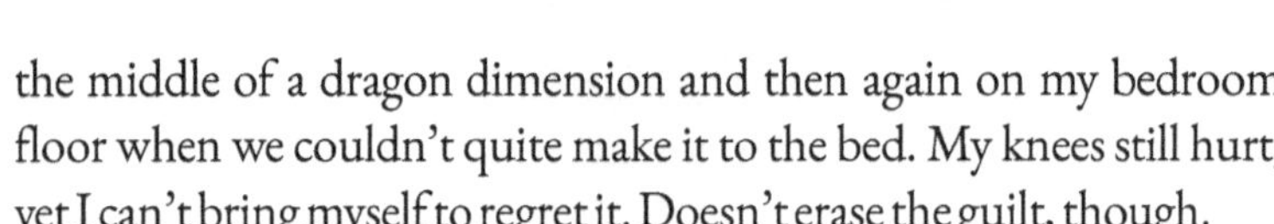

the middle of a dragon dimension and then again on my bedroom floor when we couldn't quite make it to the bed. My knees still hurt, yet I can't bring myself to regret it. Doesn't erase the guilt, though.

"Morning, spitfire," he murmurs, sleep lining his voice.

"Evening," I whisper, then clear my throat. "I'm going to go shower." Better to lie than tell him I have to pee.

He squeezes my hip, then unwinds his arm from my waist. I roll straight off the mattress, and my foot slips on an abandoned piece of clothing—underwear. His fingers brush my bare ass, and I hurry to right myself before he can "save" me. The last thing I need is a concussion.

I spend an exorbitant amount of time in the bathroom. Part of me wishes I had used the other one. I would have had to go into Lark's bedroom, and I'm not ready to face all *that* again. I'll have to before long to search for clues. I'm still trying to figure out if I should do that before or after asking Dimitri about the summoning circle when the door pops open.

Dimitri fills the doorframe, his cock out in full glory and a scowl on his face. No, not a scowl—he's pissed. Very fucking pissed. I thought I'd seen him angry when Providence popped in. This is way beyond that.

"Want to explain why you lied?" he growls, his voice duplicating—layering on top of one another until the sound echoes throughout the small space. My chest tightens and my head spins at the intensity.

Slowly, I inch open the shower door and reach for my towel. He snatches it away, and it bursts into flames. Within seconds, ashes rain to the floor, and I swallow hard. He crooks his finger, and I step gingerly onto the thick black mat.

"I don't know what you're talking about."

He jabs his finger in the general direction of the rest of the house. "You've got a whole fucking room dedicated to sorcery and necromancy. Tell me, when did you learn how to slip into Hell? Was that before or after you cursed me?"

"What? I didn't curse you. I can barely brew a healing potion, much less curse someone."

He narrows his eyes, and his form flickers. "Don't fuck with me, Mari. Is that even your actual name? Or did you lie about that, too?"

My nostrils flare and rage slowly builds within me. I try to keep my temper under control, to explain things logically. He's not making it easy. I hate when someone accuses me of shit I didn't do. Everyone in my life seems to blame me for things outside my control. I'm sick and tired of being everyone else's scapegoat.

"For your information, Mari is a nickname. Is Dimitri *your* actual name?" I plant my fists on my hips, no longer caring how dripping wet I am.

A sardonic grin takes over his face. "No, as a matter of fact, it's not."

I inhale sharply, trying to hide the hurt. I understand why he's upset, but I didn't think he'd lie to me. And then throw it in my face after...everything? I definitely didn't see that coming.

This right here is why I keep to myself. It hurts too much to let people in. They never live up to the expectations I build for them in my mind. I bite the inside of my cheek, focusing on the physical one rather than the emotional one.

"Well, fine then. I didn't lie to you, though I doubt that matters much to you. And no, I didn't curse you. Choose to believe it or not, I don't really care." I grab another towel and wrap it around my cold body. "You can go now."

His face transforms, going through a range of emotions before settling on contemplation. I don't really care. He can figure his shit out somewhere else. I have more important things to do. At least, that's what I'm telling myself. It's easier than feeling the pain. Maybe I am the liar he claims me to be.

"It's Dimitrius," he mumbles, running a hand through his hair.

"Good for you. Was there something else you needed? Or are you keeping me hostage?"

He steps to the side and allows me to pass. His fingers brush my elbow, yet I breeze by without acknowledging him. His inability to talk things through calmly isn't my problem. It's not my flaw to fix. The dark side of me, the one I keep locked away in the corner of my mind, hopes he suffers—that the guilt will eat away at him, eroding his confidence and feeling the sting of loss every time he remembers me. There's a reason I keep that side hidden from even myself.

"Mari, I didn't—"

"It's Marigold, by the way. Not that you deserve to know. Yes, my parents named me after a flower. Yes, it means not so great things. No, you can't call me it. Satisfied?"

He shakes his head, regret and shame swimming in his eyes.

Mercy doesn't cost you anything.

I mentally flip Lark off, then stop. Her advice is usually on par, even when it's in my head. I want to argue with her, but he's still looking at me. Fighting with a voice inside my head isn't exactly typical for witches.

"Fine," I snap, though whether to him or the voice, I'm not entirely sure. Maybe both.

"None of this is fine," he sighs.

"No, I mean, fine, give me your proof." As much as mercy wouldn't cost me anything, it doesn't erase my annoyance. Or the hurt.

He swallows hard and thunder rumbles overhead. If he makes it rain in this house again, I might just lose it.

"The room," he mutters. "The one behind the kitchen."

My spine snaps straight. "What about it?"

"The witchy demon things. You told me you didn't know anything about curses. You said you'd never been anywhere." His eyes lift to meet mine, but the rage is gone, replaced with something like guilt. "Why did you lie?"

I glance at the ceiling, and those damn stars stare back at me—

mocking me. "This isn't my house. I've lived here for the past several months, but I don't...this isn't my place. I lived in the city like three hours from here in a tiny-ass apartment with no elevator. This is my sister's house. She's the one who set that whole room up. I don't understand half the things in it—including the summoning circle."

His mouth parts and realization washes over him. I want to call him an asshole, tell him he should have asked questions, then waited for the answers instead of making accusations. Except the fight's drained out of me. All that's left is the sting of his words and the pain of his own omissions.

"That's...Mari, that's not a summoning circle."

"Of course it is. I saw one just like it in my parent's basement. And my other aunt's house before she vanished or died or whatever. Sure, part of it's washed away, but I figured that was normal and Lark just—"

He holds up his hand and I fall silent, realizing I'm rambling. "Lark?"

"My sister..."

"So, you're named after a flower and she's named after a bird?" He raises an eyebrow and looks at me expectantly, as if this is the most important question.

"No, we're both named after flowers. Our aunts were named after birds. My father was named after one of the moon phases, but that's neither here nor there."

"Lark isn't a flower."

"Her full name is Larkspur. Obviously, we both go by nicknames."

"Obviously," he murmurs. "Except that's not a summoning circle. That's a—"

"A what?" I ask, annoyed at the dramatic pause. When I glance down, though, he's gone. No storm clouds, no lightning, no gloriously naked demon. Just an empty bedroom and silence. Deep, bone-chilling silence.

I shiver, then rush around the room, grabbing whatever

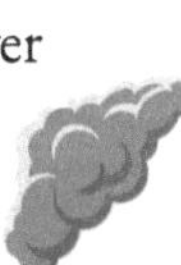

clothes I can find. There's not much I can do about his poofing back to Hell other than slam things around. Maybe curse at the floor. Nothing will change it. I try to remember what exactly he said when he was accusing me of all the bullshit. Something about Hell, but summoning circles are connected too.

Once in the living room, I dig through my sister's books. All the titles are the same as they were the last time I checked. The necromancy book lies innocently on the table, and I shake my head.

"You're no fucking help. Why don't you do something worthwhile, huh?"

I stalk away to the secret room that's not so secret. I'm surprised he didn't find it sooner. Then again, he spent most of his time here either in my bed or collapsing in the living room. What I should be wondering is why he was snooping in the first place. Except I really don't give a fuck.

"He told you," I breathe. "He told you all about how demons act when they think they're betrayed. It's not really all that surprising."

Except you like him.

I scoff as I shove open the door, then step back. The room doesn't look a damn thing like it did before. There were plants and candles and some herbs and such, but this? This screams occult and dark magic. Black walls along with blackened windows seem to suck in the light from behind me. The circle, which apparently is not a summoning circle, glows a bright gold, almost flickering like a candle. Except there aren't any.

"What the fuck, Lark."

There's more than meets the eye. Even a witch's.

If I wasn't so freaked out, I'd roll my eyes. She was always spouting that, though I never truly understood it. I figured she read it in a book and thought it made her sound mysterious. Maybe that's why my brain is parroting her words—because this is a pretty creepy situation. I shuffle forward bit by bit until my toes reach the black floorboards.

"No fucking way am I going in there." I clear my throat. "Uh, begone?" I clear my throat again. "Begone, demon."

Nothing happens, because of course it doesn't. I'm not a competent enough witch to make shit happen. Hell, Dimitri probably left the first time by chance. I've been playing at being a witch for so long, I think I lost some of my actual magic along the way. Can one of the gods or Mother Earth take it away if you're being naughty?

I snort as Dimitri's voice echoes in my mind. "Remember, he accused you of lying, Marigold. You can't just forgive him because he called you a naughty girl. Have some fucking self-respect."

Spinning on my heel, I let out a nervous laugh. My body sways, and I slam my hand into the wall to steady myself. I press my fist to my chest, willing my heart to stop racing. I drop my chin and focus on my breathing.

Mrow.

I freeze, staring at the scratched hardwood floors. If I pretend I didn't hear what I think I heard, then it didn't happen, right? That's how it works in human houses. At least, I think it does. Of course, shit has to be difficult in witchy households.

When another meow rings out, followed by a crash of glass, I spin back around. Squinting into the darkness, I search for any movement. The circle isn't glowing anymore. I don't know if that's good or bad. Both. I'm going with both.

Lark doesn't have a cat. No familiar or anything. Maybe a mountain lion broke in and is wreaking havoc on her spell room. Knowing my luck, it'll be a panther.

"A panther from Hell," I whisper, my voice wavering.

I shuffle forward until my toes line up with the threshold once more. I reach around the door frame and fumble for the light switch. Either it's disappeared along with all my confidence, or my nerves made me forget where the fuck it is.

"Just close the door and walk away. Nothing good can come from walking into a pitch-black room that's making noises."

I lean as far as I can without moving my feet, attempting to

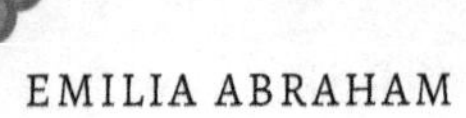

reach the knob. My foot slips and I tumble in slow motion toward the floor. I barely get my hands underneath me and save myself from a bloody nose. A groan leaves me as my knee starts to sting, and I rest my forehead on the cold floor.

Mrow?

"Fuck me," I breathe.

I pick my head up and come face to face with what's possibly the world's ugliest cat.

CHAPTER TWENTY-THREE
DIMITRI

I swear to fuck all if they don't stop yanking me around, I'm going to fucking lose it.

Yet here I am, waiting patiently for someone to reveal themselves. I'm not in the void, nor in my section of Hell. Not the dragon realm or the chicken world, or any of the normal places I've haunted before. In fact, I'm pretty sure I'm still topside.

Except the world is black and moist. My nose crinkles at the musty, swampy smell. Wherever I am, it's gross, especially while I'm naked. I cross my arms to keep them from covering my junk. If they want to summon me during what was probably the most important conversation of my existence, then they get me in all my fucking glory.

"Providence," I bellow. "One word: squids."

She doesn't show. My nostrils flare and I close my eyes. I've already tried several times to call up my magic. The curse must have gutted me. It's the only plausible explanation. The only other time I've felt this muted...

"Karma," I growl.

A tinkling laugh echoes around me, and I pull in a deep breath to keep myself in check. I can't electrocute her without magic. I can't strangle her without knowing where she is. And I can't pinpoint where she is without a little light.

"I will gut—"

"Wouldn't finish that sentence if I were you," she calls in a singsong voice.

"What the fuck are you do—"

She pops up right in front of me as the space floods with light, then dims. We're in a cave. A fucking cave with offshoots leading into the dark. She skips around, half my height and annoying as shit. She's changed her hair again. A riot of rainbow swirls around her as she spins. At least she's in a good mood.

"Karma," I snarl in warning.

She huffs with her entire body and gives me a look. "Fine. You're no fucking fun. Just because you're being a pissy boy lately, doesn't mean you can't have fun. Although..."

"Why am I here, Karma?" The sooner she gets to the point, the sooner I can get back to what's important—Mari.

"Well, I might have stirred the pot just a bit too much." She digs her bare toe into the dirt, hands behind her back as she twists back and forth.

"Spit it out."

She heaves a heavy sigh, and her form flickers. I tip my head back and wait for her to settle once more. This isn't an unusual occurrence. With her tugging at various threads throughout dimensions, she can never fully be in one place for long. It's annoying, but I can't blame her for it. She didn't ask to do this. It was thrust upon her by those ruling over us. I don't know why they skipped over me, but I'm not complaining.

"Seriously, humans need to get their shit together. Do you know how hard it is to rain down horror on all these fucking rich men? Ack. Leaves a bad taste in my mouth, and you *know* how I hate that."

"Why. Am. I. Here." It's a demand, not a question.

"Oh, I have a teeny, tiny, little, itty-bitty, minuscule favor to ask of my *dear* little brother."

"We're twins."

She waves away my words. "See, I might have meddled a little bit too much."

"You already said that."

She tilts her head, finally fixating on me. "Why are you naked? Oh! Did it work? I mean, I told her it probably wouldn't, but if it did, then maybe you'll be more inclined to help me since I'm the only reason things happened in the first place."

I scrub my hand down my face and groan. Is this what I'm like when I'm babbling about some random bullshit? Because it's frustrating as fuck. Explains why Omen tells me to get to the point when he's in a hurry. All I want to do is shake her until she tells me what the fuck is going on.

"Send me back. Now."

She purses her ruby red lips, then snaps her fingers. "I got it. You're in the middle of it and I interrupted. *That's* why you're in a bad mood. Got it. Well, I can definitely send you back if you help me with my little issue and promise me you're no longer mad at me."

"I am still mad at you."

She pouts, and I swear if she doesn't stop acting like a godsdamn toddler...her face morphs and she adopts a more serious look. Her black dress splattered with pink dissolves into a crisp business suit. Her eyes flash opaque before settling on her usual black orbs. It's as if she read my mind, which I wouldn't put past her.

"You realize I'm not actually a flighty little sprite, right? I'm perfectly capable of acting every bit of my age. Except that's no fucking fun. Do you realize how hard it is to go through my existence being shuffled around?"

"I've got an idea," I mutter, yet she continues as if I haven't spoken.

"Not to mention, everyone seems to think I can't heap *rewards* on people. *Oh, Karma will get them. Don't you worry.* I'm not a fucking genie or some harbinger of death, for fuck's sake. I thought if I was...happy, others would think I wasn't—"

"Incompetent?"

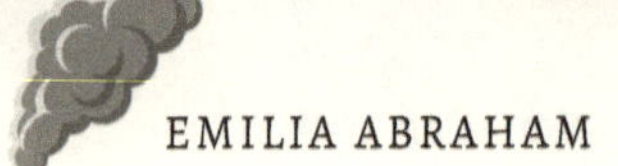

She lets out a humorless laugh. "Whatever. Are you really still mad at me?"

"Yes." I can already see the question in her eyes. "You sent me to the bottom of a volcano in Odium. Then you told everyone I was dead."

"Oh, it wasn't that big of a deal."

I throw my hands in the air. "You had a fucking funeral, Karma."

"Except you weren't really dead. You're fine. Besides, the only reason I sent you to the volcano was because you pissed me off."

"Oh yeah? And what exactly did I do?"

She purses and taps her lips. "I don't remember, but it wasn't very nice."

"You trashed my apartment. Sold half my shit. And tried to get them to demote me instead of enshrined like a demon of my station would normally be. Whatever I did certainly didn't deserve all of *that.*"

"Probably not, but you got me back. You sent me into the Mariana Trench. Do you know how dark it is down there? And the *creatures.*" Her whole body shudders.

I pace away from her, shaking out my hands. I know I'll eventually forgive her. This is always the way it is with us. One of us fucks with the other and the retaliation begins. It's never-ending and is becoming exhausting. I want off this ride. It used to be fun and quirky, but now we're just doing it out of habit. Something's gotta give or we're going to end up enemies instead of siblings.

"Can we just be done with this?" I sigh, running a hand through my hair. "And could you please clothe me?"

She snaps her fingers, and a toga drapes around my frame. Her eyes narrow. "Wait, be done with what? Us? Are you breaking up with me?"

I roll my eyes. "You're my sister, not my soulbound, Karma. We can't break up. You really need to get a grip on context clues when you watch human shows."

"So, you're just stuck with me and you hate me, then. Got it. Well, now I don't feel so bad for cursing you."

Slowly, I turn and glare at her. "It was you?"

She must not catch the warning in my tone. She's too busy off in her own head, probably thinking up the next way to torture me. All this time I thought it was some rogue witch or a demon with a grudge who employed a witch when all along it was my fucking sister. I didn't think she'd go so far as to curse me. I didn't even know she knew *how* to curse demons.

Fuck, I accused Mari of being the culprit. For nothing. I was an asshole and a vindictive one at that. I wanted to hurt her, plain and simple—inflict a bit of the same pain I was feeling. The betrayal in her eyes erased everything I'd built with her. *I* betrayed her. Shame hits me hard and fuels my rage toward Karma.

"You bitch. Do you know what you did? Do you know who you hurt?"

Her shocked gaze meets mine, and my magic flares to life. Nets of electricity encase my hands and arms. I stalk toward her as my fury alone heats the cave. Karma holds up her hands to ward me off, but I won't be stopped this time.

She's pushed too far. She's always gotten away with everything because of who she is, of what she can do. Her power's gone unchecked for too long. This time, she fucked with the wrong demon.

My wings burst from my back, and ominous thunder rolls overhead. Karma shuffles back until she hits the rocky wall. Wind whips around her, tangling her hair in the crevices of the cave. A sword forms in my fist, and sparks flicker along the blade.

"Wait," Karma screeches, straightening her arms. As if her puny hands will stop me from gutting her.

She won't die, but she'll have a hell of a time clawing her way back to this dimension. Or any dimension, really. A little time in the void will do her good. She can think about all the trouble she's caused.

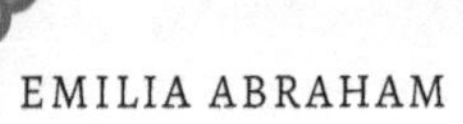

"You took *months* away from me," I growl. "Time I could have spent—"

I shake my head as pain stabs through my temple. If I'm pulled away right now because of her fucking curse, I'll make her death that much more painful. It'll be payback for the time she dropped me in shark-infested waters in Waterworld and Omen had to save my ass. Our little rivalry has gotten out of control, and I aim to end it now. She'll think twice about fucking with my life again.

Then I can go back to Mari. I'll explain what happened and beg her forgiveness. All the other issues I thought impeded us from being together wash away in the wake of my rage. I can fix this. One little swipe and it'll all be over.

"It wasn't a true curse," she yells, cringing away from me.

"I don't fucking care." I stalk toward her and flip the blade once. Twice.

"Dimitrius, please," she pleads, tears filling her eyes.

The sight gives me pause, and my feet stutter to a stop. I haven't seen Karma cry in centuries. Not since she was thrust into the role of truly being karma, deciding which way others' lives would go. Doling out rewards or punishments must be exhausting. Doesn't absolve her of all the shit she put me through.

I rest the tip of my blade against the base of her throat. "Give me one reason why I shouldn't send you into twilight."

"I'm the one who gave her the joining spell," she says in a rush, then squeezes her eyes shut and turns her head away while waiting for my blow. When I don't move, she peeks at me.

My nostrils flare and I grit my teeth. "What the fuck is a joining spell?"

She swallows hard and the sword tip bobs. "It joins two beings together. Duh."

"Who?"

"The witch?" She winces. "The one in Hell."

I glare at her, then drop the sword to my side. I haven't made up my mind yet, but she clearly has some more explaining to do. Her shoulders sag and relief floods her face.

She smirks at me. "I knew you—"

My blade whips around and slices through the leather of her satchel. Marbles scatter across the hard ground, and she cries out. When she drops to her hands and knees to gather them again, I step back. Exhaustion crashes into me, and the ache in my neck becomes unbearable. I need to get back to Mari more than I need revenge on my sister.

"Tell me what you did," I demand as my magic recedes, settling into the occasional snap, crackle, and pop.

"*Me*? I didn't do anything. I stumbled on a witch in some basement of some building in some dimension within Hell. We got to chatting and she wanted a joining spell. I *told* her it wouldn't work. She wanted to try anyways." She gathers the rest of her marbles and dumps them in the bag, then glances up at me.

"What does that have—"

"Because she needed to join someone who could protect them. I offered you up." She sighs, sitting back on her heels. "I didn't think it would work. I forgot I cursed you."

Thunder cracks overhead and she yelps. "Forgot?"

She eyes the blade. "If you put that thing away, I'll keep talking. Otherwise, I'm blipping out and leaving your sorry ass here."

My chest tightens and I suck in a sharp breath. While I'm sitting here demanding answers, my witch is wondering where I blipped off to. I'm wasting my time. Karma isn't going to give me anything of importance. I squeeze the hilt as I attempt to get my shit together. The whole sword shatters, raining sparks down my legs.

"Send me back," I whisper while I stare into the darkness.

"I thought you wanted to know—"

"I don't give a fuck. Just break the curse and send me back. Now."

"Um, well, see, I...can't." She scrambles to her feet. "I can. I just can't *here*. Plus, I can't break the joining. You've gotta do that

yourself. Might help to go see the witch. She's probably still in that cage."

My eyes snap to hers, and my mind nudges me to remember… something. Omen. The cage. Ludovic. Someone softly crying. Triton with the summoning circle. Mari. The witch. They're all connected, yet I can't figure out how. There's a block in my mind, probably brought on by Karma's curse.

"Break the curse, Karma."

"I just told you I can't. Besides, I don't know why you're so butthurt about this curse. It only sends you when someone calls you."

I dig my nails into my palms, fighting against just leaving. Staying means knowing how to deal with this so I can focus on repairing things with Mari.

Karma's face swims into view, and I realize I'm listing to the left. "Stop fighting it. You're just making it worse for yourself. Someone's thinking about you, needing you."

"Who?" I croak out.

She shrugs, glancing away. "I'll work on breaking it. I didn't know it would be painful for you."

It's as close to an apology as I'm going to get. She hops so seamlessly between worlds, she probably didn't understand how draining and disorienting it is for the rest of us. It's a small consolation in the grand scheme of things.

As the edges of my vision darken, I send a silent prayer up to whatever god is on duty tonight to take me back to Mari. I need to get back to her.

I need to make things right.

CHAPTER TWENTY-FOUR
MARI

I slam my fists onto the counter. "I'm getting the fucking food, would you shut the fuck up?"

I glare at the unexpected visitor sitting at my feet. He cocks his head and lets out an innocent meow. I roll my eyes and go back to opening the can of cat food Percy sent to me. She laughed her ass off when I told her a random cat almost killed me. Then she sent me a hundred dollars' worth of toys, food, and a fluffy bed for the thing.

"How are you even able to breathe? Your face is so squished I'm surprised you're not wheezing," I mutter. He doesn't answer, because he's a cat. As soon as I peel the top off, he jumps onto the counter. "How the hell did you get those stubby legs to work like that?"

I've never had a cat. Not because I didn't like them. I was always pretty neutral about them. As annoyed as I am, I doubt it has much to do with the feline currently trying to eat food off my hand and everything to do with a demon who's too good-looking for his own good.

"Should I forgive him, Kitty? Or should I make him suffer?"

I sigh, scooping up the cat and the bowl before placing them both on the floor. He's only been gone a few hours, yet it feels like a lifetime. Disappointment crashes into me yet again. The last

twenty-four hours were the highest of highs and the lowest of lows. I was finally letting him in, and he had to go and ruin it.

My silence probably didn't help things. Trusting him didn't come easily. Hell, trusting anyone doesn't come easy to me. I've spent my life pushing people away in the hopes I wouldn't get hurt. Then the one time I take a chance—betrayal. Except I can see how he came to the conclusions he did, which makes it all the harder to decide whether or not I should care if he comes back.

"I'd be lying if I pretended like I didn't," I whisper, and the cat gives me a look. The one only those of the feline variety seem to be able to give. "Yeah, yeah. I know that didn't make sense. Still, I need him to come back. At the very least, so I can ask him how to find my sister. He owes me that much, right?"

He winds his way around and through my legs, then trots off toward the spell room. I'd slammed the door earlier before the blackness could swallow me whole. I have no idea where it would take me. Probably some random dimension filled with elephant-sized wasps. Or sharks with legs that can breathe on land. Or spiders the size of dinner plates that can fly.

My imagination has conjured up a whole host of horrors. The cat distracted me for a bit, but not long enough to stop the thoughts. Should I be questioning a random animal showing up? Probably. I've gotten pretty used to the strange things that happen around here. Now that I think about it, there's been a lot of things I brushed off as merely peculiar. From objects randomly moving to windows being open when I was sure I closed them, the list in my head is getting quite long.

"You realize I'm not going in there, right?" I mutter as he plops in front of the door and glances over his shoulder. He paws at the wood as if it'll just pop open. "Uh, no. I mean, I'll let you in, but I'm not following."

I reach over and spin the knob and open it just an inch, then stumble back. He doesn't move, doesn't take his laser gaze off me.

"Nope." I pivot on my heel and march down the hall.

Someone's at the front door, anyway. I'm sure it's Percy. She mentioned something about coming over even though I told her not to. Normally, she'd listen, but I'm sure she heard something in my voice. She has a sixth sense about these things. Except I can't open up to her about Dimitri. It's not like she can do anything to help.

When I open the door, though, it's not Percy. Providence stands there with tense shoulders and her back to me. She spins around, her eyes flashing from silver to black and back again.

"Sorry to bother you, but have you seen Dimitrius?" She tucks her hands behind her back and rocks on her heels.

"Um, he was here earlier, then he...left. I don't know where he went. Probably Hell."

She presses her lips together and narrows her gaze. "Are you sure?"

"Why would I lie about something like that?"

"Fine. Have you seen a cat?"

I glance over my shoulder, then back at her and jolt away. She's considerably closer, crowding into my space. I'm about to smack her, or slam the door in her face, or piss myself. I haven't quite decided which one when she sniffs me—long, deep, and incredibly awkwardly. I'm so surprised, I freeze.

"Oh," she murmurs. "Oh, that's interesting."

"What's interesting?" I whisper.

She shuffles back a step and shoots me a scheming look. At least her smile feels smug and intrusive, like she knows something I don't. Obviously she's smarter than me. She's a demon...or something. She's nothing like Dimitri, but I'm pretty sure he said Providence was Omen's sister. And Omen's a demon. Unless one of them is adopted. Do demons get adopted? If she is, then we have something in common, I suppose. I shake my head, derailing my thoughts.

"Nothing. I'm sure you'll figure it out sooner rather than later. And if you don't, well, that's not my department. Now, the cat?" She raises one perfectly manicured silver eyebrow.

I hold up a hand. "Wait, whose department is it?"

"Karma's, of course. Dimitrius's twin? Now, please don't make me break into your house."

"Wouldn't be the first time," I mutter.

"I was *trying* to be polite. I've been accused of not caring about...well, whatever." She rolls her bright blue eyes, the most human thing I've seen from her.

I tilt my head. "When did you change your—I mean, how do you get your eyes—you know what? Never mind. There is a cat here. It showed up, but it went back into the spell room, which is acting very strangely, so I'm not entirely sure he's still here. I fed him before—"

"You fed him? For fuck's sake." She throws her hands up and strides down the steps. She's muttering curses under her breath as she paces back and forth.

I sag against the doorframe. I'm tired—deep down in my bones. My sister's still missing, things with Dimitri are a mess. I don't have a job, and I'm essentially homeless. Being thrust into a world I don't fully understand or am prepared for has thrown me off-kilter. Everyone I've come into contact with gives me half answers. They expect me to understand all the ins and outs of their lives. It's frustrating as fuck, and I just want to be done.

"You know what? Fuck you," I snap, and she swings toward me.

"What was that, witch?"

"Fuck. You. All you fucking demons think you're so much smarter than the rest of us. You think you can just blast into our lives, stir shit up, then vanish. And does anyone ask if we need something? Do you care about the mess you leave behind? Of course you don't. Because you're bullshit elitists. I'm sick of this. I just want—" I snap my mouth shut. She doesn't deserve to know what I want. She deserves nothing.

"I'd be careful, witch. I have more power than you can comprehend."

"As if I fucking give a shit," I snarl. "I'm not a boarding house

for cats. Or a temporary hospital for cursed demons." Her eyebrows rise higher the more I spew at her. "Or a detective. Or a savior. Or even a very competent witch. So, just...fuck off."

I slam the door, then immediately regret my outburst. I shouldn't have done that. Yelling at a demon? Bad. Yelling at a demon named Providence? Catastrophic. She could smite me off the face of the planet. Maybe she'll send me to the dragon realm. I've got some good memories there. Probably the only ones I'll have if she gets ahold of me.

Mrow.

I tip my head back and groan. "You've got to be fucking kidding me." I spin around and find the squish-faced black and white cat. "She was here for you, ya know."

He trots away, back to the damn spell room. This time I follow him straight into the darkness. Except it's no longer dark. Grey perhaps, but not pitch black. It's as if all the color's been sucked from the world. When I glance at my bare arms, I realize there's no color in *me*, either. A shudder rolls through me.

The cat saunters around the partially finished circle, the chalk seemingly embedded into the dark wood. The blood red candles stay unlit, though smoke still curls from the blackened wicks. I tiptoe closer, careful not to disturb anything. Even though there's an opening where the chalk smeared, I still give it a wide berth.

"Kitty, don't you fucking dare." I barely get the words out before he's pouncing into the middle of the damn thing.

He lands on a small book, his paws curling over the edges. I suck in a sharp breath and stumble away. That thing shouldn't be in the center of the circle. A text titled *Necromancy* which was really about plants? Yeah, fucking right. Lark probably spelled it so I wouldn't be able to read it. Then put a bullshit message in there for me to find.

Anger, grief, shame, and jealousy tangle together within my chest, making it hard to breathe. How long had she been planning this? Why didn't she talk to me? Was our fight really that bad to warrant her going off and being reckless? Or was she kidnapped

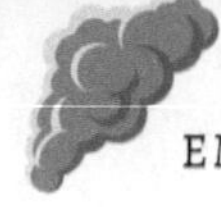

like Dimitri so flippantly suggested? Granted, he didn't know about Lark, but still. He planted the seed when I was so sure she'd merely gotten in over her head. For the first couple months, I'd convinced myself she was still in this world. It wasn't until I'd popped open this very room that I knew it was something more. Something witchy.

Just get it over with.

"Fuck you, Lark," I mutter. "I wouldn't be in this predicament if it wasn't for you."

And you wouldn't have fucked a hot demon if it wasn't for me, either.

I roll my eyes, wondering if her voice will go away once I find her. If she lives in my head forever, pointing out every ridiculous decision I make, I might...I don't even know what an appropriate response would be. Nothing good. I'd probably suffer in silence as I have been for years. It's silly, but it's how my brain operates. As soon as I say something, people either try to solve my problems or dismiss them. I learned to keep shit to myself. If I deal with my own shit, there's no one else to blame when it goes sideways.

The cat leaps toward the other side of the circle and vanishes. The book slides toward me, stopping right before it hits my foot.

"Well, that was unexpected," I mutter.

Gingerly, I nudge the thing with my bare toe, cringing as I do. It's just a book, yet for some reason I'm afraid I'll vanish along with the cat.

"Probably should be worried a Hell kitty is running around this plane, but whatever. It's fine, Mari. It's just parts of a tree repurposed into education on plants. There won't be anything in it when you open it up."

Manifesting never worked much for me, but it's the only thing I can think of other than walking away. And I've done enough of that lately. I'm sick of running and hiding and pretending I'm doing something when I'm not. Even I'm fed up with myself. I can't imagine how annoyed Percy must be with me.

I flip open the cover with my foot, then step back. Disgust

rolls through me. The fucking thing is blank. Because of course it is. No divine secrets, no descriptions of plants, no notes from my sister. Just a bunch of yellowed parchment with absolutely nothing printed on it. One of these days I'll be surprised by shit like this. Today is not that day.

Grabbing the book, I almost drop it. Except I can't. It fuses to my hand, heat searing up my arm. I let out a strangled cry as I attempt to pry my fingers away. A golden glow emanates from beneath my palm. Sparks dance along the edges of the circle, turning the white chalk black. When thunder rumbles overhead, I nearly let out a sigh of relief. Thunder means Dimitri. Dimitri means safety. And help and comfort and being seen. He'll know what to do.

The grey room plunges into darkness, and I shuffle back toward the door. At least, I think it's behind me. In the complete blackness, I'm disoriented, and the magic in the book still hasn't released me. At least the heat is bearable. Still, tears fill my eyes as the full weight of the situation settles on me.

I scream out Dimitri's name, hoping he hears my call wherever he is. My foot hits something soft—waxy. I let out one solitary keening wail as I fall in slow motion.

I never meet the hard floor. Instead, I fall into a void of nothingness. My last thought is a silent plea for Dimitri to save me. Except I know he won't come. No matter how much I might want him to, I'm going to have to save myself.

CHAPTER TWENTY-FIVE
DIMITRI

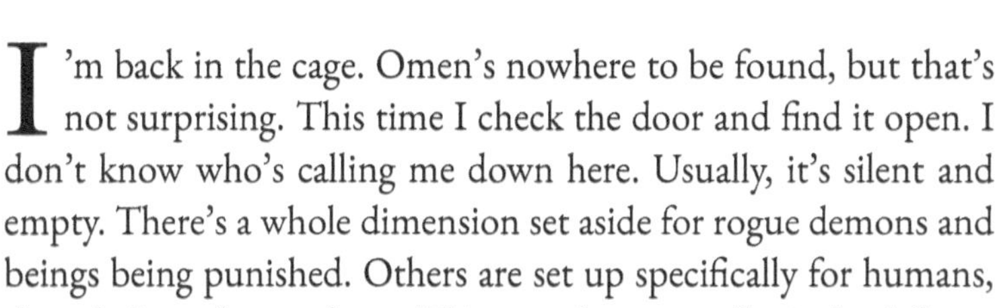

I'm back in the cage. Omen's nowhere to be found, but that's not surprising. This time I check the door and find it open. I don't know who's calling me down here. Usually, it's silent and empty. There's a whole dimension set aside for rogue demons and beings being punished. Others are set up specifically for humans, though I rarely go there. This area became effectively defunct several centuries ago.

Metal screeches as I shove the door open. My magic's been through the wringer over the last twenty-four hours. Karma's curse didn't help either. Add in the short time in the cage and I'm drained. I couldn't produce even a flicker with Karma. When it came roaring back, I was too focused on punishing my sister and couldn't enjoy it. I used up every ounce I had, and I'm lost in a sea of nothingness.

I wander about the dark space, searching for whoever summoned me. Since Karma said it was only when they call me, there has to be someone here. A heavy sigh echoes around me, and I spin around once, then twice. I know better than to call out. Even if I wasn't a demon, I've seen some of the human's horror movies. That person always dies first. I'd like to think I'd last a bit longer, but I'm not under the illusion I'd survive until the end. Not without my magic.

"You here to save me?" A familiar voice calls out, though

there's a lilt I've never heard before—an inflection different from normal.

"Thought you could save yourself, witch." I'd ask how she got down here, but it's Mari. She probably fell into the circle her sister carved into the floorboards. Why it dumps out in the underbelly of this part of Hell, I haven't figured out yet.

She lets out a humorless laugh. "I thought so, too. Where is she?"

My brows pull low as I creep in the direction of her voice. "Don't know who you're talking about. Providence?"

Omen's sister is the only person Mari's met. Unless Karma paid her a visit before sending her down here. Maybe my sister meant to send us to the same cage, though why *here* I don't know. She's capable of sending us right outside my apartment. Feels like that would have been easier. Unless this is her revenge for practically skewering her.

My fingers tingle, and I breathe a sigh of relief. I rub my fingers together, creating a soft purple glow to light my way. It's not enough to do anything significant except give me some peace of mind. A familiar cat jumps through the bars of a cage to my right, and an unbidden smile stretches across my face.

"Well hello there, Kitty." I reach down and scratch under his chin. "Not surprised to find you here. You should go home, though."

He meows before vanishing, and I huff out a laugh. When I glance up, Mari's face appears through the bars of another cage. She tilts her head and studies me as if she's never seen me before. As if we didn't spend last night together wrapped in each other's arms. As if I don't know the sounds she makes when she comes.

My mouth parts, the whisper of her name on the tip of my tongue when I'm whisked away once more. As I'm dropped right outside my apartment door, I groan, staring up at the ceiling. Except it doesn't look like the normal ceiling I'm used to. It's dotted with glittering stars with random comets whizzing by.

Whoever's fucking with the interior of our corner of Hell is

doing a damn good job of it. Unless someone took my place and moved it to some random dimension. Still, I can tell I'm in Hell. It's a weird concept and more of a certainty in my belly rather than actual knowing.

Pushing to my feet, I stumble inside and shut the door before freezing. Someone's in my house. I glance around the entryway, trying to peer into the small living room and kitchen. Nothing moves, but I can't really see anything. I should redesign everything, but I'm barely here other than to sleep. Besides, I get better sleep in Mari's bed than my own. If I could just stay up topside with her, I would in a heartbeat.

"Hello?" I call, then immediately regret it. Didn't I just go through this? Except no one has access to my place other than Omen. I doubt he'd extend it to anyone else. At least not without talking to me first.

There's a shuffling deeper in, and I prowl toward my bedroom tucked in the back. As I suspected, no one's in the other rooms. Everything's exactly like I left it. When I reach the door, I nudge it open with my foot, desperately hoping my magic doesn't fail me again. I need to get back to the cage room and free Mari. After I get her somewhere safe, I can go after whoever put her down there.

It feels like every time I'm in a situation, I'm pulled in several different directions—get info from Karma or fix things with Mari, find out who's in my apartment or get Mari out of a cage. It's all a tangled web I can't unravel.

I flip the switch and light floods the dark room. "Mari? How the hell did you get here?"

Mari freezes, then shoves her hand under the covers. She gives me a strained look, then her shoulders sag.

"Hi," she whispers.

"How did you..." It's as if my brain can't fully comprehend how she's in Hell. First in the cage and now here. None of it makes sense. Her tripping into the portal to Hell is plausible. Showing up in my apartment isn't. Unless there's some weird

loophole I don't know about, she should have been thrown into the main hall of Hell. The other demons would deal with her. A shudder rolls through me at the thought.

"I don't know. I promise I'm not stalking you."

I rear back, then glance over my shoulder, making sure there's no one else here. "Stalking? Spitfire, you're a lot of things, but a stalker never crossed my mind. I just don't understand...I suppose it doesn't matter."

"I mean, you did crash into my house. Maybe this is just payback." She lets out a nervous laugh, then drops her head.

I prowl closer, then tuck my knuckle under chin and force her to look at me. "Are you okay?"

A range of emotions runs through her eyes, too quickly for me to decipher. "I'm fine. Unless you count the book currently glued to my hand."

She pulls her arm from under the comforter and winces. It glows a strange green color, and I realize it's the necromancy book. I never gave this particular one much thought. Most witches have weird rabbit holes they burrow into when it comes to different types of magic. Mari didn't seem the type to reanimate corpses, so I wasn't worried.

When I reach out, she yanks away. "You shouldn't. It's hot."

I smirk and drop to my knees next to the bed. "I'm a demon, Mari. Heat doesn't really bother me. Let me help."

She hesitates, then nods. I trace my finger from the inside of her elbow to her wrist. When I reach the edge of the aura, she flinches. I push onward, slipping between the book and her palm. The light sputters out, and the small text drops from her hold. She lets out another nervous chuckle, and I grab her hand before she can pull away.

As I massage her sore muscles, her head hits the headboard and she lets out a moan, making my cock twitch. I focus on my task. The last time we spoke, we weren't exactly in the best place. I was a dick, throwing around accusations. The last thing she'll want to do is jump into bed with me again. Even with all the

explanations, my cock doesn't listen and soon my shaft strains against the side of the mattress.

"Why are you wearing a toga?" she murmurs, and I glance up to meet her hooded eyes.

"Karma," I grunt.

"Easy access, I suppose. And airy, I've heard."

A sharp laugh leaves me unexpectedly, and she grins. After everything we've been through, it's a glorious sight. Even if we'd been through nothing at all, it still would capture me. I don't know when it happened in our disjointed journey, but I've somehow fallen completely under her spell.

"The draft *is* quite nice." I clear my throat and drop my gaze to her hand once more. "I found out who cursed me."

"Is that an apology?"

"No. It's an explanation, not an excuse. I'm sorry I accused you. I should have..."

"Asked questions instead. That's usually the best course of action."

I sigh and my fingers still. "Yeah, that's what I should have done."

"Is your name really Dimitrius?"

"Yup. Is yours really Marigold?"

"Seems like a weird thing to make up in the heat of the moment, doesn't it? Yes, it is. My parents were...not very present. They were always off in their own little world. Only the two of them seemed to exist. Not to say they neglected us, but it was like every time I walked into the room, they suddenly remembered they had kids. Then they had a spell go wrong, and they were gone. When we went to live with our aunt, she made us go by nicknames. She was always disappointed in me on account of my name."

"Why? Sure, it's...unique, but it's not *that* bad. What does it mean?" I grimace, hoping she doesn't bite my head off for basically insulting her name.

She laughs, and I breathe a sigh of relief. "Just superstition stuff and all that. I don't really want to talk anymore."

"I can take you back," I murmur. I don't know if I actually can or not, but offering for her to stay doesn't seem like a good idea. If she says no, it'll hurt. If she says yes, I'll be hard-pressed not to rip her leggings off and devour her.

"Do you have to?"

My head snaps up, and she presses her lips together. "You can stay here. I mean, you're more than welcome—"

She leans toward me, and I freeze. "Am I making you nervous, Dimitrius?"

"What? No." My voice cracks, because of course it does.

She laughs lightly and rests her forehead against mine. "Are we okay?"

"I don't know, Marigold. Are we?"

"We will be if we forget this morning ever happened and you kiss me. If you poof out on me while you are, though, we're going to have more problems."

The hungry beast inside me roars to life, and I surge forward, covering her mouth with my own. She moans as I wrap my fingers around her neck, then slide them into her hair. I tug on the strands, and she moans again. I wrap the long locks around my fist and force her head back. Her mouth falls open and her eyes flutter shut as I run my teeth along her jaw.

"Missed this," I mumble into her skin, and she huffs out a laugh.

"Been less than a day."

"Too fucking long," I growl and untangle my fingers from her hair. I sit back on my knees, gazing up at her flushed face.

The corner of her mouth tips up. "You look pretty good on your knees, demon."

I raise a single eyebrow, then snap my fingers. Her clothes disappear along with my own. She yelps, her hands fluttering around as if she doesn't know whether to cover up or display her delicious body. I grab her ankle and yank her toward me until her legs hang over the edge of the bed. My hands land on her knees, and I give her a pointed look when she presses her thighs together.

She props herself on her elbow and gazes down at me. "I didn't mean—"

"You wanted me on my knees, and I will always give you what you want, spitfire. Now be a good witch and open your legs so I can taste my dessert."

"Dessert?" she chokes out while her chest rises and falls rapidly.

I grin wickedly and lick my lips. "I'm going to have my dessert first. Then I'll fill you up with the main course."

She snorts, then falls back. She yelps again when she hits the pillows I've stacked up behind her. Now she'll be able to watch the show, and I'll see her fall apart under my tongue. When I part her legs, she gives in easily. Her thighs twitch as I skim my lips up the soft skin. Her hips jerk, and I drop an arm over her waist while biting into her flesh.

I haven't even gotten to the good part and she's already putty in my hands if her moans echoing around us are any indication. I brush my nose along her other thigh, stopping when I reach her glistening pussy. When I inhale deeply, my mouth waters. I flick my tongue against the sensitive nub, and she jolts in my grasp.

"Intoxicating," I breathe, then wrap my lips around her clit and suck. She hisses, her hips jumping, and I concentrate on working her into a frenzy.

She moans my name and my gaze flicks to hers. She's staring at me, her eyes drowning in desire. She kicks at my chest, and I release her with a pop, then remove my hand.

"You're interrupting my meal, Mari," I growl.

She swings her legs over my shoulders and spears her fingers into my hair. A groan rips from me when she grips the strands tight and forces my face back between her thighs. I devour her, lapping up every drop of pleasure dripping from her. I plunge two fingers into her as I circle her clit with my tongue. Within seconds, she's chanting my name, her hips rocking in time with

my thrusts. She shudders and her thighs snap closed around my head. Her pussy spasms and I grin, flicking her clit one last time.

Her body goes limp, and she pants as she stares at the clouds gathering on the ceiling. She jolts when I pull free from her, and her eyes find mine when I pop my fingers in my mouth, relishing the taste of her on my tongue. Her bottom lip ends up between her teeth, and I grin again.

"Ready for the appetizer?" I ask, earning an eye roll.

I push to my feet and slip my arm around her waist before tipping her over my shoulder. She yelps out my name and squirms, so I slap her on the ass.

"What the fuck, Dimitri," she cries, and I smack her again.

"Don't tell me you don't love it. I can feel your pleasure coating my shoulder, spitfire." I march toward the kitchen, then out the back door. Her arm swings around as if she'll be able to cover herself. "Settle down. No one's going to see you but me. Unless you'd like an audience for when I make you come all over my cock."

I drop her onto her back on the pillow of clouds I gathered for this specific reason. Hell's night sky isn't all that different from topside. Stars glitter above, creating a canopy of lights. Three moons hang in various positions, allowing me to see her in all her glorious nakedness. She stares in wonder at the sight, while I do the same. Except I think my view is a whole helluva lot better. She crawls to her knees and tips her head back.

"It's beautiful," she breathes.

"Yes, it is."

Dropping to my knees in front of her, I will the clouds to cushion and support us. They gather under her and lift her to just the right height. Her arms loop around my shoulders, still gazing at the sky.

I nuzzle her neck, then plunge into her. Her head tips back and a low groan erupts from her.

"So fucking wet."

"For you," she gasps, and I surge into her.

I wanted this to be a reunion—an apology. My control sifts through my fingers, unraveling faster than I can stop it. I slam into her again and again, chasing my release. She urges me on, begging me to go faster, harder, deeper. A needy noise falls from her lips as she shatters in my arms.

When I slow, she whimpers, "Don't stop."

She clings to me as she explodes again, one orgasm rolling into the next. I groan her name as I shudder out my own release. My fingers slide into her hair, and I press her close to me as we catch our breaths.

"Don't leave," she whispers softly, more to herself than me.

"Never," I murmur and cling to her. I only hope this is one vow I can keep.

CHAPTER TWENTY-SIX
MARI

Hell was not on my wish list of places to visit when I was younger. Now that I'm here, it's exhilarating. That could be because I'm curled up next to a sleeping demon, but I'm not going to question it. I've spent enough of my life doubting my decisions, pushing others away, assuming shit would go south. I'm going to seize these moments and focus on what's important.

I snuggle closer to Dimitri, and his arm tightens around my waist. Still, my mind wanders to my sister. If she was truly in danger and didn't do this to herself, she would have told me. She would have warned me if she was about to do something that would get her killed. Trusting her not to go off the rails without a word isn't easy. I'll just have to have faith in my twin. Doesn't mean I'm going to give up my search for her.

"Deep thoughts for the morning," Dimitri murmurs, then presses a kiss to the top of my head. Every gentle touch, every intimate exchange, pulls me a bit deeper into this thing between us. The thought of losing my connection to him has a pit forming in my gut.

I slide my leg over his and haul myself on top of him. His hands land on my hips, and a grin splits his face. I dig my nails into his bare chest, relishing the feel of him underneath me. If someone had told me a month ago I'd be transported to Hell and straddling a demon, I would have scoffed, then thrown them out.

When I lean down to kiss him, his palms slip up my sides until his thumbs settle beneath my tits. I shiver, desire roaring to life within me. I grind my hips into him, and he grunts. My teeth graze over his jaw, down his neck, to his collarbone. Thunder rolls overhead and I smile against his skin.

"Horny little thing, aren't you?" he murmurs, his hands returning to my waist.

I nibble my way down to his nipple, then flick the hard bud with my tongue. I've never been one to take control before. It's a heady feeling, knowing every twitch and moan is in response to me. His cock hardens and I roll my hips, searching for the right amount of friction. A soft whimper leaves me when he hits my clit. An explosion of pleasure crashes into me, and my breath catches in my throat.

His grip falls from me, and I shove myself upright. He raises an eyebrow, his smirk firmly in place. When he tucks his hands behind his head, I glare at him.

"Do your worst, witch."

"You honestly think you'll be able to keep your hands to yourself? Doubt it. Before long you'll take over, unable to stop yourself." I squirm against him, and his arms twitch, giving him away.

His eyes narrow as I slide my wetness along his shaft. His gaze snaps down as I move on top of him. He's not even inside me and I'm already panting. I clench around nothing, hoping I can hold out longer than he can. For some reason, I want to witness him break. I need to see how much he wants me. Proof this isn't just fun and games, that I'm not just some plaything he'll discard when I'm no longer of use.

His arms slip down and I grin, knowing I won. He props himself on his elbows, and I dip my head toward his in anticipation. With our lips a hairsbreadth apart, he stops.

"Do. Your. Worst," he whispers, then flops back again, his hands back behind his head. He grins and wiggles his hips, forcing me to swallow down a moan.

"Asshole," I mutter, and his grin widens.

I push onto my knees and hover over him. Fear flashes in his eyes as if he thinks I'm going to stop. Instead, I crawl up his body until my knees rest on his arms. He tenses, his brow furrowing. I don't want to hurt him, and I watch him closely as I put more weight on him. He doesn't seem to notice, and I smirk.

One hand ends up gripping the top of the headboard and the other I slip between my legs. He tracks my movements as I hover over his face. His nostrils flare and his jaw tics. I've never done something like this before, and I'm not entirely sure it will work. Touching myself isn't anything new. Doing it while someone else watches definitely is. There's something about him that has my inhibitions vanishing. Every fantasy I've ever concocted in my head comes screaming to the forefront. They don't seem like fantasies anymore. With him, they morph into reality.

"Mari," he warns, his gaze skipping between my fingers hovering over my clit and my eyes fixed on him.

"Yes?" I mean for it to come out confidently. Instead, it's a breathless whisper of anticipation.

He licks his lips and inhales deeply once more. "You're going to have to strap me down."

"That can be arranged, sir."

He bucks underneath me, and I press my knees deeper into his muscles. A strangled cry leaves him, mingling with my moan as I slide my clit between my fingers. As much as I want to watch him lose control, my head tips back and my eyes close as an orgasm builds within me. I rub the sensitive nub in gentle circles. Part of me wants to drag this out, make him suffer. Then again, I'm already wound so tightly, I don't know how long I'll last.

I pick up my pace and glance down. He pants, his gaze fixated on my hand or my very wet pussy. His form flickers, and I wonder if he's about to get pulled into the void. I lean my forehead against my hand gripping the headboard, and my hips rock forward. He licks his lips, his black tongue morphing into something too quickly for me to see.

"Let me up," he croons. "I'll get you there, spitfire."

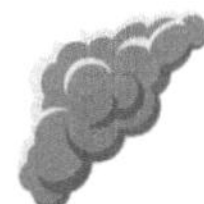

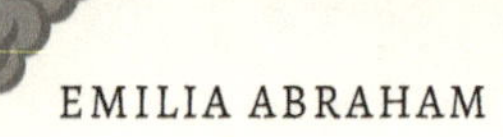

I shake my head, my hair spilling over my shoulders. I slip my hand lower, and he groans. My pussy spasms around my fingers, though it's not enough. Just a little bit more and I'd put us both out of our misery. Except I'm having too much fun. I moan as I pull out, and he bucks under me again. I'm sure he could get out if he wanted to.

"You've done so well," I murmur. "How about a little reward?"

He peers at me with a hooded gaze, his chin quivering with the effort to let me play. "Yes, please."

"Such a good little demon." I trace his bottom lip with my wet fingers. He strains toward me, and I slip them into his mouth. His tongue cleans them off, and a breathless laugh leaves me.

I rip my hand away and quiver as I circle my clit again. It's a torturous relief. Something rough, yet soft, flicks against my core, and I jolt. Dimitri grins as his tongue, long and forked, flicks toward me again. My head tips back, and a low moan reverberates through the room as he spears into me. When he hums, it vibrates within me and I spasm around him, crashing over the edge.

My legs give out, and I end up on his face. He licks and sucks at my flesh while I grip the headboard with both hands. I ride out my orgasm, grinding against his lips, his tongue, even his nose. I'm probably suffocating him, but he's a demon. I'm sure he'll figure it out. If not, well, he'll probably think it's the best way to go.

He yanks his arms from under my knees and latches onto my waist. I barely have time to yelp before I'm on my back and his face is buried between my legs again. He devours me, using his tongue and teeth to bring me to the brink once more. I writhe back and forth, my fingers gripping the mussed sheets. Within seconds, my back arches and I shudder out another release.

When he lifts his head, grinning at me, my desire coating the lower half of his face. He doesn't seem to notice or care. He crawls up my body and his cock nudges against my weeping core. I'm still floating when he nuzzles into my neck, then nips at the soft skin.

"Naughty witch, making me watch that performance. I should punish you."

He slips the tip into me and rolls his hips. I squirm underneath him, trying to force him deeper. A low whine echoes between us, and he chuckles.

"You brought this on yourself," I gasp. "Why am *I* the one being punished?"

He picks his head up, and sparks crackle across his skin. "Touché. Should I reward you instead?"

I nod my head, my breath coming in sharp gasps. If he doesn't move soon, I'll shatter into a million pieces, left bereft and wanting. I don't think I've craved anything more in my life.

He hums, then pulls away, and I let out a choked sob. As he crawls off the bed, I reach between my legs once more. Touching myself again won't ease the ache swirling inside me. It'll have to be enough if he's hellbent on edging me. Because I don't think this is anything other than that. He won't truly walk away. He's finally convinced me that no matter what happens, he'll be there. It's a scary enough thought, I shove it from my mind and focus on my fingers inching toward my clit.

He grabs my wrist and my gaze snaps to his. He shakes his head, then growls, "Did I say you could touch yourself?"

I tip my chin up, which is awkward enough while lying down. "Make me wait and I'll take care of it myself."

The corner of his mouth lifts, and a hint of possessiveness flashes in his black eyes. Purple bleeds into them, washing away the edge.

"If you insist, I'll be forced to do something drastic." He leans over me and presses a kiss to my inner wrist. "You've been warned."

He places my hand above my head, his gaze traveling down my body, and he licks his bottom lip. He drops his hold and turns on his heel. When he prowls toward the nightstand, I reach between my legs again. Thunder rumbles and the lights flicker around us. He's still digging around in a drawer, and I bite my lip.

Just before my fingers brush my clit, shadows seize my wrists and force both my hands above my head. They wrap around my ankles, leaving me spreadeagle on the bed. No, not shadows—storm clouds. He's using his magic to keep me in line.

"Well played, sir," I whisper as I tug at the restraints. They're buried into the mattress with little give.

He spins around, holding up a strip of fabric. "Didn't think I'd let you get away with it, did you?"

I attempt to shrug yet end up flopping awkwardly as the magic restraints tighten around my wrists. He tilts his head and scans my body. A thrill runs down my spine, and heat pools in my gut. I swallow hard, trying to stay still. My skin tingles in anticipation, though he makes no move to touch me.

He lets the fabric brush along my leg, and goosebumps erupt across my flesh. "You have no idea what you do to me."

I glance at his hard cock. "I've got an inkling."

He chuckles, and I jolt when the end of the strip sweeps between my legs. After two orgasms, I thought I'd be drained and ready for a shower. Instead, I'm clinging to the edge of a cliff, desperate for him to take me. I hate to admit it, but Percy was right—demons are exceptional in the sack.

As he towers over me, his horns poking from his dark hair, I should be intimidated. With Dimitri, though, I feel safer than I ever have. It's as if I'm right where I'm supposed to be, and that scares me more than anything else.

A crack of lightning snaps my focus back to him. "What's the fabric for?"

"I thought about blindfolding you. Except I'm particular to watching those stunningly exquisite eyes roll back in your head when you come all over my cock." He drops the cloth on my stomach, then smirks. "I do believe you've waited long enough."

More dark clouds gather along the ceiling and the lights wink out, plunging us into darkness. A nervous laugh leaves me, and I flinch when his fingers trail along my leg. Lightning flickers

through the room, escalating the higher he moves up my body. With every flash, I get a clearer view of him, his cracked skin revealing the deep purple underneath. His forked tongue has retreated, and I almost ask for it again. When his wings burst from his back, though, a shudder hits me hard.

"As much as I like you spread out for me, I need—" He grabs my waist and flips me onto my stomach. He tugs until my feet hit the floor and I tilt my head to the side. The clouds around my wrists embed into the bed once more, keeping me in place.

"Dimitri," I growl, and he chuckles, leaning over me.

"You wanted a reward, but your teasing drove me to the brink, spitfire. So scream all you want. In fact, I prefer it, especially if it's my name. I'll be having my fun now. Be a good girl and spread your legs."

He straightens and waits—for my compliance, my consent, my desire to continue. If I told him to stop, that it was too much, I have no doubt he would. He'd cradle me against him, probably apologizing for going too far. Except this isn't too far. It's not nearly far enough. It plays into every fantasy I've had since I realized what I wanted.

I shuffle my feet apart, and something slithers underneath my belly. I pick my head up, trying to see, and he slides his fingers in my hair and forces my face into the mattress.

"Don't worry about that. Just a little magic to keep you right where I want you. Ready, spitfire?"

There's no waiting for an answer this time. He plunges into me, and a muffled scream erupts around us. Pleasure courses over me as he thrusts into me hard and fast. My orgasm careens closer, then hovers just out of reach. I push back as much as the restraints allow, and he groans. When I clench around his length, he slows. I cry out, this time in frustration.

He grazes his fingers along my skin as if he's memorizing every dip, every hollow, every mark. He presses a kiss to the back of my neck, then my shoulder, then my cheek. When he releases my hair,

I turn my head and inhale deeply. Gone is the desperation—the claiming of my body—from seconds ago.

He whispers promises into my flesh—vows of devotion and desire. A whimper escapes me, though whether it's his words or the shallow thrusts, I'm not sure. Maybe both.

"Dimitri," I breathe, a plea weaving into my voice.

"Marigold," he whispers in return. He says it with such reverence, such care. I close my eyes, committing this moment to memory. Whatever future we're hurtling toward, I want to hold on to this.

He pulls out of me, and the restraints vanish. Tenderly, he turns me onto my back, and I push farther onto the bed. He covers my body with his, raining kisses across my chest. When he latches onto a nipple while rolling the other one between his fingers, a low moan leaves me. I wrap my legs around his waist as he surges into me once more. His wings settle over us, creating a hidden world of our own. Webs of lightning travel across the smoky expanse.

I cling to him as my orgasm crashes into me without warning. He latches onto my other nipple as he grinds his hips into me and wrings every drop of pleasure from me. When my body lies pliant beneath him, he pushes onto his knees and grabs my waist. I don't know if I'm capable of more. A weightlessness has taken over and I hum, watching him through slits.

"Oh no, spitfire. Open those pretty eyes for me," he says, pulling out of me slowly.

When I focus on him, he buries his length into me, and a needy noise falls from my tongue. He does it again with the same result.

"Perfect," he grunts, though whether he's talking to me or himself, I don't know. "Fucking perfect."

His hand slips between us and he circles my clit. Another wave of rapture hits me, and my back arches. Electricity dances across his grey skin, then sparks between us. The bite of pain is

enough to send me flying over the edge once more. He thrusts into me once, twice, then groans my name as he lets go.

When he collapses on top of me, I wrap my arms around him, holding him close as we shudder together. I cling to him as thoughts of the future try to creep in and derail my bliss. I shove the thoughts away, content to live in this euphoria just a little bit longer.

CHAPTER TWENTY-SEVEN
DIMITRI

I carry Mari's pliant body toward the bathroom. She snuggles closer to me, tucking her head under my chin. I reach for my magic, and it leaps to my fingertips. Thankfully, my apartment has already rearranged itself, placing a bathtub big enough for two in the room. It fills with hot water and steam curls into the air.

Something changed between us this morning. It was always more than sex for me. I'd hoped it was for her, too, but today I felt it. Having her in Hell, in my space, feels right. More right than anything else I've ever encountered. I've traveled through dimensions, chasing the high of an adventure I never fully understood. I wonder if I was constantly searching for her.

"I need clothes," she mumbles, her eyes closed and her hands tucked under her arms.

"I prefer you naked." I step into the warm water.

As we sink under the surface, she moans, waking up my cock again. As much as I'd like to sink into her heat once more, she needs a break. I adjust her, settling her between my legs. She rests her arms on my knees, and her head lolls against my chest. I tip my own head back and let my hands wander over her skin. She gasps when my thumb brushes over her nipple.

"What happens now?" she whispers as if she's hoping I won't hear her.

"Whatever you want, spitfire."

"Is your curse gone, then?"

I sigh, closing my eyes. "Not sure. I don't know if anyone's called me so I can't really test it."

"I don't know what that means, but I suppose it's none of my business." She tenses and I hold her tighter.

"None of that, Mari. After our...tiff—" I wince as she snorts. "It was my sister. She's the one who put the curse on me. Thought she'd be funny. Suppose she didn't realize how taxing it would be on me and my magic. She said she'd break it soon."

"How did she not think getting thrown around different dimensions at random would be taxing?"

"Well, she's karma. She can travel between worlds as easily as stepping from one room to the next. Besides, we've been escalating lately in our...revenge pranks. I think this was her way of apologizing for our fight."

She sits up and turns the upper half of her body toward me. How she's able to contort that way, I don't know. My back would snap in two if I tried.

"You had a fight with your sister, too?"

I press my lips together. It's not that I don't want to open up, but it's awkward talking to Mari about our siblings while we're naked and in a bathtub. I generally try to keep my thoughts *off* my sister while I'm unclothed.

"I got mad at her for some shit she pulled. We'll work it out. What about you, though? You've been keeping a lot of things to yourself."

She settles against me again. "I was afraid you'd walk away. It's mostly what happens when I'm not little-miss-sunshine like Lark. I open up, they meet my sister, and suddenly everything I've told them becomes ammunition. Plus, you have to remember I'd never met a demon before."

"You took the news quite well, I'd say."

"I tried to ban you from the house. I think I fucked up the spell. Glad it didn't work or I wouldn't have just had two amazing orgasms," she says, a smile in her voice.

"Four. You had four orgasms, and if you keep wiggling against my cock, it's going to be five."

She snorts again and squirms even more. I sink my teeth into her shoulder and she moans, tilting her head to give me more access to her delicious skin. As much as I want to keep going, we need to finish this conversation. I need to know what she wants to do from here—if she wants to stay with me.

I brush my lips against her temple. "What was your fight about?"

"She kept talking about our family history. It's not something I like to think about. Despite growing up in the same house, we had wildly different upbringings. We were still as thick as thieves, but part of me always resented her. When she wouldn't drop the topic of the family lore, I got mad. I said shit I didn't mean and then she wouldn't call me back." She pulls in a deep breath, then exhales slowly. "When she vanished, I knew she was still alive. I just couldn't find her. I figure she's punishing me for not helping her."

I don't know what to say. It's not like I can give her much comfort. Others don't usually open up to me like this. I have to drag Omen's problems from him since he's so locked in his own head. Everyone else seems to think I'm not capable of being serious—of helping them with their problems.

"I'm sure she's not punishing you. She probably just didn't want you to worry. Especially if you didn't want to talk about your family history."

She shakes her head and swirls her hand through her water, sending ripples across the surface. "No, she's punishing me. I know it. One of those things."

"What things? Do witches have some telepathic connection I don't know about?" I'm only half joking, but maybe it's a sister thing. Except Omen has a sister, and he doesn't have that type of link with Providence. Karma and I do, but we're twins. It's different for us.

"You should understand. You have a twin," she mumbles.

I jolt and water sloshes over the side. She sits up and glances over her shoulder, a concerned look stamped on her face. Something's sliding into place, pieces fitting into a puzzle I didn't even know was in my head. It's there, yet not quite clear. I bite the inside of my cheek, trying to force the image to focus.

"Are you okay?"

I swallow hard and shake my head. "How did you get to Hell?"

"I told you, I don't know." She slips around to face me. "One minute the book was trying to magically eat me and the next I was here."

"Where?" My hands land on her shoulders, and her eyes widen. "Where in Hell did you land? The cage?"

"Dimitri, you're worrying me. What's the cage?"

"Just answer the damn question, Mari."

"I don't know what the cage is. I ended up in your bed, fighting the book."

My breath catches in my throat and my vision swims. "I know where your sister is."

"What?" She explodes out of the water, almost slipping as she scrambles out of the tub. She searches for clothes or maybe a towel.

I stand slowly and my body sways. Magic tugs in my gut, and I reach for Mari, her name on my lips. She turns and yells just as I'm whisked away. I swear to fucking gods I'm going to kill Karma this time. It takes longer than usual to flit around the void, and I'm cussing my sister the entire time. I need to get to the cage, help reunite Mari and her sister.

My feet slam into an obsidian floor, and I glance around. This place is familiar, yet not. It looks exactly like the main halls of Hell where Omen and I work, but completely empty. It's never free of demons. Silence stretches around me, then snaps like a whip cracking through the air.

Ludovic appears in front of me, a look of disgust stamped on his face. "Dimitrius. You've become quite the problem. Shirking your duties, neglecting your paperwork, and intervening in my plans. It's become too irksome to keep you around. We're going to have to let you go."

My mouth parts as I stare at him. "Are you firing me? While I'm naked?"

He lets out a derisive laugh. "Oh no. Not firing. I'm going to need you to cease to exist, unfortunately. If you'd rather be clothed, though..."

He snaps his fingers, and a potato sack drops over my head. Fucking bastard. He might be a level higher than me, but it doesn't mean he can erase me from history. He doesn't have that kind of power. I narrow my eyes while probing for my magic. It'd better not fail me now, but I'd rather he not know. I'm stronger than him. He lost his muscle mass long ago, settling into mediocrity with his promotion. He's also neglected his magic, at least as far as I've seen. I'm healthier, stronger, and better equipped. I'd rather not fight him, though.

"Want to tell me what plans I'm apparently interrupting?"

"You expect me to give some grand speech? Fine, I suppose you can extend your life just a bit longer." A replica of the long ornate table kept in our main conference room appears, and he settles at the head. I take the other side, hissing at the cold chair on my ass, and he chuckles. "Do you know how to enter the upper gates?"

"No. They're for deities, not demons."

He smirks and wags his fingers at me. "That's where you're wrong. Demons are capable of becoming deities if they've performed certain tasks...I'll keep the details to myself, if you so please."

He's usually a hothead, flying off the handle at the drop of a hat. If I can push him hard enough, he'll make a mistake—he'll attack, and I'll be able to send him to the cages until his fate can be decided. Clearly, the power of his position, which isn't all that great to be honest, has gone to his head. I doubt they'll rehabilitate him.

"Going to give me a hint?" I lean back in my chair and smirk.

"Don't know why you're smiling. This is serious business, boy," he growls.

"Maybe I'm in the business of exploring my options, you ever think of that?"

He studies me, beady eyes narrowed as he searches for the lie. He slaps the table and grins. "I knew there was something about you. Just needed you to wake the fuck up. It won't be easy, but in a few hundred years, you might be where I am. The hardest part is finding a witch who doesn't dissolve as soon as you bring them into Hell. Once you have that, well, you'll be golden."

My eyebrows rise in shock. Thankfully, he seems to take it as surprise. "That easy, huh? Why the fuck did it take you so long?"

He huffs out a chuckle. "You say that until you start grabbing them topside. They're a feisty bunch. Plus, ya know, the dissolving bit. Don't know where they go, but ya can't get 'em back."

"So, once I've found my witch, what do I do?"

"Sacrifice them. Bleed them of their magic, discard the excess. They have to be willing, so you might have to coerce them. Convince them this is the only way they'll gain power. Now, it might not work the first couple times. You have to follow a specific ritual. There's a book and there's only one. Get your hands on that and you'll be onto the next step."

It takes everything in me to stay still. Stealing witches? Sacrificing them? Draining their magic? It sounds like a cult ritual thought up by some science fiction author. How Ludovic discovered this or thinks it'll grant him entrance into the deities' dimension is beyond me. He'll probably end up at the bottom of an acid pit. I wish I could just let him hang himself. He's got enough rope to do it. Allowing more witches to be hurt, though, isn't something I'll let happen.

"You've already drained a witch, then?" I ask, keeping my voice even.

He nods, though his grin seems forced. "Close enough. I'm

almost there, but I need the book first. Which is where *you* come in."

"Thought you were going to kill me?"

He waves his hand as if he never threatened me. "This is easier. Killing you, luring Omen out, snatching his witch, forcing her to give me the book...it's just a lot of work."

"We all know how much you hate work," I mutter sarcastically.

He booms out a laugh, and I struggle to keep my lip from curling. He's laughed and grinned more in this short interaction than I've ever seen him do before. And I've known him for centuries. We might not have come up in the ranks together, but close enough. He's always been quick to anger and a stickler for the rules. I wonder how long he's been living this double life.

"No, this is definitely easier. *You* can get Omen's witch *and* the book, then we'll do the ritual together. I hadn't planned on bringing anyone else along on this journey, but I can share." The glint in his eye says otherwise.

"How'd you find out about Cl—Omen's witch?" Omen was pretty close-lipped about it. He didn't even want to tell *me* about it. I didn't understand it at the time. He must know Ludo had this planned or at least that it was a possibility. Otherwise, he wouldn't care whether or not I know about her whereabouts. It's not like I'd steal her from him. Since they're soulbound, I doubt I could even if I wanted to.

Ludo shoves to his feet. "Enough talk. If we're going to do this, we need to do it now."

"Wait." I hold up my hand and he pauses, annoyance flashing across his face. "If you're going to drain Omen's witch, then who am *I* supposed to use? You said we'd do this together, but if it took you this long to find a witch, I doubt I'll have much luck."

"Oh, no. I'll use the one in the cages. You can use Omen's witch. Don't worry about retaliation. Once she's gone, he'll spiral. Being soulbound sounds like a fucking nightmare. Works in your favor, though. Doubt you'll even have to eliminate him."

I nod and push to my feet slowly. Ludo must have been the one to kidnap Lark. He stuck her in the cage and has been keeping her there until he can get the book. It's great to know what his plan is, but I have no idea how to stop him.

Frying him with a bolt of lightning is great in theory, not so great in execution with a demon. He'd slough off the sparks without a second thought. Clouds will only hold him for so long. Not nearly enough time for me to wade through the void for help. I don't have much more at my disposal other than typical demon powers, all of which he has as well.

None of that takes into account his own personal brand of magic. I wrack my brain, trying to remember what flows in his veins. Sorting papers? Barking orders at demons? I don't know if he's ever shown a propensity toward something *other*. He either hid it well or I wasn't paying attention. It's not like I can outright ask him.

"Ludo, what happens if they *don't* let you in?"

He swings around and his gaze narrows. "They will."

"What if—"

"They will," he screams, and I step back, immediately regretting it. He paces back and forth, his hands trembling as he mutters to himself.

"Ludovic," I say sharply, hoping to snap him out of it.

"You don't get it. You'll never get it. In the way. No. No way around it." He stops suddenly and swings to face me, a wicked shadow in his red eyes. "Time to die, Dimitrius."

The sudden flip catches me off guard and I frantically hoard my magic, feeding it as much terror and rage as I can. I'll only have one shot to get this right. I send out a silent plea to Omen to take care of Mari. The chances of it reaching him are minuscule, but I can't leave her unprotected. I whisper an apology to her, knowing she'll never understand what happened.

Electricity crackles on my palms, and sparks shoot from my fingertips. The air around us charges as Ludo lunges toward me. A portal opens behind him as I release a bolt of lightning at his chest. Time slows as Mari jumps out and swings something heavy at Ludo's head. A loud crack echoes around us, and he crumples to the ground. Despite him being down, my magic doesn't dissipate. Instead, it hits her squarely in the heart.

She stiffens, shock flashing in her eyes, and the world goes dark.

CHAPTER TWENTY-EIGHT
MARI

I should be dead.

That's usually what happens when someone's hit by lightning. Except I'm perfectly fine. A little energized, perhaps. My skin tingles and my heart thrums in my chest, but it's still beating. It could be from the adrenaline of hitting a demon over the head with a cast-iron skillet. It's not as easy to wield as the movies suggest.

I drop the heavy pan and lift my hands in front of my face. "Sparkly. Huh."

Dimitri screams out my name, anguish and despair wrapping around his words and filling the void between us. I should tell him I'm okay. I open my mouth to reassure him. Instead, black clouds swirl around me, then pour down my throat. Coughs wrack my body, and I double over until I realize I can still breathe.

I straighten and realize Dimitri's still raging. I can barely make out his shadowy form. Wood splinters as he crashes his way toward me. A chair flies through the air and I duck, though it's way off to my right.

"Would you knock it the fuck off?" I snap, brushing sparks off my arms. They just reform, creating a web over my entire body.

Dimitri freezes, squinting through the darkness. "Mari?"

"Yeah, yeah, yeah. You're welcome for saving your life. You'll be a good little demon and take care of the body, right?" I prop

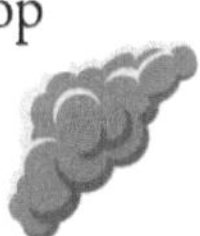

my hands on my hips and tilt my head as the smoke clears from the room.

He stumbles toward me, his gaze bouncing around. "You're... you're..."

"Electrifying? Why thank you." I give him my most dazzling smile, but he doesn't notice.

"You should be dead."

I pinch my arm and wince. "Nope. Still here. Listen, I would have cast a spell to take him out, but I was afraid of pushing it after using one to open this portal. Is *he* dead?"

I poke him with my toe, and he groans. My eyes widen and I snatch up the skillet once more. Dimitri rushes forward and grabs my wrist, stopping me from whacking the demon on the head again.

"They'll need Ludo at least a bit coherent, spitfire. I appreciate you saving me, though." He grins as he takes the pan and drops it on Ludo's head anyway.

He cups my cheeks, and he kisses me lightly. It shouldn't be enough for my body to light up like a freaking Christmas tree, but damn if it doesn't.

"You look beautiful filled with—"

"If you say cum, I'm going to whack you with that thing," I grumble, and he chuckles.

"My magic. Filled with my magic, spitfire."

"Same difference."

He kisses me again, and my eyes flutter closed. I don't know why his magic didn't take me out, but I'd rather not question it. Maybe it's because we slept together or I'm some rare badass witch. I snort and he pulls back, raising an eyebrow.

Pressing my lips together, I shake my head. I'm definitely not explaining. He'd agree I'm the least badass witch in all the dimensions, and it would hurt my feelings. Then we'd be bickering, and I'd rather not do that right now.

"Fuck," Dimitri growls and drops his hold on me. He spins to

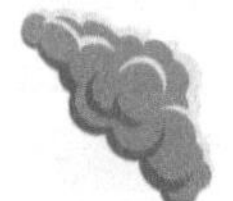

Ludo, still passed out on the floor, then back to me. He grimaces and I grab his shoulders, forcing him to focus on me.

"Explain."

"Your sister. She's in the cages. We have to—Ludo...I don't have time. I can't do both."

I nod, glancing down at the magic still skipping its way across my body. "Send me. I'll get her out. You take care of this, then come get us."

He's already shaking his head. "It won't—"

"It will work. You think I can't take care of myself?" When he doesn't answer, I grab the skillet and flames lick along the rim. It takes everything in me not to drop it and pretend this is totally normal.

His mouth flaps as if he's searching for another argument. I spin around and step toward the portal. Dimitri grabs my wrist, and I glance over my shoulder.

"Can I help you, sir?"

He scowls, though there's a helplessness in his eyes. "Don't fuck it up."

I roll my eyes and tug from his grasp. "See you soon, demon."

I step through the portal, sending a wish to pop out in the right place to any deities who are listening. I should have told Dimitri about how I used the book to open this thing. And the mess his apartment is in when it didn't work the first six times I tried. Half the place has burn marks, and his bed looks like I butchered a dozen geese on top of it. But it worked so he can't really complain.

At least this time I have some light to show me the way. A path stretches out before me, the shadowy remnants of an ancient forest rising on each side. I didn't hesitate before, letting the purple floating orb guide me. There's no orb now, no clear way forward. Just an empty road with offshoots leading into the dark. I bite my lip as I walk along, the only indication of my waning confidence.

Mrow.

"Oh thank fuck," I breathe. "Here, kitty, kitty."

I click my tongue, though I'm pretty sure that's for horses. Either way, the black and white cat with his squished face appears in front of me, and I heave out a heavy sigh. He licks his paw, then springs around. Should I be trusting a cat to lead me through a barren land in a dimension devoid of almost everything including color? Maybe not. But this is Hell and nothing makes sense down here. Actually, nothing made sense at home, either. Life should have been easier, simpler, better. Instead, I was thrust into one subtle trauma after another until life dropped a whole host of boring in my lap.

"Whatever you're doing, karma, I could really use some good vibes sent my way."

The cat hisses a second before a loud pop rings through the air. A woman with a rainbow dress and bright green hair drops in front of me.

"Hiya there, witch. Ooh, you are a cutie, aren't you? So sparkly. That's a good sign. I can definitely see why he couldn't let go. Glad I could help *that* little problem. Where ya headed? Whatcha doin'? Can I come with? I need a fucking break. Seriously, I'm never cursing anyone again. It's too much fucking work. Except...if I don't care about the suffering, I suppose it would be a really good punishment for some asshats who run their mouths." She taps her finger on her chin.

"Who—"

She sticks out her hand, then cringes, dropping it to her side. "Karma."

"Is a bitch?" I blurt out. She scowls, then smirks, and the pieces fall into place. "Oh...oh, you're...that's..."

She lets out a short laugh as I point at her. "Glad you could get there. Dimitri's my brother, and I'm the real Karma. In the flesh. Sort of. Not a bitch." A contemplative look overtakes her face. "Actually, I am a bitch sometimes, but it's always deserved. Most of the time. Sometimes not."

"Wait, what are you doing here?" I ask. "Dimitri could probably use your help."

"You called. I came. That's how it works. I ignore the summons half the time, but you're special." She boops me on the nose, and the cat hisses again. She hisses right back, then rolls her eyes. She links our arms together and tugs me along. "So, where are we going?"

"Um, to get my sister out of a cage."

She gives me an impressed look. "Why isn't Dimitri with you? He's supposed to..."

"Supposed to what?"

She waves away my question. "Is she in the basement? Or in a realm with a cage?"

"I don't know," I mumble.

She waves her hand again, and a swirling vortex opens in front of us. "That's fine. I can find her. Didn't realize you two were twins..."

She pulls me into the bright colors, and I squeeze my eyes shut. A wave of cold washes over me and I shiver. When it dissipates, I peek out, hoping we're not in the middle of a volcano or something. Karma seems a bit flighty, and I doubt she'd realize I wouldn't survive something like that. I'm greeted with a large musty room, reminiscent of a warehouse basement. Most of the cages lining the wall are empty.

When I try to rush toward the darkness, Karma digs her nails into my arm. "Wouldn't do that if I were you. Witches go missing in Hell all the time. It's why we usually have them escorted or they're soulbound to someone. I doubt your sister's accepted her bond yet. Probably waiting for you. Sometimes split souls will do that."

"Split souls?"

She nods, then grins as she laces our fingers together and skips along. I have no choice but to follow. Even though it's clear the spaces are empty, I still search them. The farther we travel, the

more my heart sinks and the electricity once coursing through my body dims.

We waited too long. Dimitri must have seen Lark last night, thinking it was me. That's why he kept asking how I got into his room. He didn't think I came from my house—he thought I was in a cage. And because I was more concerned with myself, I didn't ask. I didn't demand he help me look for her. Sleeping with him was more important.

Guilt crashes into me, and my knees buckle. My chest tightens, but the tears won't come. I cried them all weeks ago, leaving me an empty, selfish shell of a witch. I cared more about hooking up with a demon than figuring out what happened to Lark. I don't even deserve to be here. She deserves someone competent and committed and loyal. Instead, she got me.

Karma's face swims into view as my vision tunnels. Her voice calls my name as if she's miles away. I should tell her to go, to find Lark, yet the words won't come. I shudder and curl into a ball as electricity sparks from me. If it burns me up from the inside out, I won't even fight it. It's an apt punishment.

Strong hands haul me against a hard chest, and I try to shove Dimitri away. I don't deserve his warmth, his comfort. I fucked up. Over and over again, I fucked up. I let my jealousy override my love for her.

"Marigold, stop. It's okay. I've got you." He shushes me, holding me tight. Still, I thrash in his grasp. "There's a note. She left a note."

My skin turns clammy while I burn and nausea bubbles in my gut. Maybe I'll puke on him and he'll leave me be. A note means nothing. A note only says she was here, not where she is. A note does nothing to alleviate the guilt.

"Read it to her, for fuck's sake," Karma hisses.

"I'm not invading her privacy, Karma. Why the fuck are you here, anyways? You're not needed."

"Well, you weren't here and someone needed to show her the way. Besides, I wanted to meet the one who fused to your dumbass soul. Why she chose you, I'll never understand. Maybe I actually *like* her. You ever think of that?"

"You met her two minutes ago. You can't figure out if you like someone in that amount of time."

"How about two months? Hasn't it been that long since *you've* known her? You should know whether you're just fucking around or if you're actually going to keep her."

"She's not a fucking pet, Karma. Go bother someone else. Or better yet, make yourself useful and find her fucking sister. It should be easy since they look fucking identical."

Karma scoffs and her footsteps fade away. I have no idea whether or not she's left. It doesn't really matter. Neither of them is particularly helpful in this situation. If they don't know where Lark went, they're of no use to me. The thought sends a pang through my chest, and I curl into myself. Dimitri cradles me in his lap, whispering words I can't decipher.

He tucks the note between my hands and urges me over and over to read it. It's then I realize how badly I'm shaking. The paper crumples in my hand as my heartbeat pounds in my head. I pull in deep, even breaths, willing my body to calm down. I can't help Lark if I'm freaking out. Besides, it's just one more selfish move on my part. Par for the course, I suppose.

"Put me down," I croak, forcing the words from my raw throat.

He shuffles me onto the cold floor and leans me against the bars of an empty cage. I clutch the note in my hand, Lark's familiar script on the front spelling out my full name.

Dimitri paces away, then starts arguing with someone—probably Karma. His harsh words float back to me garbled and indistinct. When I unfold the paper, the edges curl and ash eats at the corners. I sit up straighter and scan the words as quickly as I can, then once more. I barely get to the end when the entire thing crumbles, turning my hands a sooty black.

Dimitri crouches in front of me, though I don't know how long I've sat here, committing her words to memory.

"Where to, spitfire?" he murmurs, his hand reaching out, then flopping to his side before he touches me.

"Nowhere," I whisper. I thump my head back against the hard metal, relishing the dull pain it causes.

"Is she...Ludo didn't..."

"She says she's as safe as she can be, but she doesn't want me to follow." My gaze meets his, and my heart cracks. "Take me home, please."

He nods, then snaps his fingers. His sad smile is the last thing I see before my world goes dark. I carry that image with me all the way home.

CHAPTER TWENTY-NINE
MARI

A blanket of murkiness has settled over the world —*my* world. My muddled thoughts aren't processing. Sounds around me are muted. No, silent. Nothing moves. Nothing breaks the silence. Nothing matters.

All because of my sister's choices. Her decision to leave me behind. We were supposed to do things together. Our fates are inextricably intertwined. Yet she still ran from me as if I wasn't enough for her. I thought I'd dealt with my inadequacy when it came to my sister. I spent too much time comparing us. Her light outshone my dark. She was always the kinder twin, the happier twin, the better twin. Our aunt used to say we were two sides of the same coin. Yet when a coin is flipped, there's always a side landing facedown.

I groan and curl into a ball, burrowing under the covers. A dry, musty smell wafts over me, and I sink into the darkness once more.

At least I try to. The void in my mind doesn't embrace me. Instead, it ejects me into reality, and a choked sob falls from my cracked lips. I clamp my hand over my mouth and swallow down my tears. Nothing good will come from wallowing. Except the words feel hollow.

Still, I force myself to sit up. It takes another five minutes for me to register the dark room around me. I thought the quiet, the

nothingness, was in my mind. Unfortunately, it was also in my room.

When I finally swing my legs around and attempt to stand, I crumple back onto the mattress. I went to the bathroom while I was lost in my emotions. My body should technically work. Then again, I might have crawled there and just forgotten. As I stumble toward the toilet, my brain clears away the cobwebs. At least enough to realize how utterly alone I am.

Lark and I haven't gone longer than a few days without talking. Except for this last time. I waited too long. It's my fault. She suffered because I convinced myself she was fine.

Dimitri said she was in that cage. How long did she waste away in there, her magic slowly draining, while I shied away from the truth? While I was running around dragon realms and fucking a demon, she was wondering if anyone out there would save her.

I don't care what her note said. None of it matters until we talk face to face. She could have stayed, waited until I was in front of her. Then she could go off on whatever adventure she wanted. Rage stirs in my gut, and I splash water on my face to shock my system out of it. The light above the mirror flickers, and my gaze snaps up.

"Dimitri?" I call softly. I close my eyes, waiting for the telltale sign of his imminent arrival. No demons crash to the ground. No feet shuffle down the hall. No thunder rolls overhead.

I clamp my lips together and swing my gaze to the ceiling, refusing to cry. No one owes me anything. Percy probably doesn't even know I'm here. Dimitri kept his promise, then his duty was done. I can't fault him for washing his hands of me. I brought nothing but trouble to his life. He didn't seem to mind me tagging along, or fucking me. Still, he didn't sign up for *this*. I glance down at my wrinkled shirt, and greasy strands flop over my shoulders.

I sigh and head back to the bathroom. Even after showering, eating, and making myself a large pot of coffee, I'm still empty inside. I end up staring out the window as the shadows from the leaves dance on the ground, then disappear with the setting sun. Minutes—hours, maybe—pass until the front door creaks open. I don't bother to look at who it is.

The light flicks on, and I shy away from the harshness. "Oh, Mari. Out of bed so soon? Thought you'd waste away, never to be seen again."

I blink at her reflection in the window. I know her, I just can't remember...

Worry flashes across her face before she plasters on a large, fake smile. She disappears into the kitchen with a bunch of bags. I'd ask if she was moving in, but I don't really care. Until Lark comes back, nothing matters. Pain hits me when Dimitri crosses my mind. No matter how much I try to forget him, he still worms his way back in. He made his intentions clear. Our time together was fun, short, and is now over.

"So, I thought about making soup tonight. Except that's all you've been eating for the last three weeks, so maybe sandwiches. Ooh, or grilled cheese. I got some homemade bread from your neighbor. And I took all your packages. Oh, and cheesecake for dessert."

Questions pile on my tongue, crowding my mouth and weighing me down. Percy. That's who it is. I'm not surprised she's here, but she seems to know I'm not sick. I'm just...dazed. She babbles on while clanging around in the kitchen. I tune her out until she says my demon's name. I wince, rejecting the idea of him being mine. We were a fling. Nothing more. Nothing less.

Percy crouches in front of me, and I finally meet her gaze. "Mari, I need something from you. Something more than sobbing or begging that demon to stay." She huffs when I pull my brows low. "Yeah, you were pretty out of it. The little lightning thief filled me in. Lark wouldn't want you to do this. She'd want you to...go on with your life until she could come back. And I'd know. I was friends with her for a long time."

I swallow hard and shake my head. Waiting for Lark is all I

have. How do I explain that to Percy? How do I put our bond into words? How do I tell her it's all my fault Lark is gone?

"I know what you're thinking. You're all wrapped up in guilt and shame. Guilt for not coming sooner—for not knowing she was in trouble. Being ashamed for shacking up with a demon while she was missing. Except you *knew*. That's why I never freaked out. After we figured out Dusty wasn't hiding her somewhere, I trusted you. If *you* weren't worried about her, then I wouldn't be either."

"I was worried," I croak. "Too scared to admit it."

She nods like she understands. She doesn't. She can't. "Listen, and I mean really listen. Lark knew what she was doing. And you wallowing like this only does her a disservice. She'd be pretty pissed at you for doubting her."

"She was in a cage."

She slaps her thighs, then pushes to her feet. "Yup. Except those cages don't really do anything other than keep you inside. At least that's what Dimitri said. Speaking of..."

"Don't," I whisper harshly, glancing out the window at the darkness. It reminds me of the void. Which reminds me of the dragon realm. Which leads back to Dimitri.

Percy holds up her hands in surrender. "Okay. I won't say anything. I won't tell you to get your shit together and go find him. I won't tell you to confess your feelings to him. And I certainly won't tell you to bring him some fries when you do it. Oh, by the way, that big black book keeps following me around. It's fucking creepy so if you could, ya know, deal with that."

She prances off to the kitchen. I'm not ready to think about her words. Digesting them would mean admitting truths I'm not ready to face. Maybe tomorrow. Or next week. Or whenever Lark deems it necessary to include me in her life once more. A familiar bolt of rage hits me, and I shove it down again.

"Okay, I know we said we weren't going to talk about it, but I need to know—did you sleep with him? Because I need to know if

my theory of them being amazing in the sack checks out," Percy calls over something sizzling in a pan.

My lips twitch, but I'm not ready to feel anything other than abject misery. She continues speaking as if I answered. I wonder how many times she's had to carry on a conversation with herself. Much like I did when my sister's voice was resonating in my head. She's silent now—beyond my mind's reach.

"You know, I was thinking you could ask Dimitri about scrying. Or maybe the other one who stopped by if you're hell-bent on not talking to him."

"What other one?"

"She speaks!" Percy flounces into the living room again, a spatula in her hand. "Yes, the tiny one with the hair that kept changing colors. She said everything should be good now. And something about soulbound, but I don't know what that is."

"It's two souls bound together through space and time," I murmur, my mind half on the conversation. Karma showing up here isn't something I expected. We don't know each other. She should be with Dimitri. Or going off and raining down consequences on unsuspecting assholes.

"Well, I was barely paying attention. She's cute. Like, *really* cute. She must have gotten all the good genes in that setup."

"I don't—"

"Because they're twins and all. Her and Dimitri. Honestly, if Karma dropped out of a closet on top of me, I'd be smitten for sure."

"How did you..."

"Oh, the gossip was hot, honey. Plus, with you not really giving me the story, I had to ask *someone*. Anyhoo, about the book? I know it's such a small thing compared to, well, everything, but it's really freaking me out. That little witchy friend of yours needs it back."

I squeeze my eyes shut and search my memories. I don't remember getting the book from a witch. I sift through each

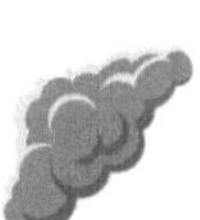

snapshot in reverse. Dimitri bringing me home. Lark's note. Hitting Ludo with the skillet. Successfully creating a portal.

There.

The return of Lark's voice has me swallowing a sob. I don't have time to worry about that right now. Dimitri disappeared and, like clockwork, a witch appeared at his door. She waltzed right in like she owned the place, then apologized. A lot. When I calmed down enough to tell her what was going on, a black book much larger than *Necromancy* appeared. She scoffed, handed it to me, then left me to my own devices—said I needed to do it on my own or it wouldn't work. That's how I created the portal. That's how I found Dimitri. It wasn't divine intervention or his curse. It was a spell, plain and simple.

Which means I need to return it. To Hell. If I run into Dimitri...I'll deal with that when—*if*—the time comes.

I stand abruptly and Percy jolts away. "I'm going to take it back. Now."

"Like, right now? Dude, you just got up. Maybe eat first?"

I shake my head and head for the bedroom. Real clothes will be needed. Especially if I plan on seeing people. As I tug on a pair of jeans, I spot the black spellbook. It's filled with all sorts of charms, enchantments, and hexes, not to mention pathways into Hell. I won't be needing those. In fact, I doubt I'll need anything from this ancient tome anymore.

Glancing toward my door, I contemplate whether or not to tell Percy I'm going. Instead, I scribble a note and leave it at that. I end up sneaking down the hallway, then through the kitchen, and finally to Lark's spell room. Percy's nowhere to be found, thankfully. This time there aren't any funny noises or strange lights. The candles wait for a spark, and the circle sits open, waiting for another victim.

A chill rolls down my spine as I hug the book to my chest. I don't know what awaits me in Hell. Probably nothing. I'll most likely be right back here in no time. Back to wallowing and

wondering where the fuck Lark went off to. And where I went wrong with Dimitri.

CHAPTER THIRTY
DIMITRI

"Get up."

Omen's voice rings through the dark room. I grunt in response only because the bastard won't leave me alone if I don't answer him.

He looms over my bed, the flame in his hand illuminating his face. "Enough moping. Time to go get your witch. Isn't that what you told me?"

"Different scenario. Different results."

He shakes his head, then glances over his shoulder. Probably at Clara. I wouldn't put it past him to invite her in to convince me to go after Mari. Not that either of them understands. I've barely told them anything about her. Karma probably ratted me out. Or Providence. They both seem to have their own issues to deal with, though.

"She your soulbound?" he snaps.

"Doesn't matter."

He huffs and I swear he rolls his eyes. "Of course it does."

"No, it doesn't. She asked to go home. I took her home. End of story."

"Sounds exactly like what I went through." He drops into a chair that wasn't there a second before.

"It's not. Go away."

His nose wrinkles, and I flip on my side, facing away from

him. I clutch a pillow to my chest, wishing it still held Mari's scent. It faded long ago. Or maybe yesterday. I've lost track of time, to be honest.

"When was the last time you ate? Or bathed?" He mutters something about dirty-ass motherfuckers, but I stopped listening. At least I'm trying to. "Did you clarify what *home* meant?"

"She spent one night down here. Can't claim it as home." Apparently I'm not done listening to him. Maybe I want him to swoop in and tell me what a shithead I've been. Maybe I want him to tell me to go get her. Maybe I want him to say she'll welcome me with open arms—that she loves me. Except that's not reality and I won't fall for fantasies.

"How do you know if you didn't ask?"

"Because I know her."

"All the more reason to—"

I explode out of bed, pillows and blankets flying everywhere. The ceiling cracks open and rain pours down on us, soaking me to the bone. I don't fucking care. If he does, he can get the fuck out.

"She's not here, Omen. She'll never be here. She doesn't belong in Hell. So, stop meddling in my business."

I gasp for breath, my shoulders heaving and my hands trembling. Movement behind him has me glancing up, and my heart stops. Clara purses her lips as Mari pushes past her, her purple hair streaming behind her in her haste to get away.

"Fuck," I snarl, then launch over the bed. Omen tips backward in his chair and crashes to the ground. Clara steps to the side as I fling myself out of my bedroom and down the hall. Her laughter at Omen's antics fades as I search for Mari. She couldn't have gone far. Unless she's mastered portals or whatever shit witches use to walk through worlds.

A glowing sigil on the inside of the front door catches my eye, and I race toward it. Slowly it fades from gold to silver, and I fling myself at the hard wood. My body disappears and I groan as I'm sucked through a keyhole. At least, that's what it feels like. I'm

compressed and rearranged, then put back together as I tumble into her world.

I'm met with a bucketful of hot water, and I sputter as my knees hit the hardwood floor. I swipe a hand down my face, wishing I had a shirt to wipe away the wetness. Being only in boxers was great while I was wallowing, but not so much for dramatic apologies.

"Well, at least you'll be clean now," she snarls. "Would you like some soap before you fuck off back to Hell?"

"Mari, I—"

"I don't want to hear it, bat-boy."

I open my mouth, then snap it shut. "I'm not a fucking vampire, Mari."

"Let's see, you have wings, you dissolve into shadows, you suck the soul out of unsuspecting people, and you don't give a damn who you hurt." She ticks each point off on her fingers. "If it quacks like a duck..."

"I'm not a duck either."

"Fuck the ducks," she cries. "That's not the fucking point, Dimitri. Just...get out. I only went because I needed to return Clara's book. I didn't realize it would drop me at your place. Go back to your...private time or whatever the hell you were doing."

"I was wallowing, thank you very much. Because *someone* drove me away when shit got hard. Instead of leaning on me like she should have."

I struggle to my bare feet, then slip on the wet floor. I manage to catch myself, but just barely. A giggle escapes her and my head snaps up. She glares at me all while her lips twitch, giving her away.

"I didn't drive you away. I asked you to take me home. I didn't say *leave* me there without a word."

"I gave you a word. I gave you plenty of words. I sat next to your bed and told you it'd be okay. I offered to go searching for her. Hell, I even made your gross coffee that's way too fucking

strong. Then when you wouldn't respond, I called Percy. What the fuck else was I supposed to do?"

"Stay," she cries. "You were supposed to stay and take care of me. Not foist me off on someone else." She pulls in a deep breath and closes her eyes. "I get it. I'm not mad."

I snort, rubbing my palms on my boxers and wishing I had a towel. "Nope, not mad at all. Totally chill."

"No, I'm really not. I understand why you left. I even understand why you didn't come back. I'm not your—"

I stab a finger in her direction. "If you call yourself a problem, I swear to fuck, I will put you—"

"In my place?" She raises an eyebrow and crosses her arms.

I step out of the circle and prowl closer. She tenses, and her nails dig into her skin. It feels like it's been forever since I've set my eyes on her. It's like waking up for the first time after a long nap. Like diving into a cold lake on a hot day. Like feeling the sun on my face after years in the dark. She tips her chin up, reminding me we're in the middle of...something. A fight? A tiff? A battle? Whatever it is, it's invigorating.

My lips brush the shell of her ear as I lean close and whisper, "I'll put you over my knee."

"You can't...this isn't...I'm not..." Her palms slap into my bare chest and she shoves me back. "This isn't a joke, Dimitri."

"Oh, I wasn't joking, spitfire. Now yell at me. Tell me how much you hate me so I can grovel at your feet. I'll confess how devoid of color my life has been. How I've wallowed for weeks, unable to leave my bed for more than a few minutes. How you were never far from my mind. You infiltrated every waking moment and most of my dreams—nightmares really, since they were all of losing you."

Her bottom lip trembles. "She left me."

A tear trickles down her cheek, and I sigh. "Oh, witch. No."

She collapses into my arms, and I cradle her against me. I don't bother with useless words she won't hear anyway. No matter how many times I tell her she didn't fail her sister, she won't believe me. I'm not the one who can help. Only her sister will be able to reassure her. She doesn't even have the note to cling to.

When her cries subside to the occasional sniff, I bury my nose in her hair and inhale deeply, committing her scent to memory. Not that I need to. It's already embedded in my psyche. Still, this might be the last time I get to hold her. I'll take whatever I can get.

She makes a noise in the back of her throat. "You left me, too. I failed my sister, and you just confirmed I wasn't good enough to stick around for. I just...I'm sorry I yelled at you. It's not your fault. I get why you went back."

I cup her cheeks and force her head up. "None of this is your fault. Your sister is an adult. She makes her own decisions. Okay?" I wait until she nods, then rest my forehead on hers. "I didn't mean to leave you. I just didn't know how to help. And I didn't know what the joining spell did to you or how the curse impacted you."

She pulls away and deep grooves appear between her eyes. "Joining spell?"

I drop my hands and put space between us—fist-swinging space. "*My* sister helped *your* sister do a joining spell. It, uh, linked us in a way? Coupled with the curse, it's why..."

"Why you showed up. A curse and a spell. That's..." She stares at my chest, and I scramble for words—something to convince her this is more than just magic. Except I can't. Magic brought us together and magic binds our souls. I'd like to think if I had met her randomly, I'd still be drawn to her, but I have no proof.

I run my hand through my hair, sending static rippling through the short strands. Magic thrums in my veins, matching my need—my anxiety.

"Do not make it rain in here," she snaps, then sniffs. "Did Karma break the curse then? Did my sister dissolve the spell? Or are we just going to continue having these awkward encounters where you don't really want to be here and I don't know how to let you go?" She presses her lips together as if she's said too much.

"She reversed the curse as soon as she stepped back into Hell. While I was dealing with Ludo."

"And the spell?"

"I don't know," I breathe. "Wouldn't be so bad."

She snorts, shaking her head. "Sure it wouldn't."

"Hate me that much, huh?"

She lets out a frustrated cry. "Hate you? How can I hate you when you were driven as much as I was by this bullshit? By other people meddling in our lives? No, I don't hate you. I hate how they fucked with us. I hate how nothing makes sense anymore. I hate how none of it was real—that magic wove our lives together until we don't know what's our own decisions and what was a trick."

"It wasn't a spell or a curse driving me when I found you while you looked for your sister." I step closer. "It wasn't magic when I brought you to the dragon realm." I move again, and she matches me step for step until her back hits the wall. "It wasn't anything other than desire when I fucked you." My hands land on either side of her head, and I lean closer. "You want real? This. Magic can't conjure feelings. It can't force me to fall for you. Magic may have been the thread, but it didn't tie us together. *We* did. Us and only us, spitfire."

She bites her bottom lip, dragging my gaze down. Indecision and hope fight for dominance in her eyes. It's killing me to wait for her to take a chance on us. To figure out what's real and what's not.

"Why me?" she finally whispers, genuine confusion in her tone.

I let out a chuckle, then rest my forehead on hers. "You match my chaos. You're resilient, loyal—no, don't do that. You are, otherwise you wouldn't have been so hurt when you thought you'd failed your sister. You find wonder in things I've long since gotten used to. You're all fire and attitude, and I swear it gets me hard every fucking time you yell at me. Your turn."

She jolts back, her head thumping on the wall. "What?"

"You think I don't need a little reassurance? After you told me to take you home? After you shut me out?" I could go on, but she's already gritting her teeth. "That hard to come up with something?"

"No, but I have a feeling as soon as I tell you, your ego will get so big it'll make the house explode."

"Oh, little witch has jokes, does she?"

She presses her lips together, fighting a smile. "I think you're funny. And even if it was the spell, I like how protective you are. Even when you're pissed off, you're still genuine. You can tell you still care. They don't see that, do they?" She studies my face, and I shrug. "I don't know...I can't turn off the part of my brain saying you'll walk away again. That eventually you'll get bored of a mediocre witch when someone more interesting comes along. You have entire dimensions to find someone else."

"I'd walk through worlds for you. Only you."

Tears fill her eyes, and she launches herself at me. I stumble back as I wrap my arms around her. Things might not be magically better, there's still shit to work through, but right here—right now, it feels like we'll get there. As long as we're together, we'll figure it out.

EPILOGUE
DIMITRI

Three Months Later

"There it is," I grumble, pointing toward the horizon.

Mari's nose crinkles and she glances around. "I don't think the volcano would bother me as much as the smell."

"Well, when your skin is being burned off while your eyeballs melt, it definitely bothers you."

She gives me a side-eye. "Except none of that happens to demons when they're thrown into fire."

"How do you know that? Thought you weren't that well-versed in demon-y things."

She shrugs. "I *may* have been doing some reading. And I *may* have been talking to Clara. She's a lot more competent when it comes to witchy things. She's also been teaching me about being soulbound to a demon. Apparently, it makes demons grumpier. At least, that's the conclusion we came to."

"Is that so?" I murmur, and she nods, a smirk playing on her lips.

I lunge for her and she shrieks, taking off down the barren rocky hill. There's nowhere for her to run, but I chase after her, anyway. Better than her tumbling headlong down the whole damn mountain. When I catch her around the waist, she shrieks again. I spin us straight into the void, then step into a dense forest.

"Shh. You'll wake them," I whisper in her ear.

She freezes and I point over our heads. Crows nest above us, sleepy and silent. They won't hurt me, and I'm banking on them leaving her alone. They're more likely to follow her around like lost puppies, begging for a bit of her attention. I befriended them centuries ago when I was a very young demon. For a while, they were my only companions besides Karma. Until Omen came along, that is.

"Where are we?" she breathes, glancing around at the dense trees. Fog weaves its way through the trunks as if it's sentient. Hell, it might be. I always found it the calm to my volatile nature.

I carry her into a clearing and plop her onto the trunk in the dead center. "Welcome to the woods, spitfire. I used to come here a lot."

"Are we topside? We're not, right? This is some...ancient dimension or something?" She can't seem to stop scanning the area, her head swiveling back and forth.

"Probably. It was old when I was young. I've never seen anyone else here, but that doesn't mean others don't know about it. I also haven't found anything truly scary hidden in the trees."

"So I don't have to worry about anything eating me?"

I tap her on the nose, and she fixes her gaze on me. "Only me."

She rolls her eyes. "It's really calming here."

"I think so. While I did want you to see it, I also figured this was the best place," I say nonchalantly.

"Best place for what?"

"Well, you want to run from me...this is safer than a world riddled with volcanic activity." I cross my arms and see the moment my words click into place.

She slips off the trunk and holds her hands up. "Whoa there, demon. I thought we were going to have like a picnic or something. Not a chase scene where you give me a minute head start, then chase after me."

"Then fuck you against a tree. And then again on a bed of soft

needles. And once more in the cave just to the north." I tip my chin toward the mountain rising over the trees behind her, then obscured by wispy white clouds.

She glances over her shoulder, then back at me. "Except I don't know where I'm going and you do. Doesn't that seem like I'm at a disadvantage?"

"I'm a demon, spitfire. You're always at a disadvantage in these cases." I smirk at her scowl.

"And what do we do about *that*?" She points behind me, and I follow the direction.

I search the trees, trying to peer through the fog at whatever she spotted. All while she attempts to sneak away. She probably would have gotten away with it if she hadn't stepped on a twig. I grin, pretending I'm still focused on her imaginary sighting.

"I don't know what you're talking about, Marigold. There's nothing there."

Her giggle, quickly cut off, comes from the west, and I sigh before settling on the worn-down trunk. I count silently in my head to a hundred. She still isn't far enough away to truly make this a chase, but she's not ready for one of those yet. Eventually, we'll explore more. For now, this is perfect. *She's* perfect. At least for me.

The last few months have been an upheaval in both our lives. With Ludo suitably punished, they have yet to find a replacement. Triton took off to fuck-knows-where, and I've been stepping in for him. It doesn't give me quite as much free time as I want with Mari. Apparently she's been putting that extra time to good use. She's still not ready to give up her life topside.

Providence and Karma have been planning something, but they won't tell me what. I suspect it's a way for us to travel freely through the dimensions. I don't really give a fuck where we end up, as long as it's wherever Mari is. I still haven't fully come to grips with the fact she chose me. Whenever I say that, though, she gives me a look and tells me to pull my head out of my ass. A smile creeps to my lips as I remember when she shoved me out the

window for telling her she could do better. Granted, she didn't know the window was open, but still. Funny as hell.

I push to my feet and close my eyes. It only takes me a few seconds to pinpoint her location. She's practically screaming where she is with how she's crashing through the underbrush. I clear my throat and tip my head back.

"Ready or not, witch," I call.

I'm met with another giggle, then take off for the tree line. I don't even need to use any of my magic to weave my way through the trunks, the fog clearing a path for me. Mari stops half a mile ahead, and her harsh breaths ring around me. Grinning, I stalk toward her. Within minutes I spot her purple hair peeking from behind a trunk. I'm pretty sure she was trying to climb the thing, then gave up.

"Better run, witch," I say softly, and the fog carries my words to her.

She gasps, then sprints deeper into the woods. She glances over her shoulder, her face a mixture of panic and desire. I launch over a fallen log and her eyes widen. The stream winding its way through the forest should stop her. It's not far ahead. And if she falls in, well, it'll be a good reason to get her naked. As if I need one.

A frustrated groan echoes back to me as the trees open up. Instead of stopping, Mari's feet fly over the ground. I open my mouth to stop her, but she's already launching off the bank and sailing through the air. I rush forward, my wings bursting from my back and ripping my shirt from the sheer force of magic coursing through me. They've gotten stronger over the last few months. Hopefully enough to carry both of us once I save her sorry ass from drowning.

Her boots hit the soft soil on the opposite bank, and I stutter to a stop. She falls forward and scrambles up the small hill while the soil erodes under her weight. When she's steady, she glances over her shoulder. A grin plays on her lips, and she blows me a kiss before taking off again.

"Fuck me," I breathe.

"Will if you catch me, demon," she yells, and I let out a laugh before I jump, allowing the wind catch my wings. As fun as it would be to continue prowling after her, my cock is straining against my pants, and I can't take another mini heart attack.

I land in front of her, and she skitters to a stop. She spins and runs back where we came. Snapping my fingers, I end up in front of her yet again. She glares at me, probably for using magic. She mutters something under her breath, then spins once more.

"I can do this all day, spitfire. You'll get tired before I will," I call with a laugh at her retreating back. My mouth drops open when a portal opens in her path and she sprints headlong into it. The last thing I see is her hair streaming behind her and her middle finger lifted over her head.

"Cheater," I whisper harshly.

I close my eyes, focusing on the thread tying our souls together. It thrums with excitement, anticipation, desire, and something else I haven't been able to identify. Focusing on the bond, I follow it all the way to her. She hasn't gone as far as I imagined, albeit in a different dimension.

Stepping into the void, I reorient myself, then step into the garden behind our house. *Our house.* The thought sends my heart fluttering. I'm still not completely convinced she's here to stay. We've expanded the apartment, the garden, our little slice of Hell. She's settled in, her touch in every room. I wake up every morning, thanking my lucky stars she's still in my arms.

"Marigold," I call in a singsong voice. "Where are you?"

"Big scary demon can't find one little witch?" Her voice echoes around the revamped garden.

"If you wouldn't have put in an entire hedge maze, it might be easier," I growl, scanning the area. "You know you'll get lost if you go in there, spitfire. Then I'll have to come save you." I freeze when a foot scuffles behind me.

"Thought you liked saving me," she murmurs.

Her nails bite into my skin between my wings, and I shudder.

She rips the rest of the fabric from my body, and it flutters to my feet. I drop my chin to my chest and force myself to stay still while she explores. She skims her palms along one wing, and my cock hardens. I swallow down a groan as she plays, tracing the veins.

"You're not very good at running from me," I say gruffly.

"I got bored waiting for you."

A growl rips from me as I spin, snatching her around the waist before she can take off again. She lets out a shrieking laugh as our clothes disappear into the void. Dark clouds coalesce behind her a second before I slam her back into a tree. I plunge into her, and her breath catches in her throat, then dissolves into a moan. Her legs wind around my waist as I thrust into her hard and fast.

She rests her forehead on mine while she flutters around my shaft. Adrenaline from the chase, from her words, from merely being in her presence courses through my veins.

"You can fuck me harder than that," she taunts, a smirk playing on her mouth.

My wings curl around us and spear into the trunk on either side of her. She tips her head against the tree, giving me access to her perfect skin. I bite into the top of her tit, and she grabs my hair. A delicious pain echoes through me as she yanks on the strands and I nip at her nipple.

"Yes. More," she breathes, then moans my name as she crashes into an orgasm. As she floats along, her eyes find mine. "Again."

"Needy witch," I snarl, thrusting into her harder. She gasps at the angle, and my magic rumbles within me as if I'm tapping into some unknown well.

My body trembles and lightning races along my skin, skipping to her, then back again.

"Fuck," she says through gritted teeth, and her gaze drops where I vanish into her again and again.

I concentrate the magic to my cock, and it begins to vibrate. She lets out a choked sob, and I press harder into her until I hit

her clit. She collapses into a limp mess in my arms as I roar out my release.

I bury my face in her neck, whispering words I've been too scared to say out loud into her skin. They're safe there, branding her as mine, linking us together.

"That was…"

"Exhilarating," I murmur. "I love watching you come. I love this." I thrust into her, and she sucks in a sharp breath.

Her hands cup my cheeks and gazes at me with adoration. "I love this, too."

"I love *you*," I whisper, then tense.

"Good thing I love you, too." She kisses me softly, then pulls back and unravels her legs from around me.

I set her down gently as I slip from her. My cock bobs, still hard even as her pleasure glistens on my shaft. The longer we're together, the more I make love to her, the more I crave all of it— all of her. She's everything I never knew I needed.

She steps away from me when I reach for her, and her lips twitch. "Care to prove how much you love me? How far would you go to convince me of your love?"

I raise an eyebrow. "I'd search through every dimension for you. I'd walk through every world. I'll always find you, witch. You're mine. If you run right now, though, I won't be gentle as I prove how much I care for you."

She grins. "Do your worst, demon."

Her peals of laughter trail after her as she takes off into the garden. As she dashes away from me, I grin. She disappears around a corner and I sprint after her. When I catch her, I'll show her exactly how devoted I am to her.

My soulbound, my spitfire, my witch, my everything.

Thank You
Thank you so much for reading Dimitri and Mari's story!

Ready for another adventure?
Check out the other works available by Emilia Abraham.

If you'd like to hear about the other stories that have been living in my head, sign up for my newsletter (including extra scenes & epilogues), visit my website, or follow me on social media visit: emiliaabraham.com

Special Thanks:
K.B. Barrett Designs-Cover Artist and Formatter
Dragon Smith Publishing, LLC-Emily Michel-Editor
Erenee-Beta Reader
Krysten-Omega Reader

ALSO BY
E. ABRAHAM

Shadows of Synd:

Under the Shadows-Book 1

Between the Shadows: Novella

Running From Shadows-Book 2

Becoming Shadows-Book 3

Shadows Within Us-Book 4

Beyond the Shadows-Book 5

Ruins of Rima: Spin-off Series

Chasing Darkness-Book 1

Charmed by Darkness-Book 2

Havoc in Harris Duology:

Phantom Betrayal

Novella:

Cadence of the Xylophone

Available on Newsletter: Extra Scenes,

Bridging Epilogues (Shadows of Synd-Book 1 & 2)

ABOUT

E. ABRAHAM

After many years of dreaming of becoming a full-time writer, Emilia Abraham took the leap, bringing her words to print. From sweet contemporary romance to spicy why choose and everything in between, she focuses on the happily ever after.

Emilia lives in the Upper Midwest with her husband (who's probably sick of listening to her expound on fictional men) and three kids (who try to steal her post-it notes). When she's not writing, she enjoys reading, playing video games, and consuming copious amounts of energy drinks.